MR. Bone's Retreat

>>>>>>>>>>>>>>>>>>>>>>>>>>>>>>>

MARGARET FORSTER

SIMON AND SCHUSTER
NEW YORK

First U.S. printing

SBN 671-20805-5
Library of Congress Catalog Card Number: 74-133092
Designed by Jack Jaget
Manufactured in the United States of America
By H. Wolff, New York

for
LORNA *and* DAVID,
who followed on

One

THE NIGHT began badly. William felt, later, that he ought to have realized how significant this was. He had, after all, put up his camp bed for thirty-seven years now, in exactly the same position, in exactly the same way, and had no trouble with it at all. It was an excellent bed. The struts supporting it were cast iron and exceedingly strong. The canvas was reinforced top and bottom, double stitched all round, and not stretched too tightly. The whole thing folded flat, into a rectangle one yard by two feet, and William was able to keep it during the day behind his easel, where it fitted most snugly. The padded sleeping bag and one gray army-issue blanket that went on top of it rolled into a cylinder ball that leaned unobstrusively in a corner. It was a happy arrangement. William could never set his bed up or take it down without reflecting on this.

But on Christmas Eve, William had trouble with his bed. At first he thought it was a human error—his error. He was tired. Wrapping presents was an exhausting business which he was growing to dread more and more. He had lost his roll of Sellotape early in the proceedings, and without it the whole operation had seemed impossible. Irritably, he had searched for it. It was not in the heap marked "Examinations," nor had it strayed into "Civil Service," nor even lodged itself in "House," which was the biggest heap of all. William had stood and looked at his heaps, arranged round the room like the upturnings of some giant worm, and wondered if after all he might have to buy a desk, or two desks. But he liked his heaps. He liked to walk round them, little mountains of industry, and often felt like designing fences —of bamboo, say—to go round them. Only the thought of Pullen's disapproval deterred him. As his architect, Pullen had rights.

The Sellotape was not to be found. William tried to be philosophical, and then to be ingenious. Since he had no glue—it was not allowed in the house—he made a paste of flour and water, as his nanny had done when he was a child, and sealed the edges of the paper with this glutinous mess. Then he ironed the narrow pieces of ribbon that the girl in Woolworth's had so cruelly bundled into a bag, and made pretty bows. He had watched the woman in Selfridge's demonstrating how to tie them—a question of winding the ribbon over and over and teasing it through and then snipping the lot at exactly the right place. Standing with his back to her, he had watched through the mirror in front of the elevator and made notes.

His shoulders ached with the intensity of his concentration. Stretching, he had gone to get his bed and bedding and had flicked the ends up with his foot and, so confident was he that the bed would now be firmly balanced, had turned away to untuck the sleeping bag. The bed collapsed with a crash. Amazed, William stared at it. Carefully, he lifted the struts with his hands and splayed the legs out. They seemed fine. Relieved, he again turned to get his sleeping bag untied, and to his horror the bed collapsed again. That was when William blamed himself. He must be very tired. He took a deep breath and walked round the room a couple of times to relax himself. He felt worked up. Dreading his next encounter, he lowered himself onto his stomach—feeling just a little pain as he did so—and examined the flattened bed. Nothing amiss. He turned it over and spread the legs apart, and as he did so he noticed the fault—the screw that held the joint was loose. William was surprised. He maintained his bed scrupulously. Thoughtfully, a little depressed, he got a spanner and tightened the screw and set the bed up. It stayed where it was, but he felt upset.

Quietly, he ran down the stairs to the bathroom on the half landing. The oil heater in the hall was smelling and tomorrow, Christmas Day or not, Mrs. Joliffe would make remarks. These remarks were unfair. It was for Mrs. Joliffe's sake that William had bought the heater. It had involved three phone calls and two incredibly wearing visits to Pullen before a design could be agreed on, and then there was the buying of it and the transporting of it and the burdensome starting and fueling of it. Now all Mrs. Joliffe did was make remarks about its smell and the low heat it gave. William knew it smelled. He often felt like saying—but of course controlled himself in time—that he had a nose, too. But it was efficient. It took the chill off the hall magnificently. The damp at the top of the front door had now completely disappeared, thanks to its warmth. Very nicely, William did not say all this to Mrs. Joliffe. He just smiled and said yes it did pong a little.

William locked the bathroom door, and then hesitated and unlocked it. He was trying to reform himself. Mrs. Joliffe, who in any case was a semicripple and would never have been able to climb all these stairs even if she had wanted to catch William on the lavatory, had her own bathroom. There was no one else in the house. Yet William, to his own annoyance, went on locking the bathroom door. It was an infuriating habit, quite maddening, and must be controlled. William peed, then washed his hands scrupulously and cleaned his teeth. Before he left the bathroom, he put the lavatory lid down. He and Mrs. Joliffe had an agreement that the lavatories in the house should not be flushed after ten o'clock. This was really William's idea. The water tank was next to his room and rumbled on for fully twenty minutes, preventing him from sleeping or having quiet thoughts. Having broached the subject, with much delicacy, to Mrs. Joliffe, William had felt bound to say that he would do the same for her, even though the water tank was a long way from her. Mrs. Joliffe had been surprisingly sympathetic, and the deal had been concluded.

On his way back upstairs, William stopped at the middle flat door. He might just pop in and see everything was all right. He pushed open the door and went into the large front room, switching on the chandelier central light that Pullen had advised. It was a very beautiful room, the proportions quite perfect. Two floor-to-ceiling windows, connected by a wrought-iron balcony—William intended to have white geraniums there—filled one wall. There was an Adam fireplace and two arched recesses. The paintwork was white and the walls pale green, but they were white and green with a difference. Nobody but William knew the secret. He had mixed one part yellow to one part cream to two parts white, and thereby triumphantly overcome the greeny glow that pure white gave. The green had gray and white in it and was a soft, subtle shade such as William knew did not appear on any color chart. Everything was satisfactory, as indeed it should be, considering he aired the room every day. He went through the door into the kitchen and, going straight to the sink, peered anxiously at the draining board, which he had spent most of yesterday treating with linseed oil. He had not needed Pullen to tell him that stainless steel simply would not do for the draining board of the sink in a kitchen in a Regency house. Nor would vitreous enamel be any better. It had to be wood, and the search for the correct wood had been long and difficult. William had at last—with a slight sense of panic—bypassed teak in favor of an African wood the name of which always eluded him. He touched it now with his fingertips. It seemed hard enough, but then it was not yet in use.

William gave the rest of the kitchen—high, light and stark—a quick look, and then went on up to bed. The problem got into bed with him. How was he to find tenants for his vacant flat? It made him tremble just to think of it. Advertising was dangerous, beset with all kinds of perils, even if, as Mrs. Joliffe suggested, he confined himself to the *Times*. All sorts of people read the *Times* these days, and William was always just about to stop reading it himself. There was, in any case, something about advertising that William could not condone. He was not an advertising man. Once, goaded by Mrs. Joliffe's remarks, he had begun to draft an advertisement and had instantly been troubled by both the limitations of space and the demands of truth. Before he had even described the house—his house—in which the flat was, William had used many hundreds of words. Perplexed, he had read them and could not find any that were dispensable, and knew finally beyond any shadow of doubt that advertising was not his medium.

There remained estate agents and personal recommendation. Pullen was for estate agents. He claimed one must go to the specialist for a specialist job. William bought his meat from a butcher, didn't he? Well, he should let his flat through an estate agent. Twice William had managed to get himself inside Gibson's, and twice his nerve had deserted him and he had run away. The trouble was, he did not know his own terms. How much was he going to charge? Pullen said the most he could get, what a damfool question, but William did not want the most he could get. He just wanted enough. But what was enough? And who would pay it? He did not want just anybody. He did not want anyone noisy, or careless, or unappreciative. He wanted the right person.

Because of these half-formed notions, William favored personal recommendation, but here too there were drawbacks. Whom did he trust enough to trust their recommendation? His circle of friends was small, very small, growing yearly smaller. It would be an embarrassment he could not afford if he had to get rid of a friend's personal recommendation. At the thought of getting rid of anyone, William's heart did a somersault. He would be incapable of it. Knowing this, he had spent some six months drawing up a list of rules which he would show to any prospective tenants and get them to agree to. It would be written into the lease that they agreed—William was quite definite about that. Then, if things turned out badly, it would be quite simple. There need be no awkwardness. It would rightly be a matter for the solicitors.

William sighed and stretched his toes inside his sleeping bag. It was such a pity the flat had to be let at all. Now that he was on the brink of such a momentous decision, he wished it need never be made. He had his top flat, Mrs. Joliffe the ground floor; did he really need any other people? His income was quite substantial but of course fixed and therefore ever dwindling, but really money was irrelevant, almost. The point was, if he loved his house, as he did, he must see that it was lived in. He could not possibly live in all of it, therefore he must agree to someone else doing so. One read, too, such dreadful things about lack of housing that even though he was most certainly not a Socialist, William felt obliged to do his bit.

He had thought long and carefully about doing his bit, ever since Mrs. Joliffe had called him selfish because he would not let Boy Scouts into his house to do bob-a-jobs. Apart from being cross at the allegation, William had also been interested in it. How was it possible to be selfish when he had at once given the Scouts five shillings and told them to do a job for nothing for someone in need? It seemed to him that though he was often self-indulgent he was never selfish. Indeed, he found it difficult to be selfish, living as he did on his own. Only his own needs and desires had to be catered for. He could not be accused of selfishness when he had no one else to consider. Mrs. Joliffe said nonsense. She said the very fact of living on his own was selfish. She said he had to consider mankind in general and what he ought to, and could, do for them. William replied, with dignity, that he had fought two very hard wars for mankind, and that was enough.

But still, William did worry about his lack of participation. He sent checks off regularly to various charities, but that was not quite the thing. He did not know how to offer his services, or to whom. If he had been religious then it would have been simple, but he was not. He had begun life as a baptized member of the Church of England. Until he was fourteen he had attended church three times on Sundays, said his prayers every night and grace after every meal, and read the Scriptures not just dutifully but with zeal. Then he had begun to think, and the progression to atheism was swift. He had never returned to the fold, though there were many who thought, because of how he lived and conducted himself, that he was a strong churchman. Naturally, he did not flaunt his atheism. He continued to put "C. of E." on forms without too many scruples, but he never attended any kind of service, marriage or funeral. Many people had told him that his convictions would return with old age, but they had not yet done so. Mrs. Joliffe thought likewise, which was a mercy. She professed herself an agnostic, not an atheist, so they quibbled gently about names and terms, but neither of them expected anything but oblivion upon their approaching demise. It was not that William expected to answer to his Maker that made him anxious to do his bit so much as his daily answering to himself.

Sighing, William returned to thinking about his flat and the problems of letting it as he had done every night before dropping off to sleep for the last two years, and he drifted into a semiconscious state of warmth and worry. He lay on his back, only his nose and the upper part of his head visible, his arms at his sides inside the bag, and his eyes closed. He may have actually dozed off, or he may not have, but whatever his true state he had immediate violent palpitations when the doorbell rang shrilly through his silent flat. He lifted his head a little, covering his racing heart with a calming hand, and listened. The horrid bell screeched again. William let his head drop back. Carol singers? No one sang. A friend? Utterly impossible. It must be a mistake, and since it was a mistake he was not going to get up. Anger replaced alarm as the bell was rung again. Somebody had their finger down hard on it. But now William's concern was not for the bell—he had already decided nothing would make him answer it—but for the telephone. He held his breath and screwed up his eyes, but his willpower had no effect. The telephone rang, as he had known it would, and since it would not stop until he answered, he would have to get up and answer it. The telephone meant Mrs. Joliffe.

"William?" she said sharply. "There is someone ringing the doorbell. They have been ringing and ringing, you know."

"Yes," said William.

"Aren't you going to answer it?"

"No," said William, and he had to repeat his refusal when the bell interrupted him.

"There it is again," said Mrs. Joliffe. "Really, this is intolerable. If you aren't going to answer it, William, what *are* you going to do, pray?"

"Ignore it," said William.

"Ignore it? Ignore that beastly noise? Well, I have my ear-plugs in and I'm finding it quite impossible to ignore."

"It will stop soon," said William. "Whoever it is will get tired and go away," he added, as the bell rang again for fully thirty seconds.

"Very well, William," said Mrs. Joliffe. "I'm sorry to have troubled you. I ought to have known your reaction. You leave me no alternative but to answer it myself."

"No," said William. "I forbid you. It is my bell."

"I beg your pardon?"

"Don't answer."

"William, it may have escaped your notice, but it is Christmas Day tomorrow. I wish to be at my poor best. How am I to cope if I cannot sleep? There—do you still think they are going to go away? Does it sound as if they are? Answer me, William."

"There is nothing they can do," said William. "The door is locked, they cannot get in. You have nothing to fear."

"I am not in the *least* afraid," said Mrs. Joliffe furiously. "How dare you suggest such a thing? I am simply enraged by the assault on my hearing, which is very precious to me. Listen to that! It is beyond endurance!"

"You will not have much longer to endure," said William. "The average person tires after ten minutes of trying to gain entry."

"I do not wish to hear about average people—average people do not knock on doors on Christmas Eve and go on knocking and ringing and banging when no one answers. It is simpler and quicker to answer."

"It would inevitably lead to a scene," said William, "which would be distasteful."

"William, stop fussing, at once. Go and open that door and tell those hooligans to take themselves off."

"Oh, very well," said William, and slammed the receiver down, glad at least to cut off one source of annoyance.

Trembling, he pulled on his trousers over his pajamas and practiced what he was going to say to whoever was at the door. He was going to be very rude. Without opening the door more than a crack he would ask them what they thought they were doing, disturbing him at that hour of the night. He would say he intended to send for the police if there was any further disturbance. His lips moving, William went to the window before he left his room and peered out, even though he knew he could not possibly see anyone standing below because of the overhang of the balcony on the first floor. All he saw was snow sweeping across Richmond Park in flurries. He dropped the curtain and ran down the four flights of stairs, a light pattering run, into the hall. The wick of the oil heater seemed very low, and William, in spite of his haste, could not prevent himself from giving it a quick, anxious look. It was on the verge of going out, not because there was not enough oil but because the wick needed raising. William patted it. He would attend to it after he had dealt with his enemy.

William opened the door without taking any precaution. The chain was for Mrs. Joliffe's sake—he would never use it, not being in the least afraid of being attacked. He had not weathered two world wars only to be afraid to open his own front door. People were apt to laugh at William's physical courage on the rare occasions he chose to display it. Once, he had told quite a large crowd to keep away while he went into a burning house to rescue a child. They had been most derisory, but William had carried out the dangerous operation and converted them. His life was studded with incidents like that, but always, of course, incognito. All that the world knew was that he had earned the Military Cross twice.

"Now, look here," began William, sharply, but even before he had time to confront whoever was there, the wind had blown the door wide open and rushed with gale force into the hall, and behind him he heard the heater plop. Hastily, William dashed to the heater and turned the fuel control off. It needed only a minute without a flame for the whole house to be filled with oil fumes. When he turned back to the door again, it had been closed. Three feet away, their backs to the door, dripping snow all over the shiny plain black linoleum that Mrs. Joliffe said was the most unsuitable floor covering she had seen in her life, stood two people.

William blinked. His head went down, like a goat's about to butt, and he could think of nothing to say. The outrage that filled him inflicted him with a familiar mental paralysis. They were no longer shapes outside in the dark, to whom he could justifiably be as cheeky as he liked, but people, standing in his hall, in his house.

"Now, look here," William said again, but everything had changed. He was weak. They now possessed an unfair advantage that they did not even know about. "You rang my bell," he found himself saying weakly, looking anywhere but at them.

"We're so sorry to disturb you," a young voice said, "but we wondered if perhaps . . ."

"We saw a light," said another voice, younger still, "in an empty flat . . ."

"We thought if it was to rent . . ."

"No," said William loudly, "it is not to rent."

Encouraged by his own words, he managed to look at the voices, a furtive look, but sufficient. A young man and a very young girl. Both were wet. The young man had his arm round the girl. His gaze now flickering lower, William saw the bulge of the girl's stomach and shivered. He had a horror of pregnant women, especially this kind of pregnant woman. William could remember his own mother's pregnancy, since he was ten when his sister was born. It had been a decent affair. His mother had worn loose flowing garments in dark colors and though her huge stomach had frightened and alarmed him, it had only in certain positions been evident. She did everything possible to avoid standing in such a way as to thrust it forward, as though she were as ashamed as he, and he had been grateful.

This girl was different. She wore a very short dress and coat, both in rich, patterned materials. The material seemed caught under her bust, emphasizing the beginning of the bulge, and clung to its outline. William was careful not to think "disgusting." He had trained himself to do this. Before he retired from the Board of Trade he had been aware of the unreasonable hostility that greeted the young clerks who dared to have long hair or sideboards or any but the most conventional clothes. William's colleagues had expected him to side with them, automatically, but he had been determined not to. These feelings of the over-fifties amounted, he thought, to a kind of hysteria. He made it a point of honor always to be polite and courteous toward these young men, though his natural feelings were not wholly favorable.

It was as well he had bothered to do so, he thought, since the young couple on his doorstep would have brought on an apoplectic fit in most of his generation. They were undoubtedly in the vanguard of fashion. The boy's hair was longer than the girl's, much curled and twisted and obviously dyed. The hair on his head was almost outdone by the hair on his face. His moustache met beard and sideboards in one giant flourish. His garments, like the girl's, were too numerous and gaudy to differentiate. But at least it showed imagination, William decided. They were not drab, nor scruffy, nor in the least dirty. All their clothes gleamed, and their hands were clean even to the fingernails. Also, they smelled pleasantly. Quite distinctly, an aroma strong enough to overcome the oil fumes came from them, and even in the middle of his distress William noted and approved. It was a musky, pungent smell, but William could tell it was neither cheap nor nasty nor covering over something unpleasant. Overcome with his own inquisitiveness, William twitched his nostrils and cleared his throat.

"We're so sorry to have disturbed you," the girl said. "We should have known it wasn't to rent."

"Do you know of anywhere vacant around here?" the young man asked. "Anywhere at all? A room?"

"Oh, let's go," the girl said, "we mustn't bother him." She had her hand on the door handle. "We're so sorry to have disturbed you."

But the young man ignored her. "There is an empty flat, isn't there?" he said aggressively. "Couldn't you let us sleep there for tonight? Please?"

"Impossible," William said, and added, pleased with himself but knowing a second later it was fatal, "there is no furniture, nothing at all."

"We don't need furniture," the young man said. "A floor would be fine—anywhere dry. We slept on a floor last night. Please?"

"Out of the question," said William.

"Let's go," the girl said, "and thank you so much."

She opened the door, and again the wind hit the hall. Clumsily, she wrapped her coat more tightly round her swollen body and turned her collar up, and held out an arm to the young man, who took it and thrust her hand into his pocket. William saw that at the bottom of the steps, his steps, there was a suitcase. The man picked it up. The girl waved her free arm at him and smiled and nodded through the dark, and then, hardly had she turned away from him, she fell. Her feet seemed to whoosh up from beneath her, and she let out a cry and fell on her back, dragging the young man and the suitcase on top of her.

William, nimble as ever, was at her side in a second, so light on his feet that he hardly touched the ice. He felt the

wind tearing at his bare throat and stabbing his chest between the buttons of his pajama jacket. He looked back,
afraid that his front door would be slammed shut, but it was
open, the light glowing comfortingly.

"Dear me," he said, "you fell. Dreadfully slippy. Are you
hurt? Can you get up?"

She was crying, naturally, but she could and did get up,
and, clinging to the young man, she sobbed against his coat,
but said, barely audibly, "Thank you—I'm quite all right—
thank you."

The young man cradled her head against his chest and
stroked her wet hair and stared accusingly at William, who
wondered if he could get back into his house now, before
the inevitable happened, get back and lock the door and
take care not to put the light on in the empty flat again.

"I say," he said, "your wife has had a shock. I think she
should come into my house and rest a little, don't you? My
name is William Ellis Bone. This way."

Two

It never even entered William's head to take his unlooked-for visitors into his own flat. No one had ever been in his flat except for Pullen and Mrs. Joliffe. Pullen he had wanted to come, shyly, and Mrs. Joliffe he had been unable to avoid. Taking one step every five minutes, she had hauled her painful way up, and he had been obliged to entertain her with tea and biscuits. It was not that he was ashamed of where he lived but rather that it was too intimate, too revealing. This had always been the trouble. Even at home, even at university, he had kept his room to himself, meeting friends anywhere but there. He did not want them passing comments, saying this is nice that is not, he did not want them fingering and touching and staring. Such behavior—which other people seemed positively to expect—reduced him to a paroxysm of nerves. It was rather as though he had been asked to strip.

The young couple were welcome to think what they liked. At a run, William led them into the hall and up the stairs and into the totally empty flat. He left them standing in the middle of the room while he spent a frantic half hour running up and down stairs carrying first an electric fire, then three chairs, then a carpet, then a bottle of port and three glasses into the empty flat. Excitedly, he grouped the chairs together in front of the fire and spread the carpet between them, and poured the port and, handing it round, said repeatedly, "Quite cozy, isn't it, amazing, in such a short time, really very cozy, though of course with the ceiling cork-lined and a fiber-glass lining in the roof one is getting twice the heat, twice the heat. To you, then, er, an excellent Christmas and may you feel no effects from your fall."

"Thank you so much," the girl said. "You're being very kind indeed. I do appreciate it."

William saw the young man walking round the flat, glass in hand, eyeing it.

"Of course, it isn't finished yet," he said, "so I can't rent it. There's an awful lot to be done, an awful lot."

"Looks all right to me," the young man said. "Do you mind if I smoke?"

"No," said William, who did mind very much and mentally made Rule 10 "Nonsmokers only."

"What are you thinking of charging?" the young man asked.

"Oh, no point in considering that yet," said William, laughing. "It's not finished, you see, very far from finished, so I haven't got round to that. More port, my dear?"

"No, thank you," she said. "My name is Sophie, and my husband is Alexander—Alex and Sophie Hill. Alex, do come and sit down. Mr. Bone will think you terribly rude."

Alex came and sat down, and William, who before had wished he would do just that, now wished he would go on walking about. He slid his eyes away as Sophie reached out and took Alex's hand.

"Well, I mustn't keep you," William said. He was ashamed when Sophie stood up at once and reached for her coat.

"You've been very kind," she said, smiling, and William blinked rapidly and thought what a very lovely girl she was, so old-fashioned and sweet.

"We're desperate," Alex said abruptly. "If you don't let us stay we shall have to walk about all night, and in Sophie's condition it might be fatal."

"Oh!" gasped Sophie. "Really—Mr. Bone—you must excuse him—Alex! How can you be so embarrassing!"

"Shut up," shouted Alex, and William flinched. "It's the truth, isn't it? Do you think I'm going to pass up the chance to kip here just because of your bloody good manners?"

"Yes, it's getting late," William said, making a lot of noise pulling his chair about.

"Can we stay?" asked Alex. Sophie closed her eyes and seemed to sway.

"So sorry I can't help," William said, his hands full, moving toward the door, trying and failing to knock the light off with his elbow. Somehow, in a blind panic, he got the door onto the landing open and stood with his foot propping it wide for his visitors to go through. But they did not come. The cane chair he was carrying cut into the palms of William's hands as he watched Alex move the carpet into the middle of the room, then remove his scarf and roll it into a pillow, then his coat, which he tenderly placed on top of the carpet. Fully dressed, he lay down and, pulling his coat up to his ears, he said, "Good night. Merry Christmas."

"No," William said, "this is ridiculous."

Alex snored.

"No," William said. "I don't want any unpleasantness, but this is my flat and I do not wish you to stay in it."

He was addressing himself to the prone Alex, but only Sophied replied.

"I do apologize," she whispered. "I am so sorry—I do wish . . ." And she began to cry again.

"Please," William said, "don't distress yourself."

"But it's my fault," Sophie said. "It was my idea. Alex said there won't be any flats here, it's much too posh, even if there was one we could never afford it, but I insisted, I said let's just walk up and down once, and then when this light came on and we saw this flat empty, I said, I insisted, I made him ring your bell and try, I wanted him to at least try, it's such a beautiful house and it would be heaven, and I'm so sorry this had to happen, are you really going to call the police, must you, right away? I promise we will go in the morning, faithfully, before you're even awake, you won't even know we've gone, it would be so kind if you could possibly . . ."

William felt wretched. He sat up and held his head in his hands and wished he had not so positively given up aspirin. Unhappily, he had previously decided to break his normal routine for Christmas Day and he could not therefore find solace, as he normally did after a troubled night, in plunging at once into his Japanese Linguaphone lesson. Nor was he going to run down to the Round Pond and back—that too he had forsworn in honor of the festivities. All a mistake. He ought to have stuck to his daily pattern and not bothered about feeling mean-spirited. Who knew? Only he.

If they had fallen asleep at once and, as Sophie had promised, disappeared with the dawn, he might have been able to put the incident at the back of his mind till the day was over. But they had not. The moment he had reached his bed, the activity had begun. There had been the thundering of feet up and down to the bathroom, the flushing of the lavatory time after time, and the singing of the suddenly wide-awake Alex, carol after carol, all loud and tuneless. Worst of all, one of them had had a bath. The water had cascaded through the cistern until William was reduced to a gibbering wreck, completely unable to shut out the noise. There were tears in his eyes when, expectedly, Mrs. Joliffe rang.

"Well, William?"

"I can't explain," he said. "Something dreadful has happened."

"Is this your house, William?"

"Yes, but—"

"Then you are master. Deal with this disgraceful noise at once."

Luckily, at that moment there was a final bang, and then silence.

"I think everything will be all right now," William said.

For Mrs. Joliffe, everything remained still for the rest of the night. William thought of her sleeping and envied her. He did not sleep. The violent noises had subsided, but now sounds more disturbing and insidious began to invade his room. There was gentle laughter—laughter, in their position!—and shushings that dissolved into giggles.

The giggles reminded him again of his sister Frances, who had giggled her days away throughout her childhood. He had envied her terribly, he who found even a smile difficult, and all laughter except the feigned impossible. There were between this Sophie and his Frances many resemblances, and William knew he was being influenced by this against his better judgment. Perhaps if Frances had not died so young the likeness would not have bothered him—perhaps if her giggles had had time to fade into the cackling of middle age he would not have found them so attractive. The whole notion made William irritable. He had had no romantic attachment to Frances. She had not been his ideal of womanhood and he had had no incestuous thoughts. His feelings when she had died at the age of twenty-five had been fury at the waste. Thinking back, he had not shed a tear. He had instead thought back to the slim, fragile, easily merry Frances and felt only sad that such miseries as himself were left. Did Sophie, like Frances, deserve enshrining in such melancholy? He could not even begin to be sure. She was perhaps stronger, freer, more the child of her age than

Frances could ever have been. Turning on his side, William tried to stop thinking of the dead, though these days if one was to think about anyone there were more dead than living to choose from. The giggles had stopped.

Then, unmistakably, though William was not conversant with them, came sounds of passion, which shocked and frightened him. Did people who were pregnant have sexual intercourse? William was immensely distressed at the thought. And on his carpet, with no curtains at the windows —it was too much. William breathed deeply and tried to be practical. It was all temporary. Looking on the bright side, as he had trained himself to do, he had learned a lot. Tomorrow—no, not tomorrow, being what it was, but as soon as was decently possible—he must ring Pullen and report that cork-lined ceilings might make rooms warmer but they were not an effective insulation against noise. Something else must be devised at once, whatever the cost, whatever the upheaval. The minute the shops opened he must also remedy another grave error—he must buy muslin and have curtains made for the empty flat so that its secret could be kept from rapacious eyes.

Feeling stiff and aching everywhere, William got up and washed at his kitchen sink. He felt shy about using the bathroom when they might come. He washed in cold water and then in hot, and shaved and combed his hair and felt marginally better. Since it was Christmas Day and he was to have lunch with Mrs. Joliffe and her daughter, Germaine, and the daughter's husband, Homer, he put on his Civil Service suit and a clean white shirt. Then he made himself a cup of China tea and went and looked out of his window. All William's windows were heavily draped, though Mrs. Joliffe wanted to know who but the birds could see in at that height? She also said William must be lying about having bought the house for the view, as he took such care to exclude it. But the net curtains were no hindrance to William.

He was able to look through them as though they were not there, and yet knowing they were there made him feel comfortable.

He stood now and looked, his spectacles misted slightly by the steam rising from his very hot tea. The sky was gray and enormous, dominating the park and squashing to nothing the houses round about. There were sky days and tree days. William had seen the trees, green and mushrooming everywhere, quite obliterate the sky, forcing it into the humiliating position of having to peep through gaps. The snowfall had been heavy. Now, at seven in the morning, the ground and bushes were covered and unmarked, and the long ledges of white so precisely balanced on the bare branches of the trees had not yet begun to fall. There was a tiny ping against William's window—a single drop of rain, and then another. William was glad he did not have to go out.

His tea, in a mug with lovebirds on it, was restoring him. He wandered through into his kitchen and looked out the window there at his garden. Once, all these gardens of this row of houses had been a rich man's orchard, and now that brick walls split it up, the fruit trees did their best to fight the artificial division. Over each garden wall branches entwined themselves with branches on the other side, and in May, at blossom time, they grew together. William was excited by this. Even now, in the snow, tree touched tree, and the walls below, hidden in any case, were forgotten. A crowd of birds were already on the bird table, even though it was not yet light. The table was Mrs. Joliffe's concern, but William contributed to its upkeep.

His bed put away, William closed the door of that room. In the mornings, it tended to annoy him. He could hear Mrs. Joliffe asking him when on earth he was going to have that carpet fitted that he had talked so much about. He did not know. Nor did he know when he was going to have the walls painted or proper curtains put up. He knew it was a joke, really—he had been getting these two rooms ready ever since he had moved in nearly forty years ago. Nevertheless, Mrs. Joliffe was mistaken in thinking he made no progress at all. He did. He had almost completed his kitchen–living room. There were patterned tiles on the floor and a lovely screen in front of the sink, and armchairs designed by Pullen in front of the fire. He didn't actually have a table to eat from yet, but he was near it, very near it. It ought to be here before another Christmas came. Had he said that last Christmas? William expected he had. Where had he said it? Here? Had he spent last Christmas here, or at his nephew's, or with Pullen? His memory of each individual Christmas was sharp, but the dates were hazy. Christmas 1968 had, he decided, been spent with Pullen, and very unpleasant it had been, too. William had thought the idea was for Pullen and him to have an old-style traditional Christmas together, but Pullen had thought quite the opposite. Apparently he intended to abolish Christmas in an orgy of drinking and dirty-story telling. Instead of the turkey and trimmings that William had a weakness for, instead of carols and all that jolly nonsense, there had been bottles of whisky and gin and disgusting unfestive snacks. William shuddered at the blatant trickery of his friend. Christian he might not be, but Christmas he loved and saw no harm in. At least Agnes Joliffe knew how to celebrate the festival. Her style was perhaps cramped now by circumstances, but the glory of her country-house Christmas parties was not quite forgotten. William remembered with excitement the large house full of guests, bursting with holly and goodies, and outside, truly, the snow coming in from the fens. He would almost rather have nothing if he could not have that.

William breakfasted off fresh orange juice, squeezed from two Jaffa oranges, wholemeal bread made by Mrs. Joliffe, and more China tea. He had it standing up looking out his window, watching the light grow stronger. All the time he was eating and drinking, he eyed the presents he had wrapped the night before, and tried, by concentrating on them, to forget what had happened since. There were four presents. One for Mrs. Joliffe—a Victorian pincushion; one for Germaine—a cameo brooch; one for Homer—a crystal paperweight; and one for Mrs. Wood who cleaned the house. Hers was the largest—a big box of biscuits. William intended to creep along to her house, or rather the house where she had a room in the basement, and leave it on the doorstep. Any confrontation was to be avoided. The other things he would unfortunately have to hand over and watch the recipients unwrap. A pity.

It was now eight o'clock and William was uneasy. In contrast to the noise half the night, there was now complete hush. It occurred to William, with a lovely warm leap, that perhaps he had not heard everything he thought he had heard, perhaps they had, after all, gone? Hesitantly, he went out onto the landing and listened. Nothing. He tiptoed down, feeling very guilty, and listened again outside their door. Why did he say *their* door to himself? It was *not* their door, it was *his* door. Very quietly, he prodded the door with his finger. It moved. They had not locked themselves in. William cleared his throat, and waited. He tapped gently. He stuck his head round the door and said, "I say?" After five minutes, during which he got cramp in his foot from keeping it half in and half out of the little hall, he stepped right inside and knocked authoritatively on the inner door. There was no reply. William pushed that door too, and fearfully looked in.

They were both quite soundly and unfeignedly asleep, curled up under Alex's damp overcoat (it was only with a great effort that William used names to himself—he always thought in statements—"They are curled up under Alex's damp overcoat"). Sophie's hair tumbled over the coat and hid her face, and both pairs of feet stuck out—stockinged—from the coat. The light in the room seemed unaccountably rosy, until William realized how very warm the atmosphere was and looked and saw that the electric fire was still on. It had been on all night. It was not their flat, nor their fire, and yet they had used his electricity, for which they could not, on their own admission, pay. If William needed any spur, that gave it to him. He shut the door, shut the other door, ran up to his own flat, snatched a piece of notepaper and a pen, and sat down at once to compose a note.

William wrote with great speed and fluency. He never felt diffident on paper. He could say anything to anyone so long as he could write it down and leave it for his enemy to collect. All his working life he had used the Note as his greatest weapon, and even now it was his main means of communication. Mrs. Joliffe resisted this, but he continued to leave notes for her on the hall shelf even if he had been speaking to her only a moment before on the telephone. When she challenged him on the patent absurdity of this kind of behavior, William giggled, wagged a finger and said, "No harm in putting things down."

He headed his note "Christmas Day 8.30 A.M.," but did not put his address. One hoped they knew where they were, though on the present showing one wondered. He went straight into it.

> I should be obliged (though I rather think the obligation is on your side) if you would vacate my rooms before midday (or earlier: you did promise to leave at dawn, however). Please leave the door open so that the cigarette fumes may escape (they darken the paintwork which, as you have probably observed, is freshly done, alas). Please unplug the electric fire. I should be glad to have a forwarding address in order that I may forward the bill for the fuel you have used, which I shall calculate on the basis that one unit costs 5¼d (which I think is the fairest way when there is not a separate meter).
>
> W.E.B.

William blotted his note and without reading it—such was his confidence—folded it into four and wrote "Alexander Hill" on the outside. Then he ran down the stairs and, through force of habit, left the note propped up on the hall shelf. Halfway back up the stairs, he paused. The note might not be noticed there, since these intruders did not know where to look. Indeed, they might not go down the stairs at all. However agonizing, that had to be faced. Quickly William pattered down the stairs again and, taking the note, ran back up again and slipped it under the middle flat door. But the hall inside—a mere square between doors—was dark. The note might get stood on. Frowning, William opened the door, retrieved his note, and rapidly pushed it under the inner door. He could do no more.

Quite exhausted, William decided after all to get out of the house for a little while. It would be politic. He was not due down at Mrs. Joliffe's until twelve-thirty, and he could not relax here until the Hills had gone. Glad that he had made the decision, William put on his jacket and raincoat and his dark-blue trilby and, picking up Mrs. Wood's box of biscuits, stole out of his house with it. At the top of the steps, he paused to pull on his gloves and snap the press-stud fasteners shut. He paused again at the bottom of the steps to look up at the front of his house, as a husband might look back at his wife. The façade had changed a great deal since William had first seen it. In 1933 the paintwork on the door and windows had been a virulent, hard green. Now it was white. The glass in the downstairs window had been cracked and filthy. William, when he renewed it, had restored the sixteen small panes that the proportions demanded. The stone was resanded, the brick repointed. The door was painted yellow and the number—109—charmingly drawn on the glass above. Two large urns stood on either side of the door, filled with seasonal flowers and plants, and the tiny front garden held a perfect magnolia tree.

Happily, William trotted off, sneaking another look before he got to the end of the street. None of the other houses
in the street had been as lovingly cared for as his, but there
was a general air of wealth and grace that William liked.
He knew hardly any of his neighbors but trusted that none
of them minded his handiwork. He had not vulgarized anything. Doubtful about his own taste—though knowing he at
least had taste—William had relied heavily on Pullen, who,
though he became testy about this reliance, had done a
splendid job. Perhaps more people, seeing and admiring
No. 109, would ask Pullen for help, and they would end up
renaming the street Pullen Street. William laughed and dis-
lodged a drop from the end of his nose. He turned the corner, walked very quickly down the next street, turned again,
crossed the road, and immediately came to quite another
area. William was now in a desperate hurry. He did not like
Mrs. Wood's street. At a gallop, he reached her house, scut-
tered down the steps, banged the biscuits outside the door
beside the dirty milk bottle, and ran away.

William returned home the long way round. His feet got
very wet going through the park, but it was preferable to
retracing his footsteps through the mean, ugly street at the
end of which Mrs. Wood lived. Mrs. Wood herself was almost excessively clean, but where she lived was filthy. William felt sorry for her, but so terrified was he of his own pity
that he never mentioned it to Mrs. Wood, who certainly
never mentioned it to him. They both pretended, it seemed
to William, that she lived somewhere else, and that was
quite satisfactory. William was unhappy enough with the
servant relationship as it was without having it more complicated. Mrs. Joliffe did not know what he was talking
about, or so she said when the subject had once come up
and William had unwisely mumbled out his difficulties. But
then Agnes had been born to have servants. Her very bearing was regal and imperious and saved her the volumes of

words William needed. It had often struck him that he looked like a servant himself—small, thin and hunched. He flinched when spoken directly to and was apt to give obsequious gestures that he could not help. He had never in his life been able to command anyone and had inevitably ended up doing everything for himself, whereas Agnes never, at one time, did anything if there was someone else to do it for her. Nor had she basically changed. Mrs. Wood, who was supposed only to clean the stairs and bathrooms and outside yard once a week, inevitably ended up spring-cleaning Mrs. Joliffe's flat. Agnes said the poor creature liked the work—it was hardly worth her while to come for what William required, especially when she found that he had usually got down on his knees and done it all himself. She was, she said, doing the woman a favor. William thought this rich, coming from a Socialist, but he did not say so because it would lead to another political diatribe that had long since ceased to interest him. All he knew was that having Mrs. Wood at all made him uneasy. The only reason he did have her was out of a vague feeling that he ought, that it was seemly, since he was a man and men ostensibly knew nothing about cleaning. Sometimes he wondered if having Mrs. Wood was not his way of doing his bit. He gave her a pound a week for the one morning she came, and since she came at ten and was gone by midday he thought she was doing well. In fact, more than well. There was no getting away from it—he ought to have spoken to her years ago about what she ought to do and what she did. The idea had been that if the body and workings of the house were thoroughly cleaned by a professional once a week, then he would be able to keep it up himself the rest of the time. But the professional turned out to be himself and Mrs. Wood the keeper-up. In order to cover up her sloppy work, William was obliged to scrub till his back ached. It was ridiculous, it was foolish, but he could not bring himself either to speak out or to write a note. The woman was a slovenly nuisance, but she was a servant of sorts, not one of his own breed—though William was in doubt as to what that was—and he could not communicate with her. He continued to say, "Ah! Mrs. Wood—ready to get down to it, eh?" when she came, and "Ah! Mrs. Wood—finished already, jolly good" when she went.

The house looked the same. William opened the door and went in. The hall was delightfully warm, and the house smelled of roast turkey. After he had wiped his feet carefully, William went on up the stairs, very cautiously. There was not a sound. He continued on his way, head down, deep in thought, and did not see Sophie until he was right up to his door.

"Good heavens," William said.

"I'm so sorry," Sophie said. "It's about your note."

William lowered his eyes. She stood directly in his way, her hands clasped high above her stomach in a position doubtless comfortable at that time but one which looked uncomfortable and specially adopted for pleading.

"There isn't really anything to be said," William said, keeping his eyes down.

"May I talk to you about it? Please? I'm so sorry," she said.

Three

>>>>>>>>

THE PRESENTS were still in his hands, though he had been seated fully five minutes, and though they were very small William looked weighed down, making Agnes Joliffe sigh. The man was such a dear, dear man, but such an irritant, such a fool. She supposed he aroused women's maternal instincts, and certainly she had always wanted to protect and comfort him. When young, of course, William had also aroused other, less philanthropic instincts, not only in her but in many others, but she did not think he knew about that. In his Cambridge days he had been so handsome— poetic, dreamlike, a shy, ruffled, gentle sprite that quite melted girls' hearts away. Seeing William in army uniform about to go off to Flanders had been one of the most anguished moments of Agnes' life. It made her see the war, instantly, as criminal while others still thought it heroic.

But there he was—old, like her. Bent and wrinkled and unromantic. Had William ever kissed a woman? Sometimes Agnes thought that without speculation boredom would have stifled her long ago. She had never asked William if he had spurned her only to give in to others. Had some frail, waiflike creature wrapped her thin arms around him and kissed him? Perhaps, but she did not think so. William would have shown it, somehow. No, she preferred to believe that he was going to his grave a virgin and that she alone had ever touched him. William would never know the joys that she had known and that even now, at a distance, Agnes remembered with pride. She had had lovers in plenty. Well, four was plenty, surely, though hardly a surfeit, she agreed. None like William, of course—all like Matthew, her husband, large and strong and domineering. William she had saved, then never caught. What would an affair with William have been like? It was only recently that Agnes had started to use the past tense. Now it was quite out of the question. Bodies had had their day. But hearts, minds, emotions? Should William propose tomorrow she would accept and glory in their marriage. Except he would not propose, nor in any way reveal the depth of his feeling for her. She was lucky to be near him at all, to see or hear him every day. She tried to smile at him encouragingly, but he dropped his eyes and would not look at her. He liked her to bully him, to take him to task, be unpleasant, and would allow her no other role. He wanted to be reprimanded, chided, but not sympathized with or soothed. And in return he gave her nothing—she was not allowed to write his part. If she should ever weep in his presence, she would never see him again.

"Now, William," she said sharply, "relax and have a glass of sherry and tell me all about it before Germaine arrives."

"Merry Christmas," William said miserably, holding his packets out.

"Thank you, William. Put them beside the tree. We will all open them later. Quickly, tell me, what silly thing have you done?"

"I have let the flat," William said.

"Oh. Have you." Agnes wanted to giggle at his air of

tragedy, but knew he required her to be a stern authoritarian figure, so she said instead, "To whom?"

"A young couple," William whispered. "A Mr. and Mrs. Alexander Hill."

"A *young* couple? In your house?" asked Agnes, horrified.

"Yes," said William, "but the lease is very short—only six months in the first instance."

"William," said Agnes solemnly, "you are fidgeting. I see you have not told me all." Really, the way in which he liked her to speak was becoming very trying.

"There is a baby due," William said, "in March."

"William! What have you done?"

William put down his empty sherry glass and shrank back into the dark-blue velvet wing chair. The wings cast a shadow over his face and relieved the glare from Mrs. Joliffe's furious eyes. She sat opposite him, elegant and severe in gray silk, her cane clasped so tightly that her knuckles were white. She sat on the very edge of her chair as though ready to spring at William. In a minute he knew she would stamp her good foot and try to make him answer, and he searched desperately for an explanation sufficiently feasible to satisfy her. He had no excuses worth offering. He was as appalled as she. All he wanted to do, in a childish, spiteful way, was to tell her that it was all her fault—she had made him answer the door, she had made him let Sophie in, and once Sophie was in, what could he have done?

But Mrs. Joliffe had not seen Sophie, and even if she had seen her she might not understand William's agony. It was not how Sophie looked—so frail and vulnerable—nor her condition, but something to do with the way she apologized all the time, so that instantly one wanted to reassure her, tell her there was nothing to be sorry for, everything was perfectly all right. She ought not to have worries, it was too upsetting even to think of her being bothered by them. There ought to be someone who dealt with them for her.

"She's a very charming young lady," William croaked. "You will like her. I hope you will be good friends, she will be company for you."

"When I wish you to choose my company I shall tell you," Mrs. Joliffe said fiercely. "Her niceness—and you are not a good judge of character, William—is beside the point. The point is, will they be suitable tenants? I thought you had decided—and heaven knows it takes you long enough to decide anything at all—I thought you had decided the flat was not suitable for a married couple?"

"I may have been mistaken," William muttered. "They seem to be delighted."

"So you have fallen a victim to flattery, William?" said Mrs. Joliffe, sneering most dreadfully, while inside Agnes squealed with glee.

Sophie *had* said many nice things. She had told him how she used to walk across the park with her father before he died, on sunny Sunday mornings, and he had pointed this very house out as the house where he had been born. William had raised his head at that, but Sophie had smiled at him most innocently. He knew the history of his house—it would be unthinkable not to—and he knew that it had passed to the two maiden ladies from whom he had bought it after the death of the previous owner, Lord Jonquil. Sophie prattled on about the romantic associations and how she had always wanted to live in Jonquil House—oh, excuse her, it was no longer called that, was it? But she felt William had made it look as it used to look then, as her father had told her it looked when he lived there, before his aunts took it over, before he and his mother and sisters moved to Gloucestershire, to the Hall.

"She is a very well-connected young woman," William said, but shamefaced. Mrs. Joliffe was so socialist he felt she verged on communism.

"What has that got to do with it?" snapped Mrs. Joliffe.

"I suppose you've let them have it for tuppence-halfpenny a week, without a thought for the consequences, just because they're impoverished aristocrats. They are impoverished, I take it, since they have to beg round the streets for somewhere to sleep?"

"Yes," said William, "temporarily."

"How do you know it's temporary? What does the young man do? You haven't mentioned him, I note. What does he do? Is his blood the blue shade you so admire? Well, William?"

"I haven't talked to the young man," William said.

"Then is the lease in the woman's name?"

"No," said William.

"In both their names?"

"No," said William.

"Then it *is* in his name?"

"It doesn't exist yet," William said defensively.

"Don't prevaricate. It is to be in his name, yet you haven't talked to him about it and you don't know his profession. It's as well, William, that it is Christmas Day or I should be obliged to be very angry indeed with you."

They sat and looked at each other, William hunched and penitent, Mrs. Joliffe upright and virtuous. Germaine, looking through the window at them, smiled. Here they are, friends for over fifty years, and yet they cannot even eat together without my presence. Always she was rung up by her mother and told, "I wish to ask William to dine with me, Germaine. Will Wednesday week be convenient?" Or William: "I say, Germaine, I wondered if you and Homer could dine with your mother and me at Overton's on Thursday?" If Germaine said no, as she had often done in exasperation, the excursion to Overton's was canceled and she had the unpleasant sense of spoiling their fun.

She let herself in with her own key and put it carefully away in her bag before she closed the door. William did not really approve of her having a key—he feared she might drop it somewhere and a stranger would then have access to his precious house. It grew yearly more precious, as far as Germaine could see. Since his retirement—what on earth had William done anyway, she must remember to ask—the house had taken on an incredible importance. Her mother had acquired the ground-floor flat only through sheer tenacity and the shameless exploitation of William's inability to say no to a direct request. It was not, as he explained to Germaine, that her mother was not the perfect tenant as well as one of his few lifelong friends—it was simply a matter of looking at the problem in perspective. Germaine had understood at once, which was clever of her. William did not want her mother to become bedridden in his flat. He did not want the responsibility for her. Who, had thought Germaine, did?

She smelled the turkey cooking and other tantalizing aromas. Her mother was doing all right. She could still cook an excellent Christmas dinner singlehanded, which Germaine certainly could not. If left to their own devices, which they had never yet been for this very reason, Germaine and Homer would have bunged a supermarket turkey into the oven, probably with its entrails still frozen inside, and hoped for the best. They did not fuss about Christmas, not like William and Mrs. Joliffe, who were like children with their presents and trees and decorations. To give them tokens of some sort or another was unkindness itself, but as usual it was all she had been able to manage.

Germaine shouted, "I'm here—won't be a minute," and went into her mother's bedroom, where she took off her coat and laid it on the bed, which was very neatly made. Germaine's own bed had been left unmade, with Homer in it. This bedroom was a boudoir, intimate and rich, full of materials that invited stroking and warm woods that glowed with polish. At the dressing table, Germaine picked up a heavy, scrolled silver hand mirror and looked at herself. Normal. The glass was loose but the mirror beautiful. She picked up her straw basket and went next door and kissed her mother and William.

"Merry Christmas, my love," Alex said, smiling, and burrowed deeper under his overcoat. Sophie stood at the window, breathing on it.

"Better get up," she said. She turned away from the window, really very happy, and went over to the suitcase in the corner.

"That's right," said Alex, "you unpack—make it look ours."

"It isn't yet."

"But it soon will be. That old bloke's so soft you can do anything with him."

"His note wasn't soft."

"You fixed that. Temper, temper, that's what that was. You're clever, Sophie love, very clever, and I shan't forget it."

"He might not like us to hang pictures," Sophie said doubtfully, holding a portrait of herself that Alex had drawn.

"Bugger that," Alex said. "If I'm going to take the lease of this place I'll want to hang my own bloody pictures on the wall."

Very carefully, Sophie hammered in a nail with her shoe and hung the portrait above the Adam fireplace.

"Christ," said Alex, "that smell!"

"They are all having dinner below," Sophie said. "The old man and whoever lives on the ground floor and a fat woman who just arrived. Turkey and stuffing and all that."

"You'd think they would invite us," Alex said. "Some people have no Christmas spirit."

"I wish I had some holly to put in this jug," Sophie said,

and set the brown pot on the mantelpiece and looked at it wistfully.

"I'll get you some," Alex said. "As soon as I'm up, I'll go into the park and nick some holly, don't you worry about that. This room will be bursting with holly."

As it had been at home, always, and not holly bought in a market but holly gathered by the gardener and brought in red-berried armfuls. They had had the yule-log bit, and the villagers-singing-round-their-fire bit, and the walking-to-church-en-masse-on-Christmas-morning bit. Huge Christmas tree, presents galore, groaning table, crackers and charades and parties. All horrible, all without feeling. When she was little she supposed she had enjoyed it, got overexcited and been sick with the rest, but then she had grown to hate it. It epitomized what she loathed most about her family—the big front, the façade that was never allowed to crack, united we stand, the perfect family, and divided we fall. All the quarrels were behind locked doors in darkened rooms, all the poison was stoppered with smiles and charm. That was what she had given up. The tension and strains had gone with the creature comforts, and now, whatever else she had, she had *naturalness*. Alex would never pretend. He did not know what humbug was. She had seen Mr. Bone hating him, watched Mr. Bone keeping his end up when what he wanted to do and say was fuck off and get out. She understood the Mr. Bones of this world—they deserved what they got. She was far happier with the penniless Alex than she would have been with any one of the legions of young men that had passed through her mother's house.

Alex didn't get up. He stayed where he was, and fell asleep again, and Sophie sang softly to herself as she went on unpacking. The case was mostly full of clothes, gay and cheerful clothes, but at the bottom were some books, paperbacks, and some picture postcards and a long frieze depicting the assassination of John Kennedy that Alex had

worked on night and day for a week. Sophie spread everything out, her brows furrowed. She was always amazed at
how many things they had after she had thought they had
nothing. For now, she hung their clothes on the wire hang-
ers Alex had borrowed from the dry cleaners and strung
them along the curtain rails, which she reached with difficulty. The postcards she pinned on the doors, and the frieze
she stuck on the longest wall with the old bits of Sellotape
that were still hanging from it. Pleased at the effect, she
went into the kitchen, half expecting to find the larder full,
such had been their luck so far. But it was empty and
smelled strongly of emulsion paint. Hungry, Sophie went to
Alex's bed and, searching in his pocket, found some peanuts
and a tube of throat tablets, and helped herself. Alex's arm
came out and pulled her down and she snuggled up to him
and slept, too, with a tablet hanging stickily from her lower
lip.

"Homer should be here," Germaine repeated. "Perhaps I
should just ring him again. I can't understand it."
William saw Mrs. Joliffe compress her lips firmly, and felt
for her. It was enough to have to endure Homer himself
without his revolting bad manners, for which Germaine
constantly found explanations. William had never known
Homer not be late, yet however much he and Mrs. Joliffe
prepared themselves for it, they were always taken by surprise and mortified accordingly.
"Shall we just start?" Germaine suggested. "Homer won't
mind. Nothing like that bothers him."
"Sitting down often makes people come," William said
nervously. "It has a magical effect."
"No," said Mrs. Joliffe magnificently, "we will wait. No,
Germaine, do not telephone. I should not like Homer to be
in any way hurried."
William, whose stomach groaned, composed himself to

wait yet longer. In principle he was with Mrs. Joliffe, and he ought not to mind the practicing of a little discipline to show himself with her. But though he entered eagerly into the conversation she chose to initiate, his inside protested. It whined that he would get another ulcer, and that brought back visions of sitting it out, which was how he dealt with his ulcers. William's theory was that the worse you felt the more vital it was not to go to bed. What he did was arrange everything he might need around a chair and then sit in the chair covered with a blanket and remain there till he was better. This treatment had never failed, but though William, having thought of it, wished to mention it, he knew it was not a suitable topic for Christmas Day.

Homer Hooper knew no such restraints. A large, creased, gray American, he began the minute he eventually arrived to describe to the assembled throng the state of his bowels, with which he had been having some trouble. William blinked rapidly, and twitched a little, and was furious. He and Mrs. Joliffe had discussed this. They knew Homer was simply trying to shock and embarrass them, and both had agreed that they must not be either shocked or embarrassed. Silently they hung on to their pact and put up with Homer and his drink until they could decently get him into the dining room, where, being excessively greedy, he would subside into his trough.

"I discovered," William said, "a fascinating thing yesterday, frightfully interesting."

"What?" asked Mrs. Joliffe agreeably.

"It was while I was booking my passage to the Algarve—" William began.

"Are you going on holiday?" asked Agnes, disbelieving. "Think of the risk, William," she added acidly.

"Yes, but these things have to be risked," said William cheerfully. "I'm going by sea to Lisbon."

"On one of those beastly ferries?"

"Some are quite reasonable, I'm told. I've taken care to choose a cabin to myself, of course."

"Of course," echoed Agnes. "It wouldn't do to mix with the rabble. A cabin to yourself—how posh."

"That's it!" said William excitedly. "That's precisely my discovery. Now, do you know the origin of the word 'posh'?"

"A nasty word," said Agnes. "I thought you would understand I spoke with distaste."

"It's P.O.S.H., you see," said William. "Port Out, Starboard Home—do you see? It dates from Edwardian times, when those who had traveled by sea knew that the most comfortable position on the outward voyage—because of the sun and winds and so forth—was on the port side, whereas—"

"We understand, William," said Agnes. "An interesting derivation, I suppose, but as usual the perversion from the original meaning is far more interesting. 'Posh' is such an absurd word, don't you agree?"

"No," said William. "I think its connotation's apt."

"Why?"

But before William could continue there was a loud crash on the ceiling above. Everyone paused and looked up, even Homer. William paled, and carefully put down his knife and fork, and began to rise.

"I think—" he began.

"No, William," snapped Mrs. Joliffe. "Sit down."

"Whatever was it?" asked Germaine.

"William has let the middle flat," Mrs. Joliffe said, "but he does not wish to discuss it."

"Well, well, well," said Homer, grinning at William in a slimy fashion, as though some rather nasty revelation had just been made.

They all began to eat again, but now there was total silence. The joy had gone out of it for William, and he could not embark on his monologue. He ate a little, out of politeness, but his senses were totally occupied with listening for further sounds of disaster above. He chewed unhappily, wincing as the feet began marching backward and forward across his head, and putting a hand over his eyes as the water began to run in the bathroom above. It was a distant roar, but caused as much anguish to William as if it had been pouring over him. Tactfully, Mrs. Joliffe left him alone, pushing plum pudding silently into his vision, and mercifully not asking him what kind of helping he wanted. Homer belched and laughed gently to himself, and Germaine fidgeted under her mother's warning glare. The bath water finished running, a door slammed, and they rose to go for their coffee.

William and Mrs. Joliffe had a glass of port while Homer slept between them and Germaine heroically did the washing up. It was her annual contribution to the Christmas dinner and made her feel better about not having shopped or helped to cook it. She sat in the kitchen for a long time smoking before she began, and the whole process took her four times as long as it need have done. Even then, she only washed and dried, and put nothing away, claiming she did not know where anything went. She liked to make claims like that to emphasize her complete separation from her mother.

Homer snored, but did not interfere with the enjoyment of the port. William very quickly felt rather drunk, and, as was his habit when drunk, he began to get time mixed up. Mrs. Joliffe looked younger at every sip, her hair growing golden again and her gray silk dress transforming itself rapidly into the kind of floating white garment she used to wear. William smiled. He enjoyed being maudlin. He enjoyed remembering tragedy, now that it was over. It made him, he supposed, a spiritual voyeur. He peered at Mrs. Joliffe over the top of his glasses and reflected that nobody would be able to tell that her husband had died of a bee's sting in twenty minutes one lovely summer's day. He had been staying with them at the time and could vouch for the authenticity of Matthew's end. It had happened so very quickly, in the middle of a strawberry-and-cream tea. There had been perhaps a dozen people there, all gathered under a tree on the Joliffes' lawn, glasses in one hand and spoons in the other. Agnes had flitted around with a silver sugar shaker, and at a table in the corner near the house two maids presided over the great white Victorian washstand basin full of the fruit and the jug to match full of cream. Already they had drunk champagne and William was feeling a little tipsy and hot and also a little frightened. Matthew Joliffe was a frightening man—tall, broad, loud-voiced, beetle-browed— and he seemed always to single William out for his heavy, jocular remarks. Poor William could have done without the honor. He would have been quite content to regard Matthew with awe and have nothing to do with him socially, but his invitations could not be refused. At least, William was afraid to refuse them, though he had worked it out that as he attended only one lecture of Matthew's a week and did not—nor was likely to—have him as his tutor, he would not come across him and have to answer for a refusal. But Matthew had died, dramatically, and it had not made any difference. He was still afraid and still accepted Joliffe invitations.

Mrs. Joliffe shifted in her chair, as though uncomfortable at William's reminiscing, but said nothing. She had thrown her profile into relief and William admired it, as he always had done. Her nose was very straight, her brow high and sloping, and her chin firm, kept permanently tilted in the air. She was all William felt a woman ought to be.

"William," Mrs. Joliffe said softly, "there is no need for you to sign that lease, you know. You are not committed."

Her skin seemed to wrinkle in an instant.

"Oh, I am," said William, recalled and aware of heartburn. "My honor commits me."

"Your honor! Really, William, you talk like someone in a

charade. Your honor is not involved. It's a question of common sense, not honor. They are not suitable. They will cause you a good deal of distress. If you sign a lease it will be for masochist reasons and quite reprehensible."

"It's very difficult," William said.

"No, it's very simple," Mrs. Joliffe insisted. "Sign nothing. Let your solicitor deal with it. If you like, I will talk to the young woman."

"No," said William sharply, "it's done. It may be for the best—perhaps what this house needs is young people. I suppose it *is* a bit like a morgue."

Climbing the stairs later, William regretted his simile. Mrs. Joliffe was not averse to dying, providing she was not informed of the process while it was under way. Unlike William, she had no plans to exterminate herself when she grew unable to fend for herself, but she had taken simple precautions against this event. All the same, she did not like similes like that and he ought to have been more careful, in view of the fact that she was now in her seventies. She had drawn her breath in and almost refused to talk to him, until Germaine came in, feigning exhaustion and reeking of washing-up liquid, and Homer woke up, in a particularly objectionable mood. They had seen themselves as flotsam, thrown up by Christmas, and had hurried to part.

William was happy to regain his own room. He closed his door softly and slipped off his stiff collar and walked about a bit. He could never bear to share his living quarters, and pitied Mrs. Joliffe, who regretted bitterly the necessity of not sharing hers. Not, he knew, that she wanted Germaine and Homer to live with her, but she would have liked someone companionable. Living alone was a grim business for her, and William knew he was most fortunate that he did not feel the same. Other people oppressed him if he had to put up with them more than half an hour—a discovery that had made him sad when he was young but was now his strength.

He made some lemon tea and stood by the window drinking it and inhaling the steam. Next year he would go away for Christmas, whatever remarks Mrs. Joliffe made. He would start mentioning it about June and build up a great enthusiasm for whatever visit he thought up. Perhaps he would go to his nephew, who was always inviting him. He had, after all, family, which Mrs. Joliffe sometimes chose to forget just because it suited her purposes to pretend he was dependent on her charity. William pursed his lips. He had noticed he was getting shrewish.

Below, Homer and Germaine were getting into their car. It seemed a long time between the doors shutting and the engine starting. Probably they were arguing, which they did all the time, with Homer swearing a good deal. William found swearing distasteful. He felt sorry for Germaine having to listen to it, though not sorry for Germaine. They were a dull, unappetizing couple, sitting staring immobile out of their stationary car windows, and they made William glad to be not a couple.

Whistling, William found the correct wavelength on his radio and listened to the news, just to see that nothing had happened. Sometimes the most extraordinary things happened between morning and evening, and Mrs. Joliffe and he often had recourse to the telephone after the six-o'clock news to exclaim to each other. This evening, nothing, which was as well, as he did not feel like being stimulated. Rather the reverse. He was eager to lapse back into his normal activities, which he loved so much that even a day away grieved him. Why did people think routine despicable? To William it was the supreme happiness—knowing what he was going to do and when he was going to do it. People did not know what they missed.

Pulling his chair up to the fire, William settled across his knees the tray contraption he had invented. Admiring it one day, Pullen had said he should patent it, but William had explained this was impossible since he was not at all

sure that he hadn't copied it, incorporating his own modifi-
cations, from something he had seen in a shop window.
Whatever its origin, the tray was a boon. It held everything
William might need in the course of an active evening. Flat
and broad, it clipped onto the sides of his chair. In the middle was a book-size flap he could raise if he wished; on either
side were deep compartments for writing paper (on the left)
and notes (on the right); in front, several smaller spaces for
pens, ink, pencils, reading spectacles, and sugared almonds
or whatever was William's weakness of the moment. Should
he wish for a drink, a cup or glass fitted into a metal holder
on the edge of the tray.

Tonight his book was *Flora and Fauna of the British
Isles,* which he was enjoying very much. His notes were
drawings of various botanical specimens that he himself had
made and wished to compare with those in the book. His
sweetmeats bowl was rather overloaded with some excellent
handmade chocolate truffles, Mrs. Joliffe's knowledgeable
present. A glass of madeira trembled near his elbow. Sighing
with content, William slowly moved his gaze round his tray,
and then onto his book, which he read steadily for an hour.
He lifted his eyes then only because the gas fire was splutter-
ing in an interesting fashion, the white cones suffused with a
near-purple glare that meant pressure was low. William relaxed when true red shot up, but he did not immediately
return to his reading. Sipping the madeira, he melted a
truffle in his mouth and looked at the shells at his feet. The
shells floated in a pretty, shallow bowl in front of the fire,
finding their lifeless way between bits of seaweed William
had thoughtfully placed at the bottom. Gas fires gave a dry
heat, the water moisturized it. Nodding at the truth of this,
William resumed his task.

At first, when he heard the light tap on his door, he was
sure he had imagined it. He often became so engrossed in a
book that he did not quite know where he was, and the

coming back to reality, however calm and quiet that reality, was painful. The knock was not repeated, so he was not helped in his transition, but he knew, after a few seconds, that someone was undoubtedly waiting outside his door. William pressed his knees together and clasped the tray with his hands and waited. He felt very agitated. The person outside could only be Sophie Hill, and nothing was going to make him admit her—he had had enough of answering doors. Gradually, when no further noises came, William breathed more easily. Evidently she had gone away, and now a valuable precedent had been established. She knew he was in. She now knew he did not answer the door even if he knew that she knew. William detached his tray, laid it carefully to one side and stood up. Quietly, he went to the door of the flat and cautiously opened it a crack and then, when he saw the landing was empty, a little wider. Nobody there, nobody lurking on the staircase to catch him on his way to the lavatory. With that destination in mind, William stepped outside and instantly knocked over a brown jug full of holly. He bent down and picked it up. Tied to the handle of the jug was a message saying "A Happy Christmas to Our Very Kind Landlord from Alex and Sophie Hill."

William slept with the holly on top of his "Examinations" pile so that he could watch it before he fell asleep and see it the minute he awoke. It gave him a pleasure out of all proportion to what it was, and he was aware that he was transforming it into a symbol—of hope. Nobody had ever given him a spontaneous present before. Nobody had ever thought of giving him flowers of any kind. The jug too he invested with great significance. It was a homemade jug, badly cast and roughly glazed, perhaps somebody's very first attempt, and it had been given with the holly without any mention of return. William's gladness made him damp-eyed and hurt his throat. His gesture of goodwill had been reciprocated, Mrs. Joliffe's cynicism repudiated. A great believer in human nature being intrinsically good, William had always felt he fought a losing battle against Mrs. Joliffe, who was a Machiavellian. He could not wait to tell her, and yet had been prevented from telephoning by the certain knowledge that she would somehow manage to sour his gift. She could not spoil it, that was impossible, it had been savored to the full, but the memory could be tainted and that William did not yet want. He had not sufficiently absorbed it to be able to withstand an attack on the motives of the givers. He wanted to cherish the holly and the deed that was done and not worry any more about what would follow. He had been right: what this house needed was some young people.

Four

PULLEN FELT the usual waves of irritation when his secretary said William Ellis Bone was on the line and wanted to speak to him very urgently. His brows automatically furrowed, his lips tightened and he grabbed the receiver aggressively, almost knocking the instrument off his desk.

"William," he snapped, "what's all this nonsense?"

"Ah," said William, "Pullen. Jolly decent of you to speak to me."

"You're a pest, William," Pullen growled, and when William's high, quavering laugh drifted to him, he shouted, "I mean it, William. What silly ideas have you got in your head now, eh? Eh? Come on, hurry up, we're not all out to grass like you, you know."

For the next five minutes Williams droned on about wanting to incorporate certain aesthetic standards into the lease he was preparing for his flat. As soon as he heard the word "lease" Pullen didn't even bother to half listen. He laid the receiver on his blotting paper and stared at his secretary. His position was ungainly. One leg, one short fat leg, was swung over the arm of his chair, and the way this called attention to his bulging crotch upset all his secretaries in varying degrees. His suit was covered with moldy carnation petals, coming from the sad bloom in his buttonhole, and was generally rather dirty and creased. In the lapel Pullen kept a special long pin which he occasionally used to un-hinge the wax in his ears or the tartar on his teeth. Neither of these was an attractive feature. His ears were huge for so small and so squashed a face, and his teeth were black or yellow with many prominent gaps.

The receiver was silent, then emitted a few squeaks. Bored, Pullen picked it up again.

"That's all rubbish, William," he said.

"Oh? Oh. Can you perhaps suggest any alternative safe-guards?"

"Safeguards, safeguards," said Pullen. "Do you ever think about anything else? Eh?"

"We have to have them," said William bravely. "We don't want all your work ruined, do we, by tasteless tenants who might spoil the atmosphere of the house."

"Be quiet," said Pullen, "you're off your head. Once I've finished a house, it's finished. I don't care what happens to it, and if you care—you're stupid enough to care—you shouldn't let your flat. Now get off the line. And see you come to dinner with me on Wednesday. Understand?"

With an effort, Pullen heaved himself out of his chair and stumbled over to the window. He was not drunk, but was suffering from a very mild form of Parkinson's disease which gave him a rolling gait and made him unsteady on his feet. It had not yet affected any other muscles, so he chose to ignore its existence. If anyone asked him if he was all right, he was quite likely to yell at them that he was a dying man, but he did not really believe it. He didn't feel as if he were dying, he felt strong and bad-tempered and gloriously impa-tient, just as he had always felt. Except on the days he came into any kind of contact with William. Then old age and disease and death took on new meanings.

Dolefully, Pullen looked out on Bedford Square, at the slush-softened railings and dripping stumps of trees. William shared his birthday—April first. They had gone to school together (Winchester) and been in the Army together (Royal Hussars) and been in hospital, shot up, together. Saving Pullen and four others had got William his first M.C. They had studied architecture together and very nearly gone into partnership. That had been a lucky escape. William had been edgy about the money and had instead become a civil servant. What a blessing! Anyone would have been driven screaming mad by William's daily presence, his overcautiousness, his uprightness, his niceness. Yet he had just invited him to dinner again. After the last farce, when he had vowed the sport was not worth the boredom.

The sport lay in the vicious teasing Pullen gave William. He teased him, nastily, about everything. He teased about sex, pretending William was a well-known poof, or about Mrs. Joliffe, pretending she was his mistress. He teased him about his running, pretending he ran in the park only to rape young girls and not to keep fit. He teased him about marking examination papers, pretending he did it only for the bribes. He teased about the house, pretending it was a worthless old dump about to fall down or lose its value or have offices built on either side. Oh, there was a lot to tease William about. It was amusing to see him blush, hear him stutter, watch him wince. But it was very easy.

The point was, it was a competition and it always had been. He was in competition with William, but William would not admit it. Pullen kept on winning and after every victory he let William know, but even though William congratulated him Pullen still felt he hadn't congratulated him enough. Every prize that had come his way, and a surprising number had, was something to beat the unsuspecting William over the head with. Every committee he was appointed to, every higher qualification he obtained, was accepted to dazzle William. Thinking it over, Pullen sighed. He didn't need a psychiatrist to tell him that this was a very sad state of affairs. William was a thorn in his flesh and he badly wanted it removed.

But he had asked him to dinner. William would arrive, dead on time, with some embarrassingly apt present, neat and dapper in his carefully pressed dark suit, his bald head shining with eagerness to please, his pebble glasses flashing with joy at the very fact of having been invited. William loved being asked to dinner. He hero-worshiped. He made it clear how gratified he was that he, Pullen, should bother. They would spend a dreary evening reliving experiences that no longer had any meaning except that which the glibly spoken words gave them. They would drink far too much and play chess, and one of them might even fall asleep. Pullen, thinking gloomily about it, supposed what kept this friendship going was the very fact that it was not a friendship. Neither of them liked emotion, both hated being involved. Their relationship had none of this disliked warmth. It was purely an animal recognition that it is good to drink and talk with others occasionally. That was all. There was no one else, in either of their lives, to fulfill this exacting role.

Then why the hell had William dragged him into this house affair? Angrily, Pullen lurched back to his desk and dictated a whole load of letters, knowing he went so fast that the secretary—it was always "the secretary" with Pullen —would not get half of them down. He liked being known as a difficult man to work for. He asked every new secretary —and his turnover was impressive—if she liked working for monsters, if she was used to coping with a genius, if she could stand up to shouting and didn't mind the odd pencil thrown at her. That had most of them in tears and on the way out before he had finished. The ones who stayed were masochists. The longer they stayed, the more exultant Pullen became and the cleverer at devising tortures. On a day when he had been in contact with William his mind was always particularly fertile . . .

William was used to Pullen. He knew it was all bluster and Pullen was a good, solid chap underneath. He was certainly a good architect, a damned good one, and naturally could not be expected to suffer fools gladly. Once, William had been misguided enough to introduce Pullen to Mrs. Joliffe. It seemed right that his two greatest friends, who heard through him so much about each other, should meet. It had been a catastrophe. Totally without genius herself, Mrs. Joliffe had thought Pullen a rude, boorish little man and had been surprised at William; totally without gentility, Pullen had been appalled by Agnes Joliffe and had pitied William. Neither of them had forgiven him for introducing them, and both felt slighted that he should have misjudged their taste so severely. Thereafter, William was obliged not to mention the rivals' names in each other's houses, and missed recounting the conversations he had had with them.

But he had to stand by Pullen, who was more often under attack from Mrs. Joliffe than Mrs. Joliffe was from Pullen. He had had a lot of practice defending Pullen. Though quiet and reserved, William had always been popular in any community, just as Pullen had always been unpopular. He had wasted a great many words trying to reveal Pullen's brilliance to others, trying to show them that the things they disliked about him were mere surface idiosyncrasies. Now, of course, that time was past. All their common acquaintances were dead. Apart from Mrs. Joliffe, who did not like him mentioned, there was no occasion to defend Pullen before anybody. Except himself. Yes, William nodded to himself over his telephone, that was vital. One had to show one did not care about Pullen's brusqueness. Pullen might collapse otherwise, and though William carefully avoided

thinking about the consequences, he would not have liked
to see that happen.

Clearly, he had caught Pullen at a bad moment. That
could happen to anyone. William himself had hated being
caught by a telephone call when he was not expecting one.
Pullen, being Pullen, could not, however, say this. Instead
he took refuge in being offensive. William understood this.
But it was a pity. He could not delay taking the lease to his
solicitors another day and he would have liked Pullen's assistance. Still, it would have to be done without, got down
to, got over. William straightened his shoulders and sat
down in front of his typewriter. He would write the accom-
panying note in longhand, but the rules of the house were
better typed so that they could be incorporated in the official document of leasing.

William cleared out of the way the examination paper he
had been marking. It had been a deplorable set of answers.
When he first read through it William thought there had
been some mistake and the candidate had answered the
wrong paper. He had spent an anxious half hour checking
and double-checking the list and numbers before coming to
the conclusion that it was a case of willful ignorance and
not a mistake. Such an event was not uncommon. It seemed
to him that every year the standard grew lower and lower,
and very soon, William thought, he would have to write to
the Board and tell them he was withdrawing his services.
What was so depressing was not that the candidates did not
know the answers to even the most elementary questions,
but also that in the process of giving the wrong answers they
revealed a total lack of understanding of the basic principles of architecture. Yet these were A- and sometimes S-level
papers, written by candidates who had supposedly gone
through a grounding and chosen to go further. William
could not understand it. Long hair and weird clothes troubled him not a jot, but these ungrammatical, illiterate,

badly thought-out, stupid examination answers drove him
frantic. His markings got lower and lower, and in this batch
he had not yet passed a single candidate, which, considering
he had marked twenty papers, was worse than in the summer.

"RULES OF THE HOUSE," William typed, in red capi-
tals.

It is felt that tenants will appreciate some guidance as
to the landlord's wishes with regard to the running of this
house in the interests of all parties.

1. NOISE.

Tenants are requested not to make loud noises at any
time, but particularly between the hours of 10 P.M. and 7
A.M. Musical instruments may be played, as long as the
volume of sound they produce is reasonably controlled.
Television sets will need particularly careful adjusting,
and tenants may feel, in the circumstances, that it is better not to have one. In connection with noise, it is better
to avoid flushing the lavatory after 10 P.M. In special cases
it may need flushing, but as a general rule putting the lid
down (there is an aerosol disinfectant attached to it) and
flushing before using in the morning is preferable.

2. THE HALL.

The hall and staircase are in common use and therefore are cleaned on a weekly rota, which tenants will
quickly learn. The black linoleum must be washed with
warm *clear* water into which two tablespoonfuls of vine-
gar have been stirred. Similarly, the sides of the stairs
need washing in this solution with a soft cloth (foam rubber washcloths are *not* suitable since they do not get into
the corners). The stair carpet is a very high-quality Wil-
ton and must only be brushed with a hard hand brush—
never vacuum-cleaned, as this eventually injures the pile.

3. DISPOSAL OF WASTE.

There are three dustbins in the garden, but since access to these is through Mrs. Joliffe's passageway, tenants are asked to deposit rubbish only between the hours of six and seven in the evening. In an emergency, Mrs. Joliffe's wishes must be consulted. All rubbish must first be wrapped in double-thickness newspaper, which makes collecting less messy and helps keep the inside of the bins clean.

4. WASHING.

Clothes may not be hung in the garden or out of the windows or any other aperture. Tenants may feel that the launderette—there are three in the fairly near vicinity—is the solution. No clothes may be hung at any time in the bathroom.

5. THE BATHROOM.

Unfortunately, owing to Council building restrictions, this must be shared. The landlord takes a morning bath in 2.5 inches of tepid water each morning. It is therefore possible to calculate tenants' hot water bill when the bi-annual gas bill for the house comes in. All accounts will be open for inspection. The bath must never be touched with an abrasive cleaner—immediate cleaning when still wet will remove all normal dirt. No towels or other effects of a personal nature may be left in the bathroom, since it is shared. Lavatory paper must be provided by tenants. There are two holders. That on the right of the lavatory belongs to the tenants, that on the door to the landlord. This need not be explained to guests whose stay is of short duration.

6. THE HOUSE FAÇADE.

The tenants will find windowboxes on the balcony of their sitting room. Flowers and plants may be placed in these, but the architect advises against blues and purples. Yellow, white and the more delicate shades of pink are felt to be more in keeping with the character of the house.

The windows of the whole house are cleaned once a month by a very reliable window cleaner. Tenants must contribute their share, in proportion to the number rather than yardage of window. Net curtains may be put up if preferred; the architect advises against nylon fabrics.

7. PRIVACY.

The privacy of all members of the house must be at all times respected. As a general principle, tenants should communicate by note, or if an immediate reply is needed, by telephone. Only in the most urgent and unavoidable cases must tenants knock on the other doors in the house.

8. FIRE.

There is a real danger from fire in old houses such as this, which tenants are earnestly begged to remember. Please close the inner hall door every night (this cuts out the risk of fire spreading). No paraffin heaters of any kind are allowed.

9. GUESTS.

Nobody in the house is obliged to answer the door if somebody else's bell is rung. The landlord does not wish his bell to be answered by anybody but himself. Tenants are asked to bear in mind the relative smallness of the house and may feel entertaining would be better done elsewhere (there are many excellent restaurants in town).

Exhausted, William paused. It all seemed such an effort telling people what ought to be obvious, but then it had always been so. Once he had come out of the Army at the end of the 1914–18 war he had found living in harmony with other people almost invariably impossible. So few people had taste. Now, William had doubts about his own taste, though none about Pullen's, and he knew how difficult it was, but the point was, if in doubt he *didn't*. Yet everywhere people *did*. House after house was spoiled by people's lack of taste. He had lived for a time in a charming flat in Regent's Park until the sheer vandalism of the front door—the original removed and a *glass* one substituted—had driven him away. In Kensington he was happy with a ground floor and garden to himself in an Edwardian villa, until the landlord had thought fit to paint the brickwork pale blue and even congratulate himself on how the house stood out. No, none of that was going to happen at No. 109. He knew the Hills were unlikely to substitute the front door or paint the brickwork, but all these crimes came from small beginnings and he did not see why, in his own house, he should have to put up with the ill treatment of what he had taken such care to see should be fitting. Fuss he was going to, in the interests of good taste, and he did not see why he should have to apologize for extending this taste to living.

William picked up his red pen and underlined what he felt to be key phrases, and then he read it all through, twice. Anxiously he looked for examples of curtness. He must not be curt. There were ways of putting things firmly but pleasantly and he must be sure that he had found those ways. These people were after all going to pay good money to live in his house and he must not appear to want to dictate to them. The sum he had finally settled on was five pounds a week, which he knew to be ludicrously undervaluing his property, but then he wanted only enough to pay his way. He felt the more realistic the rent the more inclined would be the tenants to live as he wanted them to live—peacefully, privately and harmoniously.

There was nothing else to add. Brow furrowed, eyes twitching with tension, William rang his solicitor, an elderly, washed-out creature who exactly suited his requirements, and told him that he would be bringing in the lease and its amendments that day and would be obliged if it could all be ready to sign by January first. That done, William hesitated. He must now contact the Hills and tell them when they would be getting the lease and when they would have to pay the first three months' rent, in advance. He had decided to be magnanimous and forget about the week they had already been in. Should he write a note, in keeping with the directive he had just written? Or should he telephone?

Trying to decide which was the lesser of the two evils, William did nothing for a while. He was, he reminded himself, sixty-nine. One would have thought that by that age social embarrassments would have receded a little, but instead they had grown worse. Of course, it was better in the sense that he did not worry so much afterward about how he had behaved—that agony had passed. No, his anxiety was not retrospective any longer, but purely anticipatory. Well, it was no good fretting about it, no good hoping he would change. It was his inheritance. His father had suffered in exactly the same way and had merely been more fortunate in managing to marry in spite of his handicap. William envied his father that. His mother, he thought, had proposed marriage and his father had been too much of a gentleman to refuse. If Agnes had asked him, would he not have been obliged to accept? But had she not asked him, obliquely? Ah! But obliquely was no good, not for a Bone. If she had said, "William, will you marry me?" that would have been different. "Yes," he would have said, because it would have been horrible to say anything else. They would have married and had several children and he would not now be going through these wretched difficulties. He would have been protected as his father had been protected.

William listened. It was very quiet down below. He knew Sophie Hill must be there on her own, for whenever the odious Alex was at home William's floorboards vibrated with the loud laughter and singing and stamping with which that young man punctuated every minute of his existence. The lease would sort that out, of course. But there was a great temptation to telephone Sophie, knowing she was on her own. It could all be quite simply explained and, most important of all, one could be sure the message had been received and understood. Already William knew that one could not be sure of that with Alexander Hill. He cleared his throat—he seemed to have had such a tiring day—and rang the Hills' number.

"Darling?" her breathless little voice said, answering at once, so that one knew she had been waiting, hand poised.

"William Ellis Bone here," said William, loudly, to hide her disappointment sighing down the line. "Sorry to bother you, but—"

"Oh, not at all, Mr. Bone. I love people to ring me—just anyone, you know."

"Ah. I see. Yes. Well—a little legal matter, about the lease."

"Is there trouble?"

"No. No trouble. Goodness, no. Simply it will be ready to sign on January first if you and your husband could arrange to be available that day."

"Oh, we're available any time, Mr. Bone, you don't have to worry about that."

"Ah. Yes. And the rent, of course. I trust three months in advance will suit you?"

There was a pause, and a faint crackling, as though she was moving the receiver about.

"We haven't discussed terms," went on William, "but I have decided on two hundred and sixty pounds per annum, exclusive of rates and all other bills. The rates are eighty-five pounds a year, so your share will be one third of that. Is that acceptable?"

"It's marvelous, Mr. Bone—you're terribly, terribly kind."

"One tries to be fair," William said hurriedly.

"Mr. Bone? Could you possibly spare a minute to come down now?"

"Now?" said William, shocked not that she was on her own but that people issued invitations so precipitately.

"Yes—only for a moment. It's about the lease. There's something I would like to explain when Alex isn't here— about the rent and the lease."

"Ah," said William, caught. "I could perhaps come down. Say in ten minutes? Would that be convenient?"

"Yes. Thank you, Mr. Bone. I'll put the kettle on."

"Don't do that!" said William quickly, but the line was dead. He distinctly heard the water running into the kettle in the kitchen below.

Swiftly, William selected a clean shirt and put it on. His trousers were quite respectable, which was lucky. They might well not have been if he had been doing anything but office work. He took a jacket from his cupboard, shook it, put it on and thrust a clean handkerchief into one bottom pocket and a biro and some paper into the breast pocket. It was always best to be prepared to be businesslike, especially if things became awkward or embarrassing, which he suspected might be more than likely. Looking down, he saw his shoes could do with topping up. They were not dirty, not even dull, but they did not gleam as they ought. After that, he naturally had to wash his hands and dry them. Giving himself a final inspection, William was miserable to see he had splattered himself with water in a suggestive place. Annoyed, and in something of a state, for his ten minutes were running out, he dashed back to the clothes cupboard and changed his trousers. They were his best-suit trousers and looked odd with his gray worsted jacket. Beads of perspiration stood out on his forehead and had to be mopped with a towel before he began going downstairs.

William knocked on the outside door, gently, and when Sophie shouted, "Come in!" he went in, and stood uncertainly, knees touching, just inside. Should he go into the kitchen or the sitting room? Both doors were closed. While he hesitated, Sophie shouted, "Where are you, Mr. Bone?"

"Here," croaked William.

The sitting-room door opened and the change from dark

to light blinded him. William followed her voice like a pit pony.

"Sit down, Mr. Bone, and have a cup of tea. Milk and sugar?"

"Neither, thank you," said William, who never drank anything but very weak lemon tea and was acutely aware that what was coming out of Sophie's teapot was a very cheap brand, strongly brewed. She sat cross-legged on the bare floorboards and William could not look at her, such was his absolute conviction that she must be injuring the baby inside her most dreadfully. He sat cross-legged himself, but then he was of an Indian build and had quite often affected that position.

"What I wanted to say," Sophie said, "was that Alex can't possibly pay the rent."

"Oh," said William, head down, thrown by Sophie's candor and also by the glimpses of what had been done to the room that were slowly coming to him. The words "drawing pins" flashed into his mind. Oh, God, there was not a word in the lease about drawing pins, and here they already were, great nasty goldheaded drawing pins defiling forever the smooth ice-green walls, matte finished.

"The thing is," Sophie was saying brightly, unaware of the cause of William's distress, if not quite oblivious to the fact of it, "I pay it. Or rather, my mother does. Or rather, she does but she doesn't know that she does and neither does Alex and so you will understand I'm in a delicate position."

"Quite," said William, taking off his glasses and polishing them energetically with his very clean handkerchief.

"I knew I could take you into my confidence," Sophie said happily. "More tea, Mr. Bone?"

It had happened before, William knew that. People— women—always thought that because he was shy and polite they need not be frightened of him, and that if there was no need to fear him he could be told anything. He had always objected to this assumption. There was nothing he hated more than being taken into someone's confidence. It immediately changed forever what was probably a perfectly satisfactory reletionship, and the burden was a nuisance. He did not wish to know that Alex Hill was being duped, nor did he wish to know that Sophie Hill's mother was being duped. The thought pained him and placed upon him the moral obligation of secrecy, which he found distateful. Yet people —women—did this kind of thing so readily, out the odious little secrets tripped, leaving you with no option but to smile and feign interest and inwardly groan. In this case, the implications of the secret were far-reaching. His view of the Hills' marriage was a romantic one, but already his opinion was bound to change. Was Alex Hill really so unmanly? What kind of marriage could this young couple have when the wife manipulated pursestrings and the husband did not even know that he did not provide! William was overwhelmed and wished he could disappear before further revelations were made. But Sophie sat, smiling, waiting, holding the poor mutilated teapot, asking him if he wanted more tea.

"No—no, thank you," said William, but again he was too late. The brown liquid was already spilling over into his saucer.

"Oops," said Sophie, "sorry. Just leave it, if you like. I'm not very good at pouring tea and this is a dreadful teapot." She held it high for William to examine. It was a cracked yellow pot, one with a broken spout. "We found it in a dustbin," she said cheerfully. "Weren't we lucky?"

"How amazing," William murmured, dabbing at his mouth with his handkerchief and wondering which diseases had now been passed on to him.

"You won't ever throw anything away, will you, Mr. Bone?" asked Sophie. "We'd take it, whatever it was. As you can see, it's all a bit makeshift here." She waved a hand round the room, giving William the chance to look properly. He felt dreadfully upset, and his prominent Adam's apple ricocheted up and down his thin neck. Wherever he looked, philistines had been at work. There was not a corner of his dear flat that had not been spoiled. Sadly he said, "It must be rather difficult for you, I can see. When will your furniture arrive?"

Sophie laughed very merrily. "It won't, Mr. Bone. We haven't any furniture. This is our all, you know."

Without really thinking what he was doing, William took the pencil and paper out of his pocket and began to write. "Now," he said, briskly, "what do you think are your basic requirements?"

"Well," said Sophie, "we've got them, really. We're very comfortable as we are. It would be nice to have a proper kettle, but——"

"I have two kettles," William said triumphantly.

"Really?"

"Yes. You may borrow one—there's no point in a perfectly good kettle going to waste, now, is there? Now, what else? A bed—surely you need a bed. I'm afraid I cannot help you there—but blankets, I do have blankets, only army surplus, you know, but warm, very warm. I have three to spare."

"How kind," said Sophie. "But our coats are adequate when the room is so warm."

"A carpet," William said excitedly. "I do believe I have an Indian carpet in the loft, an excellent carpet if I remember rightly—I bought it rather unwisely in a sale and the colors were too dark for my room. I shall fetch it down. And chairs—yes, I have two straw chairs that I've long wanted to get rid of, they're not suitable at all. You shall have them."

"Oh, Mr. Bone," said Sophie, "you're overwhelming me. I don't know what to say——"

"Nothing," said William, rising, "say nothing. I shall leave all these things on the landing directly. But you must not move them about, not on any account. When your husband comes in from work—"

"Oh, he isn't at work, Mr. Bone."

"He isn't?"

"No. Alex doesn't work."

"Ah. Well, when he returns, shall we say—you do expect him to return?"

"Oh, yes. I just meant he doesn't keep regular hours, you know."

"Well, regular hours aren't to everyone's liking," said a depressed William cheerfully.

"You are marvelous, Mr. Bone," said Sophie. "I wish all older people were as understanding as you. You've no idea how older people—social workers and probation officers, that kind of person—you've no idea how fixated they are about regular jobs. And with Alex being an orphan they get even more hysterical about it."

"An orphan?" queried William, terror-stricken.

"Oh, yes. Alex was left on a doorstep, you know the sort of thing. He was a Barnardo's Boy, terribly sad, that's why a happy, loving home life is what he needs most."

"Quite," said William faintly.

"Did you have a happy home life, Mr. Bone?"

"Good heavens, yes," said William. "One did—then."

"I didn't. I wasn't an orphan, but in some ways I was much more deprived. When—"

"Perhaps I'd better get those few things," said William. He knew the signs. The girl was settling down cozily again to tell him more ridiculous things that he did not want to hear.

"Oh, you are kind, Mr. Bone."

"I will put them on the landing, as I suggested, that will be the best place, but on no account touch them yourself."

"Very well," Sophie said, and her cheeks were full of dimples when she smiled. "I won't lift a thing," she promised, "and thank you, Mr. Bone."

William went straight up into the loft, an exercise he enjoyed. It meant getting the steps up from the garden shed, but he managed that without encountering Mrs. Joliffe, to his great relief. He put a pair of overalls on top of his clothes and climbed up the steps and hoisted himself up into the space above, rather pleased with his agility. Almost immediately the knees of his overalls were covered in thick dust, and William looked at them complacently. He was pleased about his overalls, they were real workman's overalls, which he had bought from a painter when the house was painted, showing, he felt, great foresight. He would never have brought himself to go into a shop and buy them. Easing himself forward, William crawled along between the rafters toward the far corner where he knew the carpet was. It had been carefully rolled and shrouded in polythene. William found it and pulled it along behind him. Before lowering it through the opening, he sat awhile in the dim, dark space and thought. He shouldn't be lending these things; never a borrower or lender be, his mother had said, and she was right about most things. It was a very expensive carpet, even if it had been bought in a sale. On their present showing, neither Sophie nor Alexander Hill was likely to be trustworthy. Hadn't they already mauled the flat about? But he was lending them this lovely carpet. Why? William stroked his overalls and tried to examine his motives. Only he could have understood them. It seemed that the more he didn't want to do something, the more something inside him took a perverse delight in doing it. Because he was shocked at the way the Hills were living, and wanted to tell them they were foolish and irresponsible, he went all out to apparently champion their behavior. Every day he became more and more involved in circumstances he wholly disapproved of. In marveling at their folly, he was becoming a party to it.

All the furniture went on the landing easily—the carpet

stacked in a corner, the two chairs side by side in front, the blankets on one and the kettle on the other. Back in his own flat, William divested himself of the overalls and sat down, a little shakily. He sat with his hands on his knees. What had Sophie said about the rent? That her mother paid it but did not know she paid it? What did that mean? Was there perhaps something *illegal* going on? He should have inquired further, at once, firmly, instead of shying away from the subject like a frightened horse. He should have demanded a full explanation of the exact way in which the rent would be paid. Now he feared he had already condoned duplicity. At the thought, William groaned aloud. He tried to comfort himself with the thought that it did not matter how the rent was paid so long as it was paid—but that did not work. That was someone else's philosophy, not his. He had tried to live like that and failed. But nothing had actually happened yet. No rent had been paid, no lease signed, nothing done that could not be undone. He had still time to get things straight, see that his ways were understood and agreed to.

After an hour's thought, William sat down and wrote out an invitation to the Hills. He invited them to dinner at The Garden on January first for a ceremonial signing of the lease.

Five

ABOUT half-past five in the afternoon, Agnes Joliffe always had a glass of sherry, sometimes two. She sat beside the window and sipped it, trying to make it last as long as possible, and always found that it perked her up sufficiently to get through the not always attractive evening ahead. Once, the sherry had been a prelude to dinner, but no longer. One meal, at midday, was sufficient, and though she liked her food, she sometimes found even that a struggle. It was, of course, the inactivity. Until her accident she had been extremely active, and, rather unfairly she felt, the desire to be physically active had not left her when she became crippled in one leg. She frequently envied William as she saw him trot off into the park for one of his runs, dressed in those absurd shorts.

Occasionally, when he was not busy running, William stepped in for a glass of sherry. Germaine liked to pretend they were never alone together and always had to have a chaperone, but that was not true. They did have the odd glass of sherry together. Not often, not regularly. She had tried to make it regular, thinking it would be a kindness to poor William who was such a lover of regularity. But rather to her surprise, William had resisted her attempt. His resistance had taken the usual roundabout form, but had been recognizable all the same, and it had panicked her for a while. William did not seem to like her sometimes. He had a way of speaking to her that was new, that hurt. When had he started those curt, hurried asides? Only recently, only since she had moved into his house. But she supposed that it was a risk she had had to take—that seeing him every day, or at least being in some kind of contact daily, she would see a William she had never seen before. It was worth it, naturally. She had tried to tell William what pleasure it gave her to be under his roof, but he had rebuffed her and run away. But it did. She woke up thinking, William will be awake now, and went to sleep thinking, William will be going to bed, and all around small sounds echoed her words and pleased her. She felt secure and warm, just knowing he was there. She did not always see him during the day, but at least she heard him, and he did take sherry with her, if not regularly. She returned again to the memory of how odd he had been when she had said, gaily, "Shall we make it a date, William?" He had said certainly not, it was out of the question. He had cleared his throat and coughed and frowned. While she had stood in front of him, abject, he had rebuked her. Firmly he had said five-thirty was a difficult time, a time when he did not always know his movements, and he could not be depended upon, even once a week. She had been hurt, because she knew this excuse to be a lie, but she hoped she had not shown it. If William thought she had been hurt it would be quite enough to keep him away forever. They continued to have their sherry date on the most casual basis—until she realized it was not casual at all. In William fashion, it was every third Tuesday.

This was not one of the third Tuesdays and Mrs. Joliffe sat on her own, looking out at the street. It was a lifeless

street on such a cold December day, a feeling of exhaustion
settled over it. No mothers with prams, few vehicles. There
was little to watch, but she watched keenly. Lately she had
begun to chart, with interest, the movements of this new
couple in the flat above. For three days now the young man
—a most un-William-like tenant—had bolted out of the
house about ten in the morning and not returned till very
nearly ten at night. The young woman, on the other hand,
never went out at all except briefly, for an hour, in the early
afternoon. This afternoon she had gone out at two and
come back at a little before three. She had, Mrs. Joliffe
thought, been purely and simply for a walk. She came from
the park, moving slowly, looking all around her with a
somewhat desperate interest, her hands pushed into her
pockets. Mrs. Joliffe envied her. She too had walked like
that when she was expecting Germaine, up and down the
Cam banks, across the meadows, round the long way home.
It had seemed a beginning, momentous and precious. She
had walked like that, daydreaming, loving her body, so important and obvious, and she had had no doubts. Once,
some wise—or perhaps evil?—friend had suggested to her
that in a way she had been lucky to be married only two
years. You kept the perfection, the friend said, you had the
glory and never the disillusionment. But she hadn't had a
marriage, that was the blow. There were so many, many
things that had never been worked out, so many corners she
would like to have gone round. Instead, as she had grown
older, she had learned that she never knew Matthew at all.
He grew fainter and fainter, until he receded altogether
into a haze of memories she was not quite sure of. Unlike
William. William grew and grew until everyone else was
blotted out. She had grown with him, suffered with him,
aged with him. To age with someone you loved was the
strangest experience.

Mrs. Joliffe looked again at Sophie, and speculated. Did

the child have staying power? Could she stay with her fly-by-night lover, or would he too, fifty years hence, be as insubstantial as Matthew? Mrs. Joliffe smiled at herself. Sophie smiled, down there on the pavement. She always had a half-smile on her face, ready, one felt, to be turned up a degree or two should someone respond. Her personality was obviously gentle and warm and undemanding, and yet, Mrs. Joliffe felt, there was a suspicion of real character in the rather noble face. The girl had a way of tilting her chin and tossing her hair back that suggested she was not wholly malleable. Altogether, she was attracted to her, decidedly.

Today they had waved at each other. Mrs. Joliffe had been rather embarrassed by this interchange, but was determined not to be William-like about it. All that really embarrassed her was that the girl might think she had been spying, since she had been standing at her window half shrouded by curtain when they caught sight of each other. But the girl had smiled so cheerfully and her wave had been so vigorous that Mrs. Joliffe had dismissed this worry as unlikely and in any case unimportant. It had, however, precipitated a train of thought that had lasted till now, sherry time, and showed no signs of abating. Simply, should she make overtures? William was clearly going to persist, out of sheer stubbornness, with these tenants. This must be accepted. Since she was the elder woman and the longest inhabitant, she ought to make overtures, if overtures were to be made. Should she ring up now and invite this girl, whom she knew to be alone, for a sherry? Would that not be the correct thing to do? The answer came pat from her inner self: correct, yes, but wise? For one who always looked before she leaped?

Mrs. Joliffe suffered from no William fears of involvement being fatal, something to be regarded with horror. She regarded it, on the contrary, as a necessary part of living. One was involved, like it or not. Her hesitation was due to a wish not to foist her company on people who might feel they had no escape. She was far from being a Uriah Heep, never for one minute thinking of herself as such a disgustingly very humble person, but she felt she knew her limitations. However much she read and listened to the radio, her world she knew was narrow. What had she to offer to someone like Sophie Hill? All afternoon she had pondered this question. Well, she had interest, which many people did not have. She was interested in the young. But might that not also be called curiosity, and if so did one offer curiosity to someone? Sipping her sherry, she grew tired of her own hesitations. It was a dreary evening, the end of a dreary day. They both lived in the same house, they were both alone, and they had waved at each other. What more encouragement did she want? Not to be neighborly would be uncharitable. Confident, she reached for the telephone.

"Hello?" she said loudly.

"Oh—hello—"

"You don't know me," she boomed, "but we waved at each other this afternoon. My name is Mrs. Joliffe and I live on the ground floor."

"Oh, yes, good evening, Mrs. Joliffe—how nice of you to ring. I've so wanted to meet you."

Mrs. Joliffe paused. She felt put off, but it was too late now. "I wondered if you would like to come down and take a glass of sherry?"

"Now?"

"Yes."

"But I'd love to! How perfectly sweet of you to ask me. I'll come straight away."

Mrs. Joliffe felt unpleasantly flustered. She moved painfully toward the corner cupboard and got out a clean glass and another, different bottle of sherry and returned to her chair exhausted. She waited with her hand on her cane, listening to the feet coming down the stairs, and felt excited and nervous. New people came into her life so very rarely. But it was not just that, it was hope. She realized that though it was a dangerous emotion at her age she was stirred by a great hope that she was about to begin a rewarding friendship, of which she was pathetically in need. It was silly. She thumped her cane on the floor to show herself how silly it was. Hadn't the girl's gushing tones chilled her? Hadn't she felt, just a minute ago, that she had made a mistake? It was ridiculous to be in this state, positively twitching with nerves as she heard the tap on the door, hardly able to croak, "Please come in" in answer, and then having to repeat it because the feeble sound did not carry.

"Please come in," she said, louder, and the door opened and the girl came in. "How do you do?" she said, extending her hand but not rising. "I'm Agnes Joliffe."

"Hello. I'm Sophie Hill."

They shook hands solemnly. Mrs. Joliffe was pleased to detect a shyness in Sophie's manner.

"Will you have dry or sweet sherry?" she asked.

"Oh, either."

"But which do you prefer?"

"I like both—really. Whichever you have most of."

Rather grimly, Mrs. Joliffe poured out a sweet sherry. She did not like people who refused to make decisions because they could not be bothered. It meant other people had to be bothered for them.

"What a lovely room," Sophie said. "Such lovely old furniture."

"It took a lifetime to collect," Mrs. Joliffe said, aware that she was being pompous.

"I'm sure it did," Sophie said. "I'm sure Alex and I will never manage to collect anything at all."

"It takes time and patience. Of course, I had a great deal more, but it all had to be sold when I moved here."

"Have you been here long?"

"Five years, from the moment William had it ready."

"Oh—I thought Mr. Bone had been here much longer."

"He had," said Mrs. Joliffe, irritably, always expecting miracles of people in conversation and never getting them. "He's been living in this house more than thirty years, in those rooms at the top—one can't call them anything else, they have no cohesion—but he only bought the house seven years ago when the occupants died. Being William, it took him two years to have it converted and modernized. It has taken him another five to let your flat. You are very lucky he has brought himself to do so."

"Indeed we are," agreed Sophie.

"Why do you suppose he let you have it?" asked Mrs. Joliffe sharply.

"I don't know. Perhaps—I think perhaps he felt sorry for us. And we so loved his flat. It was an accident, actually."

"Nothing William does is ever accidental."

"Oh. Then I don't know."

"How much rent is he charging you?" asked Mrs. Joliffe, enjoying the sensation of impertinence.

"Five pounds a week."

"Ridiculous!"

"Yes, I know—but so kind."

"William has always been too kind. His whole life has been ruined by kindness."

"Have you known him all his life?"

"No. I met William when he was seventeen and I was eighteen. He is now sixty-nine and I am therefore seventy. We are quite open about our ages. How old are you?"

"Nineteen."

"Good gracious. And your husband?"

"Twenty."

"Neither of you of age! Who, may I ask, is supporting you in this venture? Who is behind you? Who backs you, so to speak?"

"Alex is an orphan."

"But you are not?"

"No—though I would almost be glad to be. I expect that shocks you. It sounds very hard, I know."

"It is hard, but then my own daughter wishes daily to be an orphan, so I am acquainted with the reality of such a situation."

"Has she married someone you do not like?"

"She has married several people I do not like—in turn, of course. The one she is married to at the moment I like least of all. But that has nothing to do with it. We are incompatible. I expect it is my fault—I wanted a son. Do you want a son?"

"Badly."

"How honest. I was never honest. I was much too proud and had to pretend it did not matter. Are you well?"

"Very."

"When is the child expected?"

"March."

"Beginning or end?"

"I don't know—there was some confusion. The hospital think the end."

"Which hospital?"

"Queen Mary's, in Hampstead."

"But that is an hour from here, is it not?"

"Yes. I shall have to change."

"Queen Charlotte's in Hammersmith is the nearest that is of any use."

"Yes. They are full. They are all full."

"Of course, in my day one had them at home. The doctor came, and then one had a midwife also and a day nurse for the baby, not to mention a night nurse. What a fuss! What a lot of paraphernalia! I should have enjoyed much more being whisked off in an ambulance even if one has to give birth in public, so to speak."

"How many children do you have?" asked Sophie.

"One only," said Mrs. Joliffe, "to my intense regret. I should have had six at least. I can see you would like to know why I did not—no, I like curiosity, the more open the better. Well, I did not have time. I might have had another, but I had an appendix instead and then my husband died. We were only married two years, you see."

"Oh, how tragic," said Sophie.

"Quite," snapped Mrs. Joliffe, disliking her excessively anguished face, "but do not upset yourself. It was over fifty years ago and one does not remain tragic every day for fifty-odd years. Now, we were discussing your confinement—much more interesting. You were saying the hospitals are all full?"

"Yes, but I expect I'll get in somewhere."

"And afterward? Afterward is so very much worse than before. I felt simply splendid before, I couldn't imagine what all the fuss was about, but afterward—dreadful. I could not have managed without a nurse. Have you engaged a reliable nurse?"

"No—no, no nurse. We couldn't possibly afford it, and I do so want to look after him myself."

"I wonder how William will weather a child. He is positively neurotic about disturbances."

"We will try to keep the baby away from him."

"But not out of earshot—impossible. Will you have another sherry?"

"No—thank you. I must go, really, in case Alex telephones."

"Will you come again?"

"I should love to. When?"

Mrs. Joliffe smiled. "How sweet of you," she said. "To-morrow, every day, till you are tired of me and my questions, or have something better to do."

"Five-thirty, then? And I wondered—can I get things for you, ever, at the shops? It would be no trouble."

"That is most kind. Some days I would be most grateful if
you could collect small items that have not been delivered. I
never dare ask William—such things are an encumbrance to
him. I will leave a note and some money in the hall if ever I
need to take advantage of your offer."

"Do. Good night—until tomorrow."

The parting words rang delightfully in Mrs. Joliffe's ears
for the rest of the evening. She went over what they had said
to each other and was surprised that it amounted to so little,
since she had had the impression, at the time of speaking,
that they had overwhelmed each other with information.
Had she come out of it well? No indiscretions, that had
caused her so much distress in her youth? She did not think
there had been any. Faintly, she felt she might have been a
little disloyal to William, poked fun, been disparaging, perhaps. She must set that right at their next meeting—tomorrow. Cheerfully she ate some wholemeal bread and cheese
and listened to the radio. She had it on very low, quite low
enough to hear the telephone on the floor above ring, and it
did not ring. Not once. Poor Sophie had gone back to wait
in vain, and she felt troubled for her. She heard her walking
about, very slowly, up and down. It must be difficult for her
to put the days in, in her condition, in this kind of weather,
in that flat. How heavily time must hang, and she knew
about that. Moreover, Sophie, being young, would not have
had time to come to terms with the periods of waiting in
one's life. She would be impatient, weary of the clock taking
so long to go round. Mrs. Joliffe found herself nodding in
sympathy as she rose at 9:30 P.M. and wound her own clock,
and put the lights out and retired to bed. When she stopped
reading—a biography of Mary Queen of Scots that she considered so ill written she was surprised at Harrods for stocking it—that young man had still not come in. It was deplorable.

Sleep never came easily, but she had grown to live with
this problem, as with others. It was fatal to worry or get

emotionally excited, so Mrs. Joliffe deliberately took her
mind off Sophie and thought instead of something comfortingly ordinary like Germaine's weekly visit the next day.
Wednesday was the night Homer played squash—though
she did not believe he did any such thing—and Germaine
came from work for her supper. It was all very boring, but a
visitor. Germaine was one of life's visitors—as far as her
mother was concerned there was no permanent place for her
anywhere. She flitted. The jobs she had had were endless
and not a decent one among them. She had not had the
brains to go to university, easy though it now was compared
to Mrs. Joliffe's day, but she could at least have trained herself for some worthwhile auxiliary profession. Nor had her
personal life been any more commendable. Unmarried till
the age of thirty-two, she had then married a Hungarian
refugee who upped and went back to Hungary three weeks
later. Farcical. Quickly she had taken up with an elderly
insurance clerk, who had in due course married her, then
stepped in front of a tube train at Mornington Crescent.
Apparently he had been wearing bifocal spectacles for the
first time or something ridiculous. Then there had been
Homer. Worse or better than Alex Hill?

Debating the point, Mrs. Joliffe finally slept.

Sophie, in spite of promises to herself, felt much the same.
There was too little to do. All afternoon, it seemed, she had
sat at the window, conscious of the old lady below sitting at
her window, and looked out. She probably did not see what
Mrs. Joliffe saw. At first, perhaps, she too watched the tops
of the trees stretching like antennae into the gray sky, and
saw the empty street, but very soon daydreams blotted out
the landscape and she was sightless. Cold, especially her fingers and feet, she should not have sat near the window, but
sitting anywhere else emphasized her idleness. Her arms
were folded, her knees neatly together, and she leaned forward, as though to get a better view.

But she was not unhappy. Constantly she reminded herself how much more dreadful it would have been to be lonely *and* unhappy. She was happy. She had Alex and now a home and soon a baby. What did William Ellis Bone have? Nothing. She felt she ought to take her cue from him and make something out of nothing, for wasn't that what he did? He bustled. It was amusing that for someone retired with no commitments, he bustled so much. All day she could hear him running backward and forward, up and down the stairs, in and out of the house, always rushing. She longed to know what he did so that she could copy him.

Yet it was not as though she had ever been active. By nature, she was slow and lazy. When she was small, the fourth of four girls, the baby of the family, she had been one of those children who are content to watch and never participate. At first this pleased, but finally it irritated and then worried, and she was poked and prodded into proving she was not lacking, either physically or mentally. At school the tradition continued. She was obedient, she gave no trouble, she smiled and was pleasant and made no mark at all. Teachers had difficulty remembering who she was when they came to do reports. And after school? Alex. There had been no after school, and never would be, that way.

"Still waters run deepest," people had said, and "It's always the dark horses that surprise." That was when she found Alex and became pregnant and was not married or ever likely to be. She did not like pretending she was married, but Alex, whose wish it was that they should not be, had insisted on it. He bought her a wedding ring in Woolworth's and made her wear it. He never forgot to call her "my wife," whereas she found it a great strain to call him "my husband." She did not like telling people like Mr. Bone and Mrs. Joliffe that they were married, even though she saw it saved them distress and was thoughtful of Alex. The hospital did not matter, they were official.

Sophie lay on the floor, beside the telephone, a pillow

underneath her head, dreary thoughts going through her mind now that dreams had fled. There was so long one could dream and no longer. She supposed she should go to sleep, but why, when she would not sleep till Alex came, and was just as restful here on Mr. Bone's lovely carpet? Alex had not been pleased, or had professed not to be pleased, but he had carried everything in quickly enough and had it arranged in minutes. Then he was proud. He stood and looked at everything and admired it and did not take her teasing well. He had told her to take nothing else or Web—as he always referred to him—would think they had compromised themselves, which they certainly had not. Never. Even when they signed this lease on January first they would not have compromised themselves, not a jot. They would accept his invitation to dinner—a meal was a meal—and sign the silly bit of paper, but they would still be free agents.

Alex based everything on being a free agent. Sophie, mesmerized by him, smiled all the way through his exposition of what he meant and marveled at him. To think he thought so much! He had seemed to have fears that she might want to limit his freedom, as he saw it, but she did not. She wanted to love him, that was all, and be with him as much as possible, and she very quickly proved what she said. She loved him, was at his disposal, but never restricted him. The fault lay in herself. She too was a free agent, but she had nothing to do when she was free, she could not use her freedom. No good going to see other people—she wanted only to see Alex. No good seeking entertainment, not without Alex. She knew herself to be feeble and unimaginative and tried to correct these fatal flaws, but with a singular lack of success.

What she hoped, as she lay there, was that soon she would be looking back on these long empty days with sighs of envy, regarding them as periods of calm before the storm that would be the rest of her life. They would have many children, a huge brood of them, gloriously vital and noisy and demanding, with herself the pivot on which they all turned. She would be consumed and no longer know what it was to wait. Alex did not know. He had never waited for anything. Always he was up and off if he was bored, in search of something to interest him. For days he would lie around sleeping, and then for days hardly be there, except briefly for a few hours in the night. Sometimes he brought money back with him, sometimes people, and she never knew where either had come from. So far, he had at least always come home sometime in the twenty-four hours. His attitude varied. He could come in glowing and seize her fiercely and tell her excitedly where he had been and what he had been doing and touch her with his exuberance. Or he could trail in, moody, snappy, scowling, ready to take his revenge on her should she say the wrong thing. His variations were infinite, with one common theme—his need of her. So she felt. It bolstered her, gratified her, even when it was unpleasant in the form it took.

It was rare that she had any news to tell him. He never asked, he spared her that. She rehearsed her encounter with Mrs. Joliffe, trying to arrange it into a suitable shape to present to Alex, but somehow, like her meeting with Mr. Bone the day before, it would come out as a brief announcement—"I had a glass of sherry with Mrs. Joliffe," "I had a cup of tea with Mr. Bone." She was quite helpless to convey how much they had meant to her, what atmospheres there had been and how she had been affected. Then, Alex did not like the old, especially the old and useless. He would find nothing at all interesting about either Mrs. Joliffe or Mr. Bone. They had had their scene. They were past it. But they have so much to tell, she might murmur, but would be ignored or snubbed.

She shifted to a more comfortable position on the floor, over onto her left side, her knees drawn up. She ought to be doing the exercises for natural childbirth, but in spite of the ideal opportunity she didn't, never did. Around her, noises in the house indicated that the other two tenants were going to bed. Mrs. Joliffe's lavatory flushed, within the prohibited hours by a minute. The house was so quiet when it subsided that Sophie distinctly heard Mr. Bone getting out of his chair and walking, padding, into the next room. In a moment he was back, and there was a small commotion. Bump, bump, then a pause before the final bump. Something he was folding up or putting down? Another trip to the next room, then the swish of curtains being drawn, and the silence. All three of them were now lying down, in a position of sleep, but awake, listening.

Into this vacuum roared Alex. Only Sophie's heart leaped, and such was her devotion to him that the sound of him severed at once the warm closeness she had been feeling with Mrs. Joliffe and Mr. Bone. He was delivered by some kind of monstrous, backfiring vehicle, a sight of which she was not quick enough to catch though she had rushed to the window when, half a mile away, she had heard Alex's yell. What did he yell? She laughed and screwed up her face, but could not make out any words. It sounded like the shout of a rag-and-bone man, or the announcer over the Euston Station system. Whatever it was, it was exuberant and happy. When it ended, when shouts had been exchanged, even thank-yous, when the machine had snarled away, there was a stampede, a flinging open of the downstairs door, a slam as it closed, a thundering of feet on the stairs and a joyous "Sophie!" as he crashed open their own door.

They embraced, hugging and kissing. He was cold, cold and raw, his nose almost blue, his hands red as meat. He had no coat or scarf or gloves and the temperature was below freezing, but his eyes were bright and huge and started out of the frozen, stretched skin of his face like torches.

"Oh, Sophie, my love!" he declaimed, one arm outstretched. "What a day! What a night!"

"Wherever have you been?" she asked, curious, not nagging, happily entangled still in his arms.

"To the ends of the earth—and back. Back, that's the great thing. I've seen and felt and come back *knowing* it, do you see? That's the difference—it hasn't been lost. I'm inspired."

"To paint?"

"Paint? Good God, no—paint is puny, it's nothing. I'm inspired to live."

"Haven't you always lived?"

"No, I've existed, nothing else."

"Not even when we made love?"

"Oh, that. That's not worth mentioning in the same breath."

"Thanks."

"It's impossible to describe. If you only *knew*."

"So you keep saying. I want to know. Why can't I know?"

"You wouldn't approach it in the right spirit."

"How do you know?"

"You're uptight all the time—like this. You've too many hangups."

"You're always saying that to me, and it's not true. I'm perfectly relaxed. Everyone who knows me thinks I'm easygoing."

"I meant spiritual. Spiritually you're a drag."

"Thanks."

"You're like those two old biddies in this house. That's your wavelength—you think about nothing and brood and never act."

"How can I?"

"You never freak out."

"I'm pregnant."

"That's got nothing to do with it. We're talking about minds, not bodies. You never get up and go. Let's go now, up and off."

"Where?"

"See! Where? How do I know where?"

"All right. Let's go."

"I didn't mean it. It was an illustration."

"Oh," she said. "I'm glad."

He took his arms away from her and walked over to the mantelpiece and leaned one elbow on it and crossed one foot over the other, and gazed at her solemnly. She returned the gaze easily, her hands deep in the patch pockets of her green corduroy smock.

"Are you hungry?"

He shook his head, frowning as though pained at the suggestion.

"Good," she said, "there isn't much. Shall we go to bed?"

"You go," he said.

"Not you?"

"It's a waste."

"Oh. Won't you be tired tomorrow?"

"Yes. Does it matter? It's of absolutely no importance whether I am or not."

"Don't be cross."

"I came home full of what I'd seen and you talk of food and bed. You've failed me, Sophie."

"I'm sorry. What do you want me to talk about?"

"Nothing. Just be."

She went over to him, uncertain. Timidly she put her hand up and touched his cheek and said, "I love you," and that seemed to recharge his excitement and he crushed her again till she was gasping and said, "Oh Sophie, oh Sophie," and kissed her everywhere. She just a little bit wanted to laugh but did not know whether it would be all right. Her back ached.

When he was asleep, she lay awake. Again she was attuned to the others lying awake who wished for sleep. Guiltily she recalled the noise. Mr. Bone must have been very angry. But even had she thought to warn Alex, how could she have done so? He had come home in some kind of non-sensical ecstasy where even to try to absorb his mood was dangerous. She could not have said "Shhh." Silently she explained all this to Mr. Bone, begged him to understand, to excuse Alex, to appreciate that he lived on a different plane from them. Something had happened to him that hadn't happened to them, and they could only marvel at him and try not to interfere. He slept now, very deeply indeed, one arm round her, the other flung over his head. Carefully she removed the arm on which she lay and tucked it under Mr. Bone's magnificent blanket, and then she reached and pulled the other arm down, to join it with the first. Her fingers felt sticky. She held them up in the half-gloom and peered at them. Blood? She sat up and felt for the flashlight near the bed—there so that she would not fall over things in the dark if she had to get up in the night. It was blood; not much, but definitely blood. Worried, she shone the light on Alex's arm and made a slight clicking noise with her tongue when she saw the bruised vein in the crook of his arm, and the spots of blood around the half-dozen pinpricks there. She held the flashlight steady for a few seconds, and then put his poor arm away, and switched the light off and lay down.

It didn't matter, of course, though she did feel like crying, unaccountably. Alex wanted all kinds of experience. He did all kinds of things to see what they were like, and some of them he never did again. He never did anything to excess, as he had very proudly told her. It was just that it was disappointing, that was all. Mr. Bone might so easily misunderstand. You see, Mr. Bone . . .

Six

Alone in the park, William jogged on through the mist, keeping his elbows close in to his sides and his knees as high as possible. He had a slight touch of lumbago this morning, which it had been tempting to give in to but much more important to conquer. He had conquered. Hardly had he sprinted fifty yards—he always started off with a quick sprint to get the circulation going—when he felt his back joints loosening and the pain going. By the time he slowed down to a jog it had gone completely and he was able to concentrate on all the little exercises that he did as he moved. Some of them were breathing exercises, some coordination, but all of them were well thought out to keep William in trim. Sometimes people were alarmed, he noticed, when he came into view. He could tell by the way they called their dogs to heel and moved quickly off in the opposite direction. Most impolite. Even to their backs, William said good morning.

It was a little after eight o'clock and there was no one at all about. This morning William had pledged himself to the long circuit, right round the whole of the interior of the park. He had it so worked out that he did not need to cross any road, though he must run parallel to one toward the end. People often asked him why, since he made such a fetish of fresh air and so hated noise, he did not move to the country. They could see him, they said, in a gem of a Queen Anne house somewhere near Tunbridge Wells or Bath. There he would be able to run down country lanes and over meadows and along streams. The air would be purer and there would be no roads to avoid, if one chose the right place. Well, William had to admit he had once enjoyed such a dream, but fortunately he had realized in time what a dreadful mistake he would be making. He was a town mouse in so many ways. He liked London and its anonymity —the country made one so obvious. Nor would he admit that Richmond Park was a feeble substitute. Pullen spoke scathingly of jets flying over every minute, but William rarely heard them. There were plenty of places in the park where one had the illusion of being in the depths of the country, and William knew it all so well that he could make the most of it. Occasionally he would break out and go off for a hike at the weekend, but however successfully rustic his outing he always returned contentedly to his home park and loved it more for leaving it.

At the moment, he was halfway round and going well, so well that he was more than up to schedule and ready to switch to mental roadwork. Aware that the danger lay in both mind and body becoming rusty, William paid equal attention to both. He ran for his body, and while he ran he did tests in his head. One test was listing all the things he had had for dinner during the last two weeks—very tricky, unless he had dined out. Another was repeating all the tube stations on the Central line from left to right. Simple memory stuff, which he enjoyed. More difficult was total concentration. William selected a tree ahead and tried to concentrate solely on it. Very difficult. It had always been his weak spot; other things would keep intruding, and this morning other things were so big they blotted out the tree. . . .

There was the meal. All week, William had been visiting restaurants, picking and choosing his way through menus, watching the service as well as experiencing it, timing the volume of trade. He had hoped the Fantails would be perfect, and so it was, for food, but between seven and half past it was crowded. Regretfully, William had to rule it out. Crowds would not do. On the other hand, the Belle Etoile was not crowded enough at that time. He had dined alone, and he wanted there to be some festive atmosphere. He had next sampled Parke's, but it was quite the wrong place for what he wanted, and so were Chez Victoire and Bertorelli's. Nervously he had decided he must go to a totally new place, and had selected The Garden. It was a success. There might, perhaps, be difficulties avoiding having drinks in the bar place, but if one could steer them past that all would be well. It was a ladies' restaurant, William felt, and he was thinking far more about Sophie than Alexander. He wanted her to be comfortable, he wanted her to have something pleasant to look at as well as to eat. The Garden would do very nicely. There was one snag only: he was not known there. William, with wry honesty, managed to convince himself that it did not matter. Even in restaurants he had patronized for twenty years they seemed not to know him.

He was allowing one hour and forty minutes from the minute they disembarked from the car to the minute they stepped outside into the street. Not, he hoped, overgenerous. He did not want to have to worry about courses being late, or Sophie perhaps wanting several cups of coffee. He would rather have too much time than too little. If they had too much time he knew several ways of prolonging their stay until the allotted time for leaving. Very early on, William would start either delaying or encouraging tactics, as he saw how things worked out. It was his duty as host. He wanted them to arrive at the theater with just enough time to get settled and buy a program, without any of the hanging about that could prove so embarrassing.

The theater was vital, somehow even more so than the restaurant. One could, to a certain extent, depend on any restaurant in the Guide to give one a reasonable if not a superlative meal. But theaters were different. William took the *Times*, the *Observer* and the *New Statesman* and read all the reviews every week with increasing bewilderment. It was not that the critics of these journals disagreed—he expected them to disagree, he absolutely hoped they would—but that their standards fluctuated so alarmingly. William would have liked them to have criteria he could understand, but they did not. Usually they made references to plays that he had neither heard of nor seen and were useless yardsticks. But he was more than prepared to admit it was his fault. All he could now do was go to see for himself all the things that were being currently recommended.

This William did. He went to see two comedies, one thriller and a revue. A straight play did not seem to him to be apt. He did not think he ought to take Sophie and Alex to a straight play, not with their relationship being what it was. It was much more in keeping that they should go either to something light or to something classic, and since he had been to all the classics that were at that time being performed, William felt he must make the rounds of what was light. Accordingly he did. He left both comedies after the first act. One was vulgar and silly, the other revolting. The thriller he had thought good, but the plot had a dead baby in it and that ruled it out. There remained the revue, about which William was in agonies of doubt. So far, he had seen it twice. This afternoon he would see the matinée and make his final decision: to book or not to book.

William was coming toward the gate nearest to his house. There was still no one about. Standing beside the last clump of bushes, he touched his toes twenty times, and then ran across the road. Very quietly he let himself in and went for his bath, hurrying so that he would have it over before anyone was up. When the water had drained out, he rubbed the inside of the bath with a soft cloth and removed any hairs from the plug. He listened at the door for a second, then, reassured, ran up his stairs and into his flat, where he rewarded himself with scrambled eggs on toast. His enjoyment of the eggs was marred only by the busy day ahead of him. He did not like busy days of this variety, full of anxious moments of decision. In the morning he was going to the travel agent's, in the afternoon to the revue, and in the evening for dinner with Pullen. He would have preferred to have all these things spread out, but they had gleefully concertina'd themselves together.

It was, however, no good putting it off. Firmly William put down his teacup and began to prepare himself for the ordeal. He dressed with care, choosing a shirt with a soft collar so that his neck would not become chafed as the day wore on. So tender was this neck that even the most carefully starched stiff collar bruised and scratched it until it resembled an inexpertly strangled chicken's. His hat too was large and soft, since he had hardly less trouble with his scalp. Over his gray suit he pulled on an overcoat. He really preferred a raincoat, but was afraid it was not smart or warm enough. His overcoat he did not like. It was enormous —long and heavy, made of some very durable black material. The minute he put it on William felt tired and bowed down. But it was an overcoat day and he must get over his distaste.

Before he left his flat, William closed the curtains and lit a lamp. He would not be back until very late and he did not relish the thought that intruders might see his flat in darkness and take advantage. True, there were other people in the house, but William would have been surprised at nothing. He therefore took this small precaution and felt more secure during his absence. What he feared, he reflected as he closed his door gently behind him, was not what the intruders would do or what they would take, but simply the intrusion. To see that someone had been there would sicken him more than any possible damage. He did not even like the window cleaner going in without him being there.

Down the stairs William went, pulling on his gloves and clicking the press-studs shut at the wrist. He stopped a moment in the hall, where there were two letters propped up on the shelf. He scrutinized them and put them down very quickly. Neither was for him. As he proceeded to the door, thankful that this had been the case—he would not have liked going back upstairs with letters, nor carrying them about all day, nor being distracted by their contents—he heard Mrs. Joliffe's voice saying, "Oh, William?"

William stopped, but did not turn. His nerves were suddenly on edge. He could not bear interruptions on a day like this.

"William, are you going out?"

"Yes," William said, laughing. "As you see." He still did not turn. "Bit of a hurry," he said, blinking furiously, hand on the doorknob.

"I won't keep you a moment. William? I said I won't keep you a moment."

Furious, William was obliged to turn. Mrs. Joliffe stood at her door, holding it open for him to pass through. For a moment he thought of pretending he didn't understand and rushing out of the house, but then he would be too upset for the rest of the day. Concealing his anger, he followed Mrs. Joliffe and made a great show of consulting his stopwatch.

"Good heavens," he said, "is that the time? Goodness, I must rush or I will be late."

"William," Mrs. Joliffe said, "I want to talk to you very seriously."

"Ah," said William. "I must dash."

"The noise last night," said Mrs. Joliffe, "was quite un-speakable. Are you going to do anything about it?"

"It's all in the lease," William said. "Once the lease is signed it will be quite all right."

"Are you sure, William?"

"Yes," said William. "Now I really must go."

"Are you going to town?"

"Yes, I am."

"And dining out?"

"Yes, dining out."

"I shall not see you for sherry, then?"

"No."

"Have a good day, William."

He was glad of the long walk to the tube station. Head down, encased in his protective overcoat, William strode on down the hill at a cracking pace, seething with resentment, seething so literally he almost choked with the amount of saliva gushing into his mouth. Mrs. Joliffe was always using pretexts. She would ask him about one thing in order to reveal what he thought about another, just as his mother had done. William still had a clear picture of his mother saying, so many times, "Oh, William, have you a minute? It's nothing important." She would smile and beckon him, and unreasonably his heart would pound. For perhaps twenty minutes she would ask silly little questions and he would give grave answers, waiting to recognize the question she really wanted to ask. Mrs. Joliffe was not quite so bad, but then he was not afraid of her as he had been of his mother. There was nothing she could find out that he would rather keep hidden. William had forgotten the things he did not want his mother to find out—no dreadful revela-tions, certainly, just more inadequacies, making him the sort of son she did not want to have. He had not been freed of this oppressive inferiority until she had died. All he had felt was relief that no one could now take him to task for being what he was. Agnes Joliffe might try, but she did not succeed. He had held his own in this encounter as in any other of a similar nature.

Returning to her ostensible reason for delaying him, William bit his lip with vexation. The truth was, she had had something to complain about, there was no doubt about that at all. There *had* been a noise the night before, but that was not why she had tried to detain him. She wanted him in her flat. She wanted to talk to him, or rather to get him to talk and tell her where he was going and why. She pried, and thought he did not see beyond her subterfuge. As for mentioning sherry, he had said she could not count on him, he had gone to great trouble to teach her not to expect him, ever. Yet there she was, pretending he had rudely broken an appointment and let her down, when he had quite clearly gone to great pains not to enter into that kind of undertaking.

The tube was soothing. William settled himself behind a newspaper which he had no intention of reading and tried to order his thoughts. It was important to be businesslike at the travel agent's. The staff in these establishments were nowadays wanting in intelligence and turned surly at any demonstration of incompetence. One might think it their job to instruct the ignorant, but William had found they responded only to the knowledgeable. He must march in as if he knew exactly what he wanted, and obtain the leaflets and details about the Algarve that he needed. Hesitation would be misconstrued. He must not say he was only thinking of going there, but must appear to be quite definite about it. He must not say he wanted to know what kinds of hotel were available, but appear to know them all intimately and just want to check up.

Choosing a place for one's holidays was a frightful business, so frightful that William had not had a proper holiday for eight years. He disliked any element of risk, and however much he sifted the available facts he could never be entirely sure that this had been eliminated. If it had not been eliminated, he did not want to go. It became harder all the time, and he could foresee a time in the near future when even personally recommended places would not do. For several years he had gone to a small hotel in the Lake District, but now that was out. Last year, in April, he had had to pack up and return home on the second day because a television set had been installed in the sitting room directly beneath his bedroom. This was to be a last attempt to travel where he wished. Always, during his working years, he had been sure that his retirement would be spent traveling to all the countries that had intrigued him during his reading. He had the time, he had the money, he had the interest. What he lacked was certainty—he wanted to be certain the place of his choice was his sort of place. Disappointments were dreadful, and being so far away from home would make him feel even more committed than he already felt. It would need an elaborate security system of telegrams to himself to make him risk plunging into new territory. William sat and thought about them lovingly.

The first telegram he had ever sent himself was on his own twenty-first birthday. Actually, he had sent two that day—one in the morning at Cambridge saying "Come home at once father very ill" and the other in the afternoon, when he had reached home, saying "Return Cambridge vital." It had seemed so much simpler to be complicated. The point was, there were parties planned for him at both ends and he hated parties more than anything in the world. The thought of being centrally involved in one scared him. So he sent the telegrams, each leading to absurd repercussions, and spent a happy twenty-first-birthday evening on his own in Bletchley Station.

Now if he went to Portugal and it turned out dreadful he

would send himself a telegram saying "Mother dying please return immediately." This in hand, there would be no awkwardness about canceling his reservation. The hotel would be sympathetic. He would not have to say that his room was dirty, the noise dreadful, the food atrocious. It wouldn't get him out of paying for what he had not had, but then he did not mind that—his deviousness was not an attempt to resort to financial trickery. No, he would pay willingly, as long as there was no fuss, as long as he did not have to go through the embarrassments the truth necessitated.

A small man in a large overcoat, William was swallowed up the minute he stepped out of the tube train. He trotted rather than walked, his back hunched but his head upright, nose twitching, eyes blinking, a mole searching for the light. But he was tenacious. The crowds disgorged from several trains fought their way up the escalators, jostling for position. William didn't jostle. Quick and nimble, he slipped in and out, knowing instinctively where there was a space that could accommodate him. Once on the pavements aboveground, he traveled swiftly to the agency in Regent Street, unhindered by traffic or pedestrians, arriving at its swing doors pink-cheeked and invigorated by the race. His stay was not long. Authoritatively, not seeming to care much, he asked for and received leaflets on the Algarve and timetables of planes and trains and boats. Such was his aloofness, he almost dropped what he was given in his haste to get it into his pocket and be off.

There was then the matter of lunch before the matinée. Since he was dining with Pullen, he required a light lunch, but somewhere quiet where he could give the brochures a preliminary going over and see if he needed to go elsewhere to get more. The anonymity of Lyons' Corner House appealed to him, as well as the nostalgic overtones. When he was a boy, he and his sister had regarded Lyons' as the treat to end all treats. Brought up to town by their nanny to visit the dentist or be measured for school uniform, they had gone there with her and eaten sickly chocolate éclairs and greasy doughnuts and crisps and fizzy bright lemonade. They had been bound together by guilt. The nanny felt guilty that she was allowing them to eat such unwholesome fare, especially after a visit to the dentist, and the children felt guilty that they enjoyed it so much. They were reared at home in an atmosphere of asceticism, and the warm, brassy vulgarity of Lyons' was something they felt they ought to be repelled by but were not.

William went upstairs to the grill room. He had not the courage to patronize the memory-ridden snack bar. Here he sat on a leather sofa, at a table laid for one, most thought- fully, and after he had ordered Dover sole and a green salad he brought out the travel literature. After a little while he sighed. It was not literature. It was not even plain factual information, but a hodgepodge of facts, many inaccurate, wrapped up in crude language that offended him. He could not abide deplorable hyphenations like "sun-kissed." The pictures were hardly better, lying in their own Technicolor way. The only snippet William could find that gave him hope was a mention of state-run *poussadas* that were simple but comfortable. The next move must be to track down a *poussada*. How? Then he saw the address of the Portuguese Tourist Board and determined to visit that.

Eating his sole—unhappily a tomato had found its way into his green salad, thereby contaminating it with juice and making it unfit for his consumption—William won- dered about when he should take his holiday. He had thought the spring, but now this was out of the question. The house required his presence. He could not leave it with new tenants still adjusting, just as he had not been able to leave it for any length of time with tenants still to choose. Autumn would be best, possibly late September, certainly no later than late October. Come November, no householder wisely left his house, whose claims over the winter months were heavy. Neatly William copied down the address of the Portuguese Tourist Board into his diary. His morning's work had not been in vain. He hoped, as he drank some coffee, that he would be able to say the same at the end of the afternoon about his afternoon's work.

The theater was more than half empty, which was disturbing. William occupied the same seat as he had done before—the middle of the front row of the circle. There was no one else at all in his row. Extremely conscious of this, William kept his eyes riveted on the stage and moved his finger uneasily round his neck inside his collar. It was fortunate he had seen the revue before or his distress at his conspicuousness would have made him totally incapable of judging it. As it was, he reached the interval still undecided, and concentrating too much on the possibility of moving his seat to really consider anything else. Moving was attended by all sorts of hazards. Someone might come in for the second half and be very cross at being assumed entirely absent. Or there might be a bylaw of the theater forbidding the sitting in any seat not specifically paid for. William mopped his brow. When the lights went down again, he scurried to the end of his row and sat there. Instantly he was more relaxed. The adjoining row was almost full and he felt part of it.

Perhaps because of this, the second three quarters of an hour seemed preferable to the first. William laughed out loud twice—not very loud, but audible, sufficient to be joining in the merriment all about. The sketch that had seemed to him very rude, about the Queen, no longer seemed so. He now thought it affectionate. He followed the words of the songs much better and even thought them clever. On the way out, he stopped at the booking office and booked three tickets for January first. The Hills would enjoy it. They would have a pleasant evening. A good dinner at The Garden and then this fashionable show. William was pleased. He felt he was going to do them proud, and that had been his avowed and sole intention.

William's pleasure, and his anticipation of the Hills' pleasure, made him reckless. He stopped at a florist's and ordered a rather beautiful cyclamen to be dispatched at once to Mrs. Joliffe. She had had such a cyclamen for a whole year, but it had been struck by some vegetable plague and had died unaccountably before Christmas. It had remained in her sitting room a whole week, bare and shriveled, before she had thrown it out. This would make her very happy. William did not include a card and would deny all knowledge if asked. That way her enjoyment would be trebled: as well as loving to look at and tend the flourishing plant, Mrs. Joliffe would pass many hours speculating about who could have sent it. She would think of friends, which was always pleasant, and her view of the world would be all the kinder. So much did he dwell on the blessings he was bestowing that William had to tell himself off for being smug. He had no cause for smugness. Self-interest lay behind his gesture, he assured himself. He wanted, at the moment, to deflect Mrs. Joliffe's attention from the house, at least until the lease was signed. She was strong and had great powers of persuasion, and he feared her should she get to work on him. His fear was because he knew she was right: he should not let the flat to the Hills. Decidedly not. The noose swung in front of him, quite visible.

William banished the image with a quick shake of the head, and made his way toward the Design Centre in the Haymarket. Here he spent a very happy hour and felt he had come considerably nearer being able to choose light fittings for his sitting room. He took copious notes and filed the information away with the travel folders in his inside pocket, which was by now bulging—indeed, bulging so much William wondered if anyone might think he was carrying a pistol. The idea amused him and he went off to meet Pullen with a smile on his face.

Pullen always had to be met in his office, or at least in the building in which he had his office, which William found strange. He had never let anyone meet him in his office or anywhere near it. Not that his office was anything to be ashamed of, particularly in the last five years of his working life, when he had had a green carpet entirely covering his twelve-foot-by-five room. Anyone who knew anything about the Civil Service knew how to value that. He had kept it very neat, of course, and had several plants there worth seeing, but had never invited anyone to see them. No, business and pleasure had never been mixed. He had always met friends at the place where they were going to eat or in the foyer of the cinema or theater.

Quietly William climbed the stairs. There were no lifts in the building. Several people passed him on their way down as he was on his way up, and he recognized the paraphernalia of work—the briefcase, the mackintosh and umbrella you had thought at 8 A.M. you were going to need, the carrier bag you had nipped out to fill at lunchtime. There had been a certain contentment in the orderliness of office life, but William did not find himself experiencing more than a faint and quickly passing nostalgia. It was good to be free to be really orderly.

There was a lot of shouting coming from Pullen's office. William stopped at the end of the corridor, hand still on the curve of the stair rail, and waited for it to subside. After another burst of vocal gunfire, the door at the end of the passage was opened and hurried footsteps came toward him. William quickly ran down a dozen or so stairs and started to go up slowly again, as though he were tired after the long haul. His subterfuge was unnecessary. The girl who ran past him was crying and had a handkerchief clutched to her mouth. William frowned. Pullen expected too much. These creatures who typed and cleared up for one did not have either the mental ability or the emotional capacity to understand what one wanted. But Pullen went on bullying them in this sadistic fashion, to such a degree that William had almost been moved to speaking to him about it. There had been nothing like that in his own relationships with staff. He wanted to tell Pullen that familiarity, of whatever kind, never paid.

William was in the corridor again. Softly he padded along it toward the open door at the end. When he was almost there he stopped, hoping that something would happen to resolve the dilemma of how to announce himself.

It did. "William," shouted Pullen, "is that you skulking outside?"

"Ah—yes," said William, giggling, still not knowing how to get through the half-open door.

"Then for God's sake come in."

Gratefully William went in, one finger raised in some embarrassment over whether to extend his hand to be shaken or not. One never knew with Pullen. Once, William had not proffered his hand and had been asked, sharply, if he no longer knew how to behave like an English gentleman. Once, when he extended his hand eagerly, Pullen had turned it aside and said, "Oh, you homosexuals."

"Good God," Pullen said, "you look like the Wandering Jew in that getup."

"Ah," William said, smiling gamely, "my overcoat."

"Good job my girls have gone home," Pullen said, "or you'd have frightened them to death. You look as though you're going to do an indecent exposure any minute."

"I met one of them," William said mildly. "She seemed rather upset."

"Silly bitch," said Pullen. "I'm glad to see the back of her. What I want is one like that eunuch you had, William. What was her name? Stitch? Snitch?"

"Miss Stitt," William said.

"That's it. Where did you have her neutered, eh? Well, come on, if I've landed myself with you for dinner, as it seems I have, we'd better go and eat it and get it over. How's that ridiculous house of yours? Well, I hope, not suffering, in good shape?"

"Excellent health," said William jovially.

"Better than mine," grumbled Pullen. "I've forgotten what good health is, I can tell you. I'm going to die any minute. You look well, William. What's the secret? Do you drink cow piss or ox blood or some other bloody stupid concoction?"

"Oh, I keep fit," William said. "I get about, get plenty of fresh air."

"Well, you're not going to get any tonight," said Pullen. "We're waiting right here until my car is brought round, and then we're not getting out of it till we get to my nice centrally heated house. I don't live in an igloo like you, William. If I'm going to die I'm going to die warm, and full and comfortable."

William tittered and they descended the stairs together to Pullen's car, which was chauffeur-driven. Pullen liked to drive, but had been disqualified the previous year. William, who did not like driving and could not himself drive, was glad about the chauffeur. Cars were convenient but abominations and William saw no real reason why they could not be abolished altogether. Conveniences were not important. He smiled as he said that to himself, and Pullen jabbed him in the side with his elbow and asked him what dirty joke he was keeping to himself now. William's protests lasted till Pullen's house and put Pullen into good spirits.

Pullen lived in Cheyne Walk in a house once much coveted by William. The reason he no longer coveted it was because he now knew it was leasehold. Pullen had taken, twenty years ago, a thirty-year lease. This filled William with horror. In ten years' time Pullen would still be only seventy-eight and would have to find somewhere else, since it was extremely unlikely the lease would be renewed. There therefore seemed to William no point in it at all. At seventy-eight one would just be settling down to the enjoyments of one's house—and out one would be put. Pullen, of course, thought different. He spent a fortune on his house quite cheerfully and said that if he ever got to seventy-eight he deserved to freeze to death under London Bridge.

Pullen did not live as William lived. The door was opened by his housekeeper, a Mrs. Elspeth Morley, a neat efficient lady of sixty or so who had stayed with her master the whole twenty years in spite of his foul temper. This fact always pleased William. He had been foolish enough to express his pleasure to Pullen once and there had followed a stream of invective against Mrs. Morley that had upset William for days. It seemed that she was a gin-sodden, crooked, lying lesbian whose sole ambition was to murder her benefactor. Nevertheless, William observed, this monster meantime looked after his friend very well. She prepared delicious meals unless specifically told not to, kept the house clean and full of flowers, and ordered Pullen's chaotic life so successfully that he was not even aware it was being done.

They dined and drank and William was happy to be in such lovely surroundings. What Pullen did not realize was how much of a *home* he had. His house was beautiful, full of beautiful things, but it was used and worn at the same time. William never liked returning to his house, to his little flat, after a visit to Pullen's. His affection seemed temporarily to have faded and he felt sulky and grumpy. Flat-living seemed squalid and unworthy. He felt restricted and cornered and longed to have a dining room and drawing room and patio and library and music room like Pullen.

Knowing he was going to feel like this, William made the most of his evening. He walked about a lot—Pullen asked if he had ants in his pants—and fingered things and tried to feel the space and lightness of it all. He hardly listened to a word his friend said, and Pullen certainly never listened to a word he said, but to both the predictable evening was something to hang on to, something solid, something—however unsatisfactory—that had gone on for a long time and need not be worried about.

Seven

>>>>>>>>>

IN THE ORDINARY course of events, Mrs. Joliffe had no dealings with Alexander Hill—she did not agree with abbreviations even when they were offered to her and would never have referred to him as "Alex"—but by what she at first considered a most unfortunate occurrence she was thrown into contact with him and could not thereafter entirely avoid him, since she felt some sense of obligation. It was Germaine's fault, or, more precisely, that wretched Homer's. They had come to visit her in their car, in spite of the dreadfully treacherous roads and the age of this vehicle, and when the visit was over they could not start the car. She had grown tired of waving from the window and was about to go to the door and ask if she should telephone a garage when Alexander Hill came bounding down the stairs and started the car for them. Mrs. Joliffe felt her daughter had thanked him less than effusively. Also, his hands were covered with grease. Accordingly, she thanked him herself and gave him an old towel to wipe off the worst of the dirt. He had, she thought, nice hands—square, long-fingered, brown. He had a pleasant voice, too. Twice after that she met him in the hall and they passed the time of day, and so it seemed quite natural, the day following, to ask him how he had enjoyed his evening out. "Great," he said, "it was great."

Mrs. Joliffe pondered this statement all day. The young man had said it with such flatness, even if what he said was complimentary. He had, she remembered, said the same thing when she had handed him the towel to wipe his hands on. "Great," he had said, carefully wiping the grease from between his fingers, "that's great." It was more than likely that "great" equated with "nice" in her vocabulary and was used in the same way. Then they hardly knew each other, so what else could he have said? No, his verdict was not of value, except perhaps to show that nothing very noteworthy had happened and good-mannered harmony had prevailed.

Sophie's visit was eagerly awaited to fill in the details. She came, as she now did daily, at half-past five for a glass of sherry, and Mrs. Joliffe did not try to contain her impatience but said, before the girl was seated, "Well, how did you enjoy yourself last night?"

"Very much," said Sophie.

"Did William behave himself?"

"He was very thoughtful and kind."

"He takes a great deal of trouble," said Mrs. Joliffe. "It is not a simple matter to William, you know—he finds it impossible to be casual."

"I can see that," said Sophie. "It must make entertaining such an effort."

"All entertaining is an effort," said Mrs. Joliffe severely, "as I know. The hours I have spent preparing menus and matching guests—quite exhausting. After my dinner parties I used to have to spend the next day in bed."

"It seems a bit pointless," ventured Sophie, "unless you enjoyed it?"

"Of course I enjoyed it!" said Mrs. Joliffe sharply. "Good heavens, I wasn't doing it for money, child. Why else should I do it, if not for my own pleasure?"

"I thought perhaps out of duty," suggested Sophie.

"To whom? You forget, for most of my life I have been a widow. I had no husband to wish to promote or please, and I certainly did not do it for Germaine's sake. I banned her from my dinner parties the minute I realized what a social liability she was. In any case, she did not enjoy social intercourse—like William. It is an ordeal for him. Taking you to dinner will have cost him sleepless nights."

"I'm sorry about that," said Sophie, flushing.

"No need to be sorry—he is silly and that is that. All that is important is that you should appreciate the final result and be sure to thank him properly."

"Oh, I have," said Sophie. "I wrote a note the minute we got home and left it out for him."

"Good," said Mrs. Joliffe, "that will please him. Now tell me everything that happened. Remember, I wasn't there. Miss nothing out, however trivial."

Sophie did her best, though feeling Mrs. Joliffe hardly deserved it after presuming to tell her how to thank Mr. Bone. She said they had had a very pleasant meal. Mr. Bone had chicken, she had veal and Alex had steak. They had had two bottles of wine, and she had had two puddings because they were so delicious and Mr. Bone had pressed her. They had finished eating at seven-thirty and arrived at the theater just in time to buy a program and get settled in their seats. The revue had been funny. Mr. Bone had laughed a lot, sometimes a little before the joke, which had puzzled them. They had ice creams in the interval and Mr. Bone told them about a revue he had been in at Cambridge. Afterward they had come straight home and gone to bed.

"And when," asked Mrs. Joliffe when she saw Sophie had finished, "was the lease signed?"

"It wasn't," said Sophie.

"I thought this celebration was to mark the signing of the lease?"

"Mr. Bone thought it better Alex should go to his solicitor's office to sign it."

"What an extraordinary idea. Has he been?"

"He has gone this morning."

"How very fortunate your husband does not work."

"But he does," said Sophie.

"He has found employment? I am very pleased to hear it. What, may I ask?"

"Digging tunnels for the Victoria line."

"Good heavens—digging tunnels. Does William know this?"

"I don't think so. He never asked."

"Then don't tell him. It would upset him terribly. This is for money, I presume?"

"Yes." And Sophie had to laugh.

"You find it funny?"

"No, Mrs. Joliffe, I find you funny. What's so scandalous about digging tunnels for money? We need money, so Alex digs to earn it. When we have enough, he needn't dig any more. It's quite simple and sensible."

"Simple it may be," said Mrs. Joliffe sharply, "but not sensible. It is a most precarious way of providing for one's family."

"Alex has always provided, that's the point."

"For how long?"

"Oh, months."

"Months?" queried Mrs. Joliffe.

"For as long as we've been together," said Sophie hurriedly. "There is nothing strange about it."

"I am glad you have such confidence," said Mrs. Joliffe, "for I would find it difficult. So would William, if he knew." She paused. "Did he not ask your husband about his prospects at all last night?"

"Not really," Sophie said.

"He is the most exasperating man," said Mrs. Joliffe.

"The whole purpose of the dinner, as he explained it to me, was to lay the foundations of a good understanding. Yet how can he have done this without finding out fundamentals?"

"I think we have a good understanding," said Sophie, hesitantly, but determined to say it.

"You do?" asked Mrs. Joliffe grimly. "You understand William and what he wants?"

"I think so. He wants us all to be friends and not like landlord and tenants."

"Rubbish."

"I beg your pardon?"

"William knows what he wants, but he is afraid to tell you. He wants peace and quiet and everyone to go about their own business."

"Then why ask us out?"

"Typical. He did it to show you how civilized he is, in the hopes that you would respond also by being civilized. In fact all he did was thoroughly complicate matters. Now he will find it harder than ever to be firm and you will find it easier to take advantage."

"But we have no intention of taking advantage," said Sophie indignantly. "We like Mr. Bone very much."

"Of course you do," said Mrs. Joliffe, "and so you should. But you are no more prepared to abide by his wishes than you were before, are you? You will go on disregarding him in exactly the same way."

Without realizing it, Mrs. Joliffe had started to bang her stick on the floor, and Sophie watched as the pile of the carpet was dented and then sprang back and then was dented again. She looked up at Mrs. Joliffe's face and saw it was contorted with temper—red, eyes bolting out of her head, mouth trembling.

"I don't think we disregard him," she said, very calmly and slowly, "not intentionally."

"The evidence suggests otherwise," shouted Mrs. Joliffe, still banging. "Who flushed the lavatory at midnight last night, the very night you had dined with him?"

"It was an accident," protested Sophie, "easily done—"

"Not by William."

"He is used to his rules—they are his. We have to have time to get used to them, too. Surely you would agree?"

"I see no prospect of you ever getting used to them," said Mrs. Joliffe. "You lead a different way of life to William and cannot be expected to conform to his exacting standards. No one except yourself thinks you could ever change. But it is wrong of you to exploit William's kindness and make him endure this torture—no, it is not too strong a word, noise is torture to William. You are sadists. You come into his house because it suits your purpose, and you are determined to make him suffer as long as it goes on suiting your purpose. It is shameless."

She found she had agitated herself quite ridiculously and saw by Sophie's distressingly heightened color that she had upset her too. Horrified, she got up and went over to the girl and, laying her hand on her knee, said, "I do beg your pardon. I was very rude. Forgive me."

"Nothing to forgive," said Sophie shakily. "But you meant it, that's what's worrying."

"Have another glass of sherry," pleaded Mrs. Joliffe.

"I shouldn't. Alcohol doesn't agree with me at the moment."

"Wait," said Mrs. Joliffe. "I have something for you."

Sophie watched her drag herself across the room and felt sorry at the resentment she had harbored, but even while she was experiencing this regret it came into her head that Mrs. Joliffe was perhaps putting on something of a performance. Did she always drag her leg quite so markedly? Sophie thought not. But then, if it was deliberate, how pathetic and how much more sorry she ought to feel for the old woman. It seemed a long time before she reappeared, and Sophie felt uncomfortable sitting with her empty glass on her own. She rose cautiously and put the glass down on one of the small pedestal tables, and then rather self-consciously went and stood in front of the bookcase and scrutinized the books. They were mostly historical novels and collections of letters. Presently she heard the uneven footsteps of Mrs. Joliffe and returned to her seat, where she busied herself picking threads off her dress.

"It isn't much," Mrs. Joliffe said, "but I can't get out, you see, and I can't ask William or Germaine, they don't like to be bothered, so I thought you might like something home-made."

"Thank you," said Sophie, and she took the tin box, "but you don't need to give me anything—"

"I know I don't need to," Mrs. Joliffe said crossly. "I want to, and it's nothing. You haven't looked yet. Look."

Sophie, with something of a struggle, for it was very tight-fitting, lifted the lid of the box. Inside, the contents were covered by a white-and-yellow checked tea towel. Gently Sophie lifted the towel, and there underneath lay a perfectly baked loaf of wholemeal bread.

"I'm a silly old woman, aren't I?" said Mrs. Joliffe. "I don't suppose you like brown bread. I don't suppose home-made tastes any different to shop-bought to you, and who am I to say you're a fool?"

"You're a darling," cried Sophie. "It's the most beautiful present anyone has ever given me!"

"It isn't a present. I was baking and I made two, that was all. I can't compete with William and his splendid dinners."

Sophie took no notice and said, "Will you teach me?"

"To bake bread?"

"Yes."

"I bake every week, on Thursday at eleven in the morning. I shan't mind you looking over my shoulder. But there's a knack, you know. William hasn't got it. He's made hundreds of dratted notes and he still can't get it right."

"I never thought," said Sophie, "you would be the sort of woman who baked bread."

"And why shouldn't I bake bread?" demanded Mrs. Joliffe fiercely.

"For the same reason I have never done," challenged Sophie. "It's never been required of me. I was not brought up to know how to bake bread and I should not have thought you were."

"My dear child," said Mrs. Joliffe, "I have long ago forgotten how I was brought up. I am seventy and my upbringing has faded to nothing."

"I hope mine does," said Sophie.

"When I was sixteen," said Mrs. Joliffe, "I determined to make myself a rounded character. I sought every kind of accomplishment, both intellectual and physical. I read all I could get my hands on, I did postal courses in judo, I learned how to mend a fuse, I learned how to drive and maintain a car, I learned how to sew and to cook. I learned how to make bread."

"How marvelous," breathed Sophie.

"It was all," said Mrs. Joliffe proudly, "quite in vain. I married. I lost myself, utterly."

"But you still bake bread," said Sophie.

"That is not the point," said Mrs. Joliffe, banging her stick. "You have not understood. I did all those things so that I might be independent and lead a life without shackles, gloriously different from all the other women around me. I married. I shackled myself. That was that."

"But marriage makes me free," said Sophie earnestly.

"We shall see," said Mrs. Joliffe. "Your generation may be different. William thinks so—he admires it."

"What does he admire?"

"Oh," said Mrs. Joliffe, with an impatient wave of her

hand, "you must ask him the next time he takes you out to dinner."

"We must have him to dinner first," said Sophie, frowning, "if I can think what to give him."

"He has a delicate stomach," said Mrs. Joliffe. "He was shot in the war, and also he has ulcers, though I am sure they result from his inadequate diet. William eats foolishly. He drinks wine at every meal, but sometimes that meal is revolting tinned tuna fish or crackers and meat paste."

"I thought perhaps he might be rather a good cook," said Sophie, relieved.

"No," said Mrs. Joliffe, "he is not a good cook. He rarely cooks anything at all and for that very reason ought to have either married or had a housekeeper."

"Did he never want to marry?" asked Sophie, nervous of Mrs. Joliffe's easily aroused wrath, but unable to resist asking when presented so direct an opportunity.

"William wished to marry only once," said Mrs. Joliffe.

"Did she turn him down?"

"No. He did not ask."

"But why not?"

"He did not think he had sufficient security to offer."

"But who cares about security—if he loved her?"

"The two are inseparable to William," said Mrs. Joliffe, smiling. "It was because he loved her, I presume, that he thought it wrong to involve her in his own precarious life."

"I can't believe Mr. Bone has ever been precarious," said Sophie. "He's so careful and orderly."

"On the contrary," said Mrs. Joliffe, "he is a scatter-brain."

"Did you know the woman he wanted to marry?"

"I knew her."

"Did she want to marry him?"

"Yes, I rather think she did."

"What a waste," said Sophie. "He might have been so happy if only he hadn't bothered about money."

"It wasn't only a question of money," said Mrs. Joliffe. "It was his whole future. William was never clear what he wanted to do and he would not ask anyone else to join him in a gamble."

"Life is a gamble," said Sophie.

"That is your generation," said Mrs. Joliffe. "That is what William admires—this cool assessment and willingness to take a chance. Your plight, for instance, terrifies him—he cannot understand a couple marrying and bearing a child without security of occupation or abode—yet he at the same time admires you."

"But you don't," said Sophie.

"No," said Mrs. Joliffe, "I do not. It is one of the many things William and I disagree about."

"I must go," said Sophie. "Thank you for the sherry and the loaf. Now we will have some supper."

"Wouldn't you have had otherwise?"

"Not unless Alex brought something in. I was counting on him bringing something. I expect he will, but now we will have this lovely bread even if he doesn't."

Mrs. Joliffe told William this the next day. "She did not know," she said, "if they would have any supper."

"One does not always need it," said William, who did not like gossip. "This is excellent sherry. May I ask where you got it from?"

"From the self-service in the High Street," snapped Mrs. Joliffe, who divined the rebuff, "where I always get it from. If you weren't such a snob you would go there."

"They have many good things," William agreed, "but one has one's loyalties."

"To shopkeepers who have none to you?" asked Mrs. Joliffe. "Make no mistake, William, those establishments you patronize do not need your support."

"Perhaps," said William.

"I don't think *she* shops at all," said Mrs. Joliffe. "I've never seen her come back with anything much in her basket, and they certainly have nothing delivered. Your dinner must have been a godsend to them, William. I shouldn't be surprised if it's the first decent meal they have had in months."

"A very nice meal," said William, as though he had not heard the rest. "You must go there someday."

"Pigs might fly," said Mrs. Joliffe bitterly.

"The chicken was nevertheless not as good as yours," said William.

"One wouldn't expect it to be."

"No, quite. However, a most enjoyable meal, I thought."

"Not marred, I hope?"

"Marred?"

"By any incidents—your guests were up to your own high standards of behavior?"

William hid his confusion in his glass. It was a small glass, but he thrust his nose into it until the tip was tickled by the sherry and it looked as if he might inhale it. Alex Hill had smoked throughout the meal. Further, he had stubbed his strangely thin cigarettes out on his side plate, in spite of the large ashtray in front of him, and once he had missed the plate and stubbed it out on the tablecloth. If a waiter had not been quick there might even have been a fire. He had not put his knife and fork side by side at the end of a course but left them zigzagging across the plate so that the waiters did not know whether he had finished or not. He had used his own spoon to take the sugar, but then he had stirred the coffee and stuck the wet spoon back into the sugar for more and taken instead the dry sugar spoon. William was thereafter obliged to go without sugar. In the theater cloakroom he had not tipped the attendant, and all the way from the foyer to his seat he had combed his hair. He had got into the taxi home first, not even holding the door open for William and Sophie, and had taken up more than his fair share of the seat. He had opened the window without asking them if they wanted it open and had thrown a paper handkerchief onto the floor. William took a deep breath, took his nose out of the sherry and firmly protested, "My standards are not high."

"But were they up to them?"

"Of course. They were most polite, most agreeable."

"I am glad of it. What did you talk about?"

"Oh, I can hardly remember—this and that, as one does. We talked about food."

"Very elevating."

"It was relaxing. We were out for a pleasant evening."

"Then you did not get round to discussing more important things?"

"No. There was neither the time nor the opportunity."

"You will do it later?"

"I don't know. All that was important was some degree of understanding. This, I think, was achieved."

"The lease has been signed?"

"This morning."

"And the rent paid."

William paused. "The young man had mislaid his checkbook. I await the check."

"You are very unbusinesslike, William. I hope you get the check, and when you get it I hope it does not bounce."

"There is no question of that," said William, "but in any case I feel it is wrong to discuss it."

"I am sorry. Have another glass of sherry. Germaine and Homer may come soon."

"Ah," said William, happy to move away from the Hills, "and how is Germaine?"

"Irritating as ever," said Mrs. Joliffe. "She has changed her job yet again and her life is even more disorganized than ever. I can hardly bear to listen to her tale of woe. Now they are talking of emigrating to Australia. Not that they would ever do anything so energetic—I wish most fervently that they would."

"You would miss her," said William shyly.

"Indeed I would not. I find Germaine as much of an encumbrance as she finds me. She seems to think she is a comfort to me in my old age, but I find her most uncomfortable. We have nothing in common but blood."

"Which is thicker than water," said William feebly.

"I don't care what they say. I find I have more affinity, after two weeks, with young Sophie Hill than I have ever had with Germaine."

"Ah, yes," William said vaguely, "Sophie Hill," as though he wondered who she was.

"But she is apparently estranged from her mother," said Mrs. Joliffe, "so here am I, in loco parentis, and another poor woman somewhere daughterless."

William nodded sympathetically and regretted he could not possibly probe Mrs. Joliffe's statement further. He knew Sophie came in regularly, and had worried about it, thinking she might be bothering Mrs. Joliffe unduly. Now that he thought about it, he clearly ought to have worried about the opposite, since Mrs. Joliffe was stronger than Sophie. He could tell she was proud of her new friendship, and though he was glad for her there was an air of conspiracy about her that he did not like. Mrs. Joliffe, given half a chance, was possessive. She might try to possess Sophie Hill and an awkward situation would arise, the thought of which made William shudder and gulp his sherry hastily.

"I was thinking," Mrs. Joliffe said, "that really we ought to do something about the side entrance. I know you will be happy to have the subject changed, you see, William. We can talk animatedly about inanimate objects at least."

"The side entrance?"

"Do not echo me, William. Yes, the side entrance. It is there. We have never used it. It is time it was put into use. Am I being succinct enough?"

"But why?"

Because we are now three households and we are getting in each other's way. The Hills could come in and out by it quite easily, thereby avoiding wearing that hall linoleum to a shred. Since they came, it is always filthy. You must either clear the side entrance or get your Mrs. Wood to clean it daily. The very sight of it is driving me insane, and soon it will be worse. Soon, William, there will be a perambulator to contend with—large rubber wheels coming in and out, leaving wet, muddy tracks. Have you thought about that?"

"No."

"Well, think. Besides, it is ridiculous to have that entrance blocked up with junk."

"I will ring Pullen."

"You will do no such thing."

"He is the architect and as such—"

"And as such has nothing whatsoever to do with whether you throw away a lot of rubbish, put down a path and unlock a door."

"It is not as simple as that," said William. "The door, for example, is not painted, if I remember correctly. As it was not visible, Pullen thought it unnecessary."

"Then paint it."

"There is the question of the color. Pullen feels strongly—"

"Paint it white and put down a path and stop making such an issue of it."

"But what kind of path? There are many choices—cement, or pavingstones, or tarmac. These are not easy decisions; I should not like to make them without Pullen's assistance."

"Then we may as well forget it—it would take an age. You will just have to have your hall ruined and I shall not make any more helpful suggestions."

"I wonder whether Sophie Hill would consider leaving the pram outside?"

"Certainly she would not!" said Mrs. Joliffe, outraged, "I can speak for her."

"You have discussed a pram and its parking?"

"No, we have not, we do not descend to trivia, but I know Sophie's mind and I can speak confidently for her on any subject. She would not leave the perambulator outside. It would deteriorate in the wind and rain."

"Perhaps a temporary cover could be erected?"

"No. Sophie would not consider such a thing. Her pram must be brought into the house. I know her mind."

William sat, silent and glum.

"I know what you are thinking, William," said Mrs. Joliffe, "and there is no need. Sophie comes and goes as she pleases, under no kind of obligation. Believe it or not, her life is as lonely as mine and she is less practiced in making the best of it. You need have no fear that she is in any way constrained."

"I was merely thinking of the problem and admiring your plant," William stuttered.

"Lies, but you may admire it. It must have cost you a great deal, and it has given me a great deal of pleasure. I should have thanked you before, but my intuition told me you would not like it."

"You are mistaken," William began. "Some other friend—"

"I have no other friends, as I have told you many times," said Mrs. Joliffe severely. "They are all dead or in nursing homes or in any place but London. And in any case, nobody but you has ever sent me such a profusion of flowers out of pure kindness. Did you think I was not aware of that? I remember the very first ones you sent me—four dozen yellow tulips on Saint Valentine's Day 1923. They drove me frantic. I went to see the florist who had delivered them personally and asked him to describe the gentleman who had placed the order. He could not remember, he believed one of his assistants had taken it, but he managed to find the piece of paper on which you had written the address. I did not recognize the handwriting, but I took it home and com-

pared it with every letter I had ever received. You had written only one note, when my brother died, but it was
enough. William sent those flowers, I thought. You have no
idea how much it meant to me. Now I have embarrassed
you. I am sorry, William."

"Not at all," mumbled William.

"Matthew, of course, never sent me a flower in his life."

"He was a busy man."

"He was an insensitive one. He believed husbands had no
need to send flowers."

"Quite right," said William.

"Quite wrong—they have most need. I suspect Alexander
Hill labors under the same illusion—he takes Sophie for
granted already, which is very foolish. I shall have to speak
to him."

"Oh, no—is that wise?" blurted out William, startled.

"William, I was joking," said Mrs. Joliffe gently. "I have
hardly passed the time of day with Mr. Hill. You must know
him much better already. What do you make of him?"

"Charming young man," said William.

"Oh, come, William! There is no need to be so disapprov-
ing. Why cannot we talk about your tenants?"

"It's unfair," said William.

"Why? Where did you get that notion from? What harm
can it do?"

"I think," said William, "I hear Germaine and Homer."

He heard aright, and after staying to bid them good evening and inquire after their health, he made his escape. As
he was closing the door of Mrs. Joliffe's sitting room, he
thought he heard already the names of Sophie and Alexander on her lips and he went upstairs deep in thought, fretting still about side entrances and prams.

The evening before had not been a success, but he was not
going to tell Mrs. Joliffe that. As he sat and ate some cheese
and crisps, William thought how such a confession would

have pleased her, then instantly chided himself for being unfair. She would not gloat over his social failures. If he had said to himself that she would be pleased, what he had meant was that she would not be surprised and people like Mrs. Joliffe enjoyed not being surprised. But it had passed off reasonably smoothly, and that was quite an achievement. The moments of awkwardness had been few and not too hard to gloss over. The Hills had helped to gloss over them and that was the only thing he really regretted—that they had been as much aware of the awkwardness as he. Sometimes he comforted himself after such occasions with the assurance that it was all in his head—everything had been perfectly all right, everyone perfectly relaxed. This time he could not. The Hills had sensed his nervousness and tried to be kind.

Only, William reflected, pouring himself another glass of wine, only when he was on his own was he a gregarious animal. It seemed to him that he talked incessantly to all the people he knew as he ate his solitary snacks. Indeed, he hardly had time to snatch a bite, so busy was his tongue. When he actually was with these other people, the same tongue chattered on, but sounded foolish. He found he was alone so often, and was so used to his own pace and style of conversation, that he was bewildered by the reality of other people's. All the time he was saying "I beg your pardon," forever leaning forward, his hand tugging desperately at his earlobe, saying "I'm so sorry, I didn't quite catch that." People thought he was deaf, but he was not in the least. It was just that he could not cope with any speech that was given in the modern idiom. If, in addition, the speaker had any kind of regional accent, he was seriously handicapped. Alexander Hill spoke some kind of Scottish dialect that was completely incomprehensible to him, even though he had heard Mrs. Joliffe refer to the young man as having "the merest trace of Ayrshire" in his vowels.

Still, one must not be too depressed. They had managed.
All his little prepared anecdotes had been very well received
and he thought he had shown them that he was not too far
behind the times. That, of course, was another point. Prepared anecdotes were all very well, but it was spontaneity
that mattered and in this he was totally lacking. It was not
that things to say did not spring into his head—they did,
frequently, but he did not have time to censor them before
the conversation had moved on. He would find himself with
his mouth open, strange strangled sounds coming from his
throat, his brain teeming, and the onlookers so appalled by
his difficulties that they competed with each other to prevent him speaking at all. Women were particularly adroit at
sparing him what they imagined to be agonies of shyness.
They either jumped in quickly with some chatter of their
own or finished off whatever he had started to say. No one
was content to wait.

William finished his snack, leaving half the cheese and an
apple he had peeled. He did not feel very hungry. An enormous dinner lasted him several days, even when he ate with
restraint. Mrs. Joliffe said his meals were a permanent picnic, but he thought he balanced them very well, paying
great attention to protein and so forth. He hoped the Hills
did the same, since she apparently put them in the same
bracket. He did not need much food, because he did not
expend much energy, but they did, particularly Sophie. It
would be dreadful if she was not getting enough to eat, but
he could see no evidence of malnutrition or even an un-
healthy diet. She had looked very lovely last night—not so
much her clothes, which he had an idea hardly varied, as
her person. Her eyes were very bright and light, always as
though they had just been washed with tears, and her
cheeks were as pink as a child's. He had been proud to be
seen with her—with them both, really, since Alex had gone
to the lengths of wearing a suit and a collar and tie, marks

of respect which William, knowing he was meant to notice them, gratefully had done. It had made him, as they got into the taxi, very hopeful.

Those hopes had not been fulfilled. No, he could not say they had. He was exasperated that he could not, having enough sense to realize that to a large extent it was his own fault. He had not been able to steer the conversation in the right direction. Rather the reverse. Recalling what they had talked about, he seemed to have gone to a great deal of trouble to steer it *away* from the right direction. He had shied away like a frightened animal at any mention of money or jobs or noise or the future. At one point, Sophie had leaned across the table and said to him, very earnestly, "I do hope we haven't been disturbing you, Mr. Bone?" He had said not at all. He had actually said, "Not at all." William shook his head at the memory. How could he have had the stupidity? Then again, she had said later, on the way home, when their faces were all in darkness, which ought to have helped, "It's very good of you to charge us so little rent, Mr. Bone. When we can afford it, we would like to pay more." He had told her not to mention it. Why had he not also outlined the reasons for such a moderate rent, explaining he wanted certain things in return?

They had asked him in for coffee, but he had refused, saying he never drank coffee after eight, as it kept him awake. As he was going to bed, sad, the radio was turned on below and pop music blared out. He heard Sophie shout, and it was turned down to half volume, but half volume was still loud enough for William to make out every banal word. He sat on the edge of his bed, listening to the dreadful music and the shouts and laughs that occasionally rose above it from the young man who all evening had sat so correctly at his side. He felt utterly miserable. The noise below was an expression of relief—relief that they had escaped his restricting presence. Or was it more than that?

Was it indicative of their dislike? Was it a slap in the face? Had they been longing to deal such blows, but remembered which side their bread was buttered on? In bed, tossing restlessly, William had tried to argue that it was only thoughtlessness, only the difference in generations. Quite suddenly, only half an hour after the din began, there was complete silence. There. Usually they continued till well after midnight. They were trying. William had slept happily.

Now, his few scraps of food put away, he took out the lease that had been signed this morning. No check. The lease said the first three months' rent was payable on signing. No payment. Already he must use the law as a big stick. Sighing, William pulled his writing pad to him and wrote a note.

Congratulations on signing lease! One small point: my solicitor forgot (silly chap) to point out that the first cheque is now due—Section 1.b (iii). Just pop it in an envelope and leave it in the hall.

W.E.B.

Eight

RATHER to her own dismay, Mrs. Joliffe read the notes that passed between William and the Hills. It was, she knew, quite wrong, every bit as shameful as stealing or lying, and she was very cross with herself. The notes were, however, irresistible temptations. They were notes, not letters, and consisted of small pieces of paper, sometimes very small pieces, folded over once and left with the initials "S.H." or "W.E.B." on top. They would have been quite easy to read without touching if one had been prepared to bend low and look up where the paper had sprung out of its fold. But Mrs. Joliffe was not prepared to be so underhanded. She stood in the hall quite boldly and lifted the notes up and read them. They were not of a personal nature. They were full of long-division sums she did not understand and was sure Sophie did not understand, either. They were full of silly suggestions and complaints so ambiguously worded that they emerged as encouragements. How William twitted on, Mrs. Joliffe thought, and how her hand ached to write scathing comments across the bottom of his messages.

After reading these notes for a month, Mrs. Joliffe came

to the conclusion that Sophie Hill was cleverer than it might at first appear. There was no doubt that she was playing William at his own game very adroitly. But William did not see this. Instead, he got worse and his notes more and more fussy and ridiculous, so that she wondered at Sophie for not tearing them up in exasperation. One day there were five notes in rapid succession about hot water. Mrs. Joliffe could not believe her eyes. The first said:

Greetings from the Water Board! I have just received last quarter's bill and I thought you might appreciate advance notice that the thermal charge has increased to 1.05d, thereby making my original estimate out by .002d. Bear this in mind.

W.E.B.

Sophie's reply said:

Very interested in calculations re. water. At our present rate of consumption can you roughly calculate our first bill?

S.H.

To which William, after an hour, replied:

Enclose specimen calculation, but for accuracy need approximate depth of bath. Would you say frequency 2.7 per week?

$$12 \overline{\smash{\big)}\ 1.05 \times 35}$$
$$= \quad 13675$$
$$64.05$$
$$4 \overline{\smash{\big)}\ 13611.05}$$
$$= \quad 14.2\tfrac{1}{2}$$

Sophie came back with

Thank you! Are we so dirty?! Suggest average of 3.5 nearer.

And William:

Perhaps. By the way, it would be cheaper to have baths in morning rather than ten in evening (or after—see lease, if handy) as electric light would not be necessary, though perhaps it would as mornings are dark but one does not need much light to bathe. This (free) soap specimen not needed by me, you may like to use it.

W.E.B.

That last note was wrapped around a gift Palmolive bar of soap which had been put through the door the day before, to William's fury. Mrs. Joliffe knew that if he had been in when it was delivered, he would have run out into the street and rammed the free sample back into the bag from which it had come. He did not like what he called commercial trickery. Now he was unloading it on the Hills, and should they show willing they would become the recipient of all the things he was given.

The water correspondence perhaps went on. Mrs. Joliffe did not know. The notes made her so irritable that her curiosity was quite quenched. She listened to the two of them going up and down those stairs and pressed her lips tightly together. Sophie was to blame, because she knew William was a fool and she was enjoying exploiting his foolishness to entertain her during the long empty days—though heaven knew what she found entertaining in that kind of thing. William was to blame for starting notes in the first place, part of his total refusal to do things man to man, as they should be done. Both of them needed a good shaking, and

Mrs. Joliffe was determined to give them a verbal one even if she could not manage to chastise them physically. Unfortunately, she chose to start on Sophie first, and the minute she began she realized she was up against something she did not understand, something both amazing and alarming.

"Well, and how are you today?" she asked Sophie when she appeared for her daily sherry. The girl, as ever, was wearing the same green corduroy maternity smock, now much patched and darned after months of continuous wear. Only what was underneath varied—today a white polo-necked jumper, yesterday a long-sleeved black shirt.

"Fine, thank you," Sophie said, as she always did.

"It's all the running up and down stairs collecting those notes from William," said Mrs. Joliffe. "Every time I go into the hall there is another note for you. I am quite jealous—you seem to be enjoying a most passionate correspondence."

Sophie blushed. "Very dreary, I'm afraid," she said. "Just business."

"And what business interests do you and William share, if I may ask? I never mind being told I *can't* ask, you know. You must remember that."

"Of course you can ask," said Sophie, annoyed that she was being teased and Mrs. Joliffe did not think she had the wit to see it. "It's house business—this house."

"Really?" said Mrs. Joliffe, raising her thin eyebrows very high so that the top of the arches disappeared into her white hair. "I live in this house, too, but I must say William doesn't treat me to a constant flood of notes. He seems to manage to send me my share of the bills and that's all. I'm more intrigued than ever."

"Honestly," said Sophie. "You can see them if you like— they were about water today, about how much our baths are going to cost. Mr. Bone wants us to understand how he works the cost out."

"He doesn't," said Mrs. Joliffe, "he just ties himself in knots with higher mathematics. Quite absurd."

"I think it's very nice of him to take so much trouble," said Sophie. "Most landlords would just slap the bill in front of you and that would be that."

"Most landlords would be wise," said Mrs. Joliffe.

"Why?"

"William's notes about these trivial matters are an expression of nerves. They are meaningless so far as content goes. It is a means of trying to find out if he can trust you, if he can find a wavelength to communicate on. In short, they are a waste of time."

"I don't think so."

"You don't think what? That they are nervous tics or that they are a waste of time? Be explicit."

"They may be partly nervous, but I really think Mr. Bone does want us to see he is honest and not charging us too much. You said yourself he's meticulous about these things. He can't say them to us, because he finds speech difficult— why shouldn't he write things down if he wants to? I like writing things down, too. And it isn't all a waste of time."

"Of time, ink and paper," asserted Mrs. Joliffe.

"No," said Sophie decisively.

Mrs. Joliffe studied Sophie with interest. The girl had gone quite charmingly pink in William's defense. Was she in love with William? Mrs. Joliffe had spent a lifetime watching for signs that girls were in love with William. Usually her observation was so acute, her premonitions were so strong, that she had removed them from William's vicinity before they knew what was happening. Oh, yes, she had saved him from quite a few clutches and he had reason to be grateful to her. He could never have been happy with any of these designing hussies. All they were after was his bachelorhood—he was simply another scalp to them.

But Sophie? Ridiculous. She was in love with Alex. She might dote on William, but never love him. The idea of her nursing a passion for William was almost as absurd as the idea of Germaine doing so. Absurd now, that is. Mrs. Joliffe reminded herself that once Germaine had been very seriously in love with William. Hadn't she once, fifteen and silly, burst in upon them, in the middle of eating roast duck, and declared as much? William had dropped a dish and been in a terrible state, and she had had to make Germaine return and apologize and kiss Uncle William good night or it might all have got out of hand.

Sophie must nevertheless be told a few home truths so that her opinion of William did not go unchallenged. Doubtless she considered herself firmly placed in his affections and gaining ground all the time. She must be shown that this was wrong and that there was no reason for self-congratulation.

"William is not a sweet old man, you know," she said. "You mustn't think he's harmless. Behind everything William does is guile. He is hard too. Don't flatter yourself that he likes you. William likes nobody. He is afraid to." She paused. The vermilion in Sophie's cheeks had flamed to scarlet. "Now you think I am a nasty old woman running people down behind their backs. Well, give me credit—I do it to their faces too. I have told William he is devoid of all the normal human emotions. He quite agrees with me and lays the fault at the door of his parents, which is quite the fashion nowadays. No, you must not get involved with William, my dear."

"I haven't *got* involved," said Sophie, quite angrily for her. "I've simply replied to his notes."

"Why does not your husband reply to them?"

"Alex can't be bothered, it doesn't interest him. He leaves all that to me."

"What does he leave to you?"

"Oh, the flat, everything to do with the flat—all the bills and things like that."

"You pay the bills?"

"Yes."

"Does William know this?"

"Obviously."

"Don't go cold, Sophie. I mean well."

Sophie looked at Mrs. Joliffe, who was attempting a hang-dog expression, and simultaneously they began to giggle. They giggled until they cried, and Sophie clutched her stomach and Mrs. Joliffe mopped her eyes.

"Oh," gasped Sophie, "you don't mean well at all—and trying to look saintly!"

"No, I was never very good at that," agreed Mrs. Joliffe, "but you're wrong—I *do* mean well. I have everyone's best interests at heart, but people will never accept that I do know best about some things. I do know about William and where it is all likely to lead."

"Where?" asked Sophie.

"To total ruin. He will misrepresent himself and on the basis of his misrepresentation you will make an irrevocable decision and he will let you down."

"I can't imagine Mr. Bone ever letting anyone down."

"Not directly. Obliquely."

"You sound as if you read tea leaves with all these prophecies."

"Of course I read tea leaves, and hands. They are very interesting but of course no real indication of events. They help in judging character and personality, but that is all."

"Tea leaves?"

"Certainly."

"You amaze me again. I thought you were too intelligent and sensible for that kind of thing."

"I am not sensible. My heart rules my head, whereas William's head rules his heart. You need not look so doubtful. Most people find it hard to believe."

"You think a lot about Mr. Bone. He comes into all your examples and comparisons."

"Is that strange? Until you arrived, he was the only person with whom I was in daily contact. And I have known him more than fifty years. You do not yet appreciate what a very long time that is."

"Oh, I do. I can't think of any friend I've known for more than five, and they've all disappeared."

"To where?"

"Nowhere. I meant I never see them now."

"Why not?"

"I never visit them, they never visit me, it's simple."

"My child, I know that. Don't treat me as a senile fool. The point is, why has this visiting ceased?"

"I don't know. I suppose both sides have given up bothering—it's just sort of faded out. Alex doesn't like entertaining and he doesn't like my friends either, now that I think about it. No, he doesn't."

"Visit them on your own, in the daytime."

"I couldn't. I don't want to."

"Which?"

"Both."

"You are worse than William. He was at least faithful to the few, and still, I think, to one. A revolting man, I might add."

"But I have Alex, and the baby soon. Mr. Bone has no one, has he?"

"Neither have I."

"You have a daughter."

"Nothing."

"I would love to meet her."

"Then you shall. The very next time she honors me with her company I shall ring you and invite you down."

"Does she look like you?"

"No, alas. She looks like her father—a fine-looking man, but a man. She has his large features and a cleft chin. I took one look at her and shuddered."

Sophie remembered Mrs. Joliffe's expression when she was called down to meet Germaine later in the week. There was indeed something about the woman that made one shudder, and even though she had been determined to like Mrs. Joliffe's daughter, mostly because Mrs. Joliffe did not, she found it difficult. Germaine was uncouth and rude. Introduced to Sophie in the most elegant terms, she chose that moment to belch and neither stood up nor extended her hand. Sophie, feeling sorry for the unfortunate belch, was prepared to be particularly sympathetic, but she was ignored and Germaine went on talking to her mother as though no one had come into the room. Quietly Sophie settled herself down and waited until Germaine thought fit to include her in the conversation. That moment never came. Never once did Germaine address Sophie or look at her, and Mrs. Joliffe, obviously delighted at an exhibition that suited her purposes so well, did not interfere. A full quarter of an hour went by while Germaine droned through a minute-by-minute account of her day, and Sophie had not even been given a glass of sherry.

"Germaine," exclaimed Mrs. Joliffe at last, "poor Sophie has not been given a drop of sherry."

"That doesn't matter," said Sophie sweetly.

"Oh, we're very humble, are we?" sneered Germaine, not turning round.

"Do get Sophie some sherry," urged an unruffled Mrs. Joliffe.

"I would have thought she could get it herself," said Germaine. "She seems to practically live here."

But she got up and found the decanter and put it at Sophie's elbow with a glass.

"Help yourself," she said. "I don't suppose I'd give you the right amount."

Sophie poured out half a glass.

"Mother can afford more than that," said Germaine. "Don't stint yourself."

"Thank you," said Sophie, "but I can only manage a little at the moment. It doesn't seem to agree with me."

"Your delicate condition, you mean? My God, I thought that ridiculous attitude to pregnancy had gone out with the Victorians. Where's your pink knitting?"

"I don't knit," said Sophie, "pink or otherwise."

She left very quickly after that and thought Mrs. Joliffe a wicked old woman and Germaine a bitter middle-aged one and spent an evening dreading becoming either. Naturally, a postmortem on the encounter had to be held the next evening, when Mrs. Joliffe did a spirited imitation of her disgruntled daughter and they both ended up laughing till the sherry danced in their glasses. This led Mrs. Joliffe on to anecdotes about Germaine as a child that were so cruelly funny Sophie was appalled at the old lady's disloyalty. Mrs. Joliffe had no such scruples. Ringing up William that night after the news, she even related to him the saga of Germaine's meeting with Sophie, improving considerably on the actual dialogue, and told him how she and Sophie had laughed afterward.

"We laughed so much," Mrs. Joliffe said, "twice I thought I should burst a blood vessel."

"Jolly good," said William heartily.

"She is a very sweet girl. You could not have a nicer tenant, William."

"I think it's all working out quite satisfactorily."

"You are a little thoughtless, William, all the same."

"I? In what way?"

"Your notes. Do you not think what all this running up and down stairs is like for a girl in Sophie's condition? It is not good for her blood pressure. I will go further—it is exceedingly bad."

"But picking my notes up does not involve special trips," protested William. "She collects them whenever she happens to be passing through the hall."

"Rubbish. Sophie does not pass through the hall more

than twice a day and then only in the afternoon. Yesterday you exchanged three notes in an hour. Did you not notice? William, I asked you a question."

"Yes, yes," said William testily.

"Then take care, in future. Confine yourself to one note a day and leave it out in the afternoon."

"Thank you," said William, "I shall take your advice. How very kind of you to have gone to all this trouble."

"There is no need for that tone, William. You have no reason to be offended. Naturally Sophie found it difficult to broach the subject herself, so I felt it was up to me, as we are such old friends."

"Quite."

"Good night, William."

"Good night."

William put the telephone down feeling sad and trembly, even near to tears. Quite what had induced this state he was not sure. Not Mrs. Joliffe's interference alone, though he hated it, but more the blight she had cast on the happy intercourse he had been enjoying with Sophie Hill. She had responded so delightfully to his gentle jokes, sharing them, but solemnly. He had rushed down with eagerness to see what she had to say. Now it must stop. Mrs. Joliffe had said so—ah, that was it, that was why he was upset. It appeared that it was not Mrs. Joliffe but Sophie who had said so, who had complained to Mrs. Joliffe, who had got her to deal with him. It had all been done with pounds of tact. His old, tried, trusted friend had taken on the job, with, he was sure, alacrity. A lot was made of the age of their friendship, and yet William wondered about it. Were they such old friends?

He had met Agnes Joliffe fifty-three years ago and fallen instantly in love with her. She was married to his tutor's brother, himself a don, and had dazzled scores of other undergraduates. They had become "friends"—that is to say, he was frequently invited to Sunday lunch during his years at Cambridge, and afterward they sent each other Christmas cards and wrote letters whenever they read about each other in the *Times:* William wrote once to Agnes, when he read of her brother's death, and Agnes wrote three times to him —once when he was reported wounded, once each on the occasions of his decorations. No continuous correspondence had resulted, and yet they had imperceptibly moved onto the plane of higher friendship before they met again.

William recalled very clearly the beginning of their more intimate friendship. Not, of course, that it had ever been the least intimate. He had not been intimate with any woman, ever, and at times the thought appalled him. Anyone hearing this confession would, he knew, imagine him to be in some way abnormal, but he was not. It was only in the last ten years that he had ceased to suffer the agonizing pains of normality. It was just that with his principles it would have been impossible to seduce any woman outside wedlock, and because of his principles wedlock had been a responsibility he could never undertake. Perhaps if he had lived fifty years later, in the permissive society of the Hills, he would either have married or had a mistress. But he had not, and would go to his grave chaste.

Mrs. Joliffe knew all about this. When they had both come to live in London two years after the first war, William had quickly established the old Cambridge habit of Sunday lunching. At first there had been lots of other people there, too—men who William realized were hoping to marry Agnes Joliffe, and women who were hoping to marry these suitors when she should reject them. There was no doubting her attraction. As well as being very beautiful, she was lively and clever and a brilliant conversationalist. Although she was virtuous, there was in addition something daring about her that men found exciting. Unhappily, she found nothing exciting about them. William watched the numbers dwindle, year by year, and felt sorry for her, though she gave no indications of regret. Soon he alone came for Sunday lunch, sometimes taking a friend along, sometimes not. Occasionally there would be a cousin or an uncle there, but more often than not there would be William, Agnes and Germaine. They would lunch, and take a walk, and have tea, and then, if it was winter, William would find that he had somehow not departed and was sitting by the fire drinking sherry and talking.

He had never, that he could remember, talked about himself, but inevitably Mrs. Joliffe must have learned a good deal about him. Enough to worry about him. That, William reflected, ought to have been the end. He could not stand her worrying about him—worrying about his health, and then his profession, and soon his future. But he had gone on faithfully dancing attendance and playing up to the role of errant son, which, considering there was only one year between them, was absurd. It was a kind of protection for them both, this pretense. Often he wanted to tell her to stop it, but never did, out of embarrassment as to what their position would be if he rejected that one. He had watched Agnes age, not so much losing her looks as concealing them with wrinkles and all the other artifices of age, and had felt relieved. The older they both got, the safer and simpler everything became. Then came the accident.

William took off his spectacles and pressed his knuckles into his eyeballs. His distress had now receded, but only at the price of being caught up in a tangle of memories, and once you were in this tangle you were forced to wind your way out thread by thread. The fact was—oh, he had acknowledged it long ago—the fact was that he had had something to do with Agnes Joliffe's accident. They had gone, the three of them, for a picnic in the New Forest, where Agnes had a small cottage. William had taken a train down very early one June Saturday morning and was met by Agnes and Germaine in their car. They had driven off at once deep into the country and had finally picnicked in a glade sheltered all round by trees. Agnes had brought a splendid picnic, all beautifully packed in a wicker basket, and they had eaten and drunk very well. After this, Germaine, who was sixteen at the time, had fallen asleep, and he and Agnes had moved a little way from her so that they would not waken her with their talking. But they had not talked. The heat and food that had made Germaine sleepy had made them—well, restless. No. William slapped himself. Always, at this point, he cheated. It had made them more than restless, it had made them amorous. Yes, amorous. Agnes, who was thirty-five and in her prime, had lain back in the grass and not quite closed her eyes as she looked at William, who was thirty-four and romantic as ever. It was all very painful. He had struggled for composure—had he? It was useless trying to re-create his emotions, as useless as trying to feel past suffering. All that he truly was sure of was that he had felt very peculiar, had done nothing, and by doing nothing had in some way hurt Agnes.

He remembered sitting up and turning away from her and looking instead at the green haze all around them. At some point he must have removed his spectacles—no, she had removed them. It had been rather funny—they had slipped onto the end of his nose as he leaned over her, and gently, smiling, she had taken them off and laid them on the grass, her breast grazing his thin-shirted arm as she stretched to do this. Without them he was helpless. The green was only green, though he knew that somewhere out there were hundreds of trees with millions of leaves and beneath them so many blades of grass it was impossible to count and all of them, though green, were different. He blinked. His head felt very hot. He had almost kissed her, but, poised a fraction above her, he was so attracted by the mere thought of all that softness on which he was about to descend that it was unendurable. He had either to give way and ravish her or to get up. He got up.

For a while, until he had his feelings under control and

his body too, he stayed quite still. Then he said, "I'm sorry, Agnes." She did not reply, and he looked down and saw she was crying. "Oh, dear," he said, "don't let it upset you," and his mind was confused, wondering if perhaps he was mad and had after all given way and attacked her. He took hold of her hands and squeezed them and said, "There, there." He lay in the grass at her side and wiped the tears away with his handkerchief and patted her cheeks and said again, "I'm sorry."

"William," she sobbed. "Oh, William!"

"I'm sorry—"

"No, I don't want you to be sorry. Don't you love me, William? Why don't you kiss me? Don't you want to? Didn't you want to then?"

"I'm afraid I did."

"Then *do,* William, for God's sake!"

But he couldn't. Desire had quite left him and he felt dried up and embarrassed and she was blotchy and miserable and the haze had gone. Suddenly, with another sob that was almost a hiccup and that to his horror made him smile, she got to her feet and began running through the glade shouting, "I want to die!" He ran after her, still without his glasses, feeling foolish, and then, as they both stumbled on, both blind for different reasons, his anger at her melodramatic behavior grew until he too was shouting— "Stop this at once!" and "Pull yourself together!" She ran faster than he did, crashing through bushes, leaving strips of white muslin floating behind her, and he cursed and sweated and finally stood still. He stood and mopped his brow and in the distance heard twigs snapping and the undergrowth tearing as she went headlong on, like an animal, headlong on, straight into the large steel trap meant for a badger.

William put his head in his hands, shaking. He might not be able to totally recall the day that had gone before, but thirty-odd years later the accident still brought vomit into his mouth. The blood had been quite dreadful, and her screams tore him more than the steel teeth her poor leg. Germaine, a mile away, had woken and run to her mother and she too had screamed and screamed, so that the sunny glades had been an inferno of screaming. There was no help of any kind near. Sweating, William had prised the trap off the mangled leg, working so gently but causing Agnes to faint. At last, pulling cruelly while she was unconscious, he had freed her and, ripping his shirt to shreds, bandaged the wound to stop some of the blood. He had had to leave her with the hysterical Germaine. He had run five miles before he had come to a house, though if he had run in another direction he would not have had to run one. There had been hospitals and operations and convalescence and then, at the end, the limp. After that, they were bound together.

Sophie must have presumed rightly, Agnes spoken correctly: they were very old friends. Could friends be bitter? Agnes had never got over her bitterness. She did not blame him for the accident—it was, she said, her own carelessness, she had plunged off into the undergrowth without thinking where she was going. William had never been quite sure what she did blame him for, but something, certainly. His own wound in the second war had not helped to purge either his guilt or her bitterness, but afterward she had kept very close to him. Before, he had gone to her house freely, because he wanted to. Now he went because he was summoned. When he bought the house he had been living in and turned it into flats, the last thing in the world he had wanted had been Agnes Joliffe as a tenant. But it had happened. He had been tricked, in a way he did not like to think about, and now she was with him for life, his friend.

Exhausted, William made himself a cup of hot chocolate. Sophie and Mrs. Joliffe were now very great friends. They saw each other every day. They laughed uproariously together—he had actually heard them at the top of the house. They liked each other. Where did that leave him? William had seen, in his time, a great many elderly people become childish about such things, and he was determined not to be one of them. He was not going to be jealous, either of Sophie or of Mrs. Joliffe. He was not going to imagine they were joining forces against him. No, he would be pleasant and civil as usual to both of them, but he would bear their friendship constantly in mind. He would avoid getting hurt, that was the point. With Mrs. Joliffe he was ever on his guard, having their relationship well worked out, but he supposed he was not sure about Sophie Hill. She seemed to want his advice, she seemed genuinely interested in the trivialities of the house that interested him, she seemed, in short, to like him. But did she? And what did he really know about her? Perhaps he had been saved in the nick of time from exposing himself too much, something he had always taken great care not to do.

There was, for the rest of that evening, an air of peace and contentment in William's little flat. He washed and dried his lunch and supper dishes exulting over his independence, and, moving around the kitchen as he put them away, he sighed frequently with relief. Every now and again he was aware that he experienced an emotional brainstorm in which the very center of his world seemed to rock hideously. But once questioned, once tested and reaffirmed, his values were all the more shining and inspiring at the end. He valued himself—not because he suffered from any delusions that he was either good or great, but because he knew himself. He did not know other people. His flirtations with their worlds were always doomed to end in catastrophe. He knew himself, he was happier alone. To remain impregnable was his ultimate aim.

William nodded frequently at the rightness of these thoughts. He nodded as he pulled his curtains, he nodded as he sat down to do his written Japanese exercises, and he continued to nod till he had finished. By the time he put up his camp bed, he was humming Sibelius and thinking about his coming holiday, which he allowed himself to do only when he was very happy. Progress had been made. The Portuguese Tourist Board had put him in contact with a *poussada* at Sagres which sounded just what he wanted, and he was now enjoying a lengthy correspondence with them. It was all coming along very nicely, and if all went well he would be making bookings in a month or so. He would leave the house in good hands—Mrs. Joliffe was a dependable caretaker and the Hills were settled in. He could relax.

Sophie heard Mr. Bone go to bed and decided to go herself. Alex was on night shift and there was nothing to keep her up. Besides, she felt very tired. She realized as she climbed the stairs from Mrs. Joliffe's how tired she was. Her head and back both ached and little shooting pains went through her legs. As she undressed, she looked down at her belly and thought it had grown enormously in the last three weeks—so much so that she was beginning to have difficulty seeing her feet and when she sat down her breasts rested on it. Frowning, she lay down and worked out that there were still at least six weeks to go, and that reminded her that she had not kept her last hospital appointment. It seemed so far to go, and yet so much trouble to try to transfer somewhere else. But she must. She had not even registered with a doctor in the district. On Monday morning, first thing, she would do so.

This decision did not make her less tired. Even lying down, as comfortable as it was possible to be, she was weary. Everything seemed difficult, that was the trouble, and indeed everything *was* difficult. She had had a letter that morning from her mother, forwarded in dizzy circles round all the addresses she had ever stayed at. The postmark was six weeks old, which in view of the contents was horribly significant. Her mother said, at some length, that she was no longer going to pay her allowance as from January first. There were many reasons given, but Sophie had not bothered to plow through them. No doubt her mother sincerely believed all the rubbish about condoning her irresponsibility and it being for her her own good—it was irrelevant what she believed. Sophie knew what she would do for her own children: give. What was hers was theirs, and when it was finished it was finished. She was not giving birth so that her offspring would respect or admire or feel that strange thing called a sense of duty, but out of love. She had conceived out of love, would give birth with love, and rear them with love. Her mother was loveless. All she was interested in was a points system—ten for a good husband, ten for a career, ten for healthy children. It was revolting. She was well free of it. Still, true though this was, Sophie did not feel released but more chained than ever. Mr. Bone's check would bounce. She had signed it on the assumption that her normal monthly allowance of twenty-five pounds would have been paid into the bank on January first. Now that it had not, she was five pounds–odd in the red. Alex had no bank account, having no money, which simplified her calculations.

What was to be done? She could ring up her mother and plead. Probably that would be effective. She could rush to the bank, put in all the money Alex had given her—fifteen pounds—for his week's work. That would be partially effective. She could borrow. From whom? Heavily Sophie said it: from Mrs. Joliffe. Not pleasant. Even if Mrs. Joliffe agreed —and it was absolutely impossible to predict her reactions —how could they continue to meet every day afterward? Sophie could imagine only too well what it would be like. Already she felt an uncomfortable constraint with Mrs. Joliffe, since she was aware that she took pains always to agree with her, even when appearing to disagree. She saw when the old lady wanted her to disagree a little, and she obliged, only to come to heel the more quickly. It was all a game and she played it with less and less conviction every day. If she borrowed from Mrs. Joliffe, the game would become reality.

There was one other alternative. She could throw herself on the mercy of Mr. Bone. She could flout the rules of the house and go and knock on his door and explain. Mr. Bone, my mother has stopped my allowance. Mr. Bone, I am temporarily embarrassed. Mr. Bone, will you wait for your money, oh, will you, kind, good, gentle Mr. Bone. Sophie rehearsed and knew she could do it. Of all the alternatives, the least honorable appealed to her most. For, of course, to throw herself on Mr. Bone's mercy would not be honorable. It would be wicked. Mr. Bone could not say no—he could not say no to anything or anyone even if he very much wanted to. His confusion would be so great and his agony at her distress so acute, he would agree at once. The most wonderful part about it all would be that, unlike the consequences of asking Mrs. Joliffe, they would both be able to go on as before. Such an arrangement would compromise neither of them, but in a way help them because it would provide a bond where there was none. Sophie wanted that bond. She had become bound to Mrs. Joliffe when she did not wish to be, and would much rather be bound to Mr. Bone.

Alex had not been taken into her confidence. There was no point in telling him her mother had stopped her allowance, since he had never known that anything so grand and Victorian was going on. He thought they existed entirely on the amounts he earned during his short snatches of work, and she had encouraged him to believe she was the financial wizard this would have implied. Her deviousness could not be undone. All she could do was cajole him into working a little longer, pleading the expense of the baby, and economize frantically and pay Mr. Bone in dribs and drabs.

The thing was, Sophie decided sleepily, it was impossible to be frightened by Mr. Bone. He was the only one did she not need courage to approach.

Nine

GERMAINE, sorting out clean nightdresses and bed linen, was not comforted by the recollection that exactly the same thing had happened before. That was beside the point. Her mother was now seventy, and with each month illness took on a deeper and deeper significance. She could not now imagine why she had thought death imminent during the influenza scare five years ago. She ought to have seen that a trivial disease like flu could not conquer Mrs. Joliffe. Except, of course, death was not—never had been—the worry. Germaine longed for a phone call telling her that her mother had died peacefully, in her sleep, in the night. She would cheerfully look after the funeral. No, death was not the point.

Between the nightdresses were lavender bags, and each drawer was lined with rosebud-striped wallpaper. There were handbags everywhere—black leather ones with big, knobby brass fastenings, slim brown suede ones, white satin evening pouches, and even a Hessian one with wooden handles that was so fashionable Germaine immediately appropriated it as her own. Her mother was past needing handbags, except as receptacles for old letters and souvenirs. Was she past needing anything?

"She needs you so much," that odious girl had whined on the telephone. Typical busybody, ringing up like that, so self-righteous, boasting about how much she had done for Mother. She had done nothing. What was a few hours' chatting and drinking sherry? Nothing. A free drink, which was all she probably did it for. Nothing at all compared with the hours and hours Germaine had put in at the bedside, all the running about and organizing. Trying to teach her her duty, after all these years. She had been curt. "I'll come when I've had supper," she had said, "and you needn't have bothered ringing, William's already got in first. I suppose you couldn't resist the temptation."

"Couldn't you come now?" the girl had said. The impudence! And as if it made any difference when she got there, with all of them clucking around like a lot of hens. "Some of us have had a hard day," Germaine said, "some of us work. I'll come after supper, in an hour. You and William can keep your haloes bright managing till then." But she hadn't had any supper, not that any of them would care. She had left the steak half cooked and the potatoes chipped but unfried, and had come round at once, just so those sanctimonious hypocrites wouldn't have anything over her. She'd cut them short, she didn't want to hear their exaggerated accounts, all glorifying their own actions. The doctor was the only one worth listening to.

Closing the drawers noisily, so that the delicately wrought gold handles tinkled, Germaine sighed. The fall had not been severe, only a ligament had been torn, though since it was in the good leg this meant her mother was now totally crippled. Naturally, her heroic determination not to bother anyone had made sure she was going to be a damned nuisance to everyone. The doctor said that by dragging herself the full length of her hall she had strained her heart and that was what he was really worried about. She had never had a good heart. He had been prescribing digitalis for some years past and telling her not to do too much.

Her arms full, Germaine went into the bedroom. Her mother lay on the bed, still fully dressed, though her skirt was up to her thighs and her stocking removed for the bandages. Her eyes were closed and she looked dreadful. Germaine felt the utmost distaste and no affection or pity at all. Duty was what brought her here. Duty, and other people's interpretation of it. She began to undo her mother's blouse, already half unbuttoned by the doctor.

"Leave me," Mrs. Joliffe said, distinctly. "I can undress myself."

"No you can't," Germaine said, and yanked the blouse off. As if she *wanted* to do this! Her mother made no more protest, but kept her eyes closed. Blouse and skirt came off easily, and Germaine dealt equally efficiently with the underskirt. The rest she could not touch. The nightgown went on over knickers and vest and—absurdly—girdle and brassiere. An old woman wearing such unnecessary articles, an old woman lean and flat and emaciated, with nothing to uplift or flatten or control.

"There," Germaine said, "you'll do. Now is there anything you want?"

"Peace," her mother said.

"I'll leave this lamp on," Germaine said, "and some water on your table. What about—you know, spending a penny? What shall I do about that?"

"Nothing," her mother said, turning her head away.

"Well, I'll come tomorrow, before work," Germaine said, "and we'll decide what's to be done. All right? Good night. Sleep well."

She gave her mother's hand a squeeze, since to kiss her seemed both impossible and offensive. Leaving the door open, she went upstairs and into the main hall, where she paused to fasten her coat and pull on her sheepskin mittens.

"Ah, Germaine," William said, appearing from nowhere

so that she knew he had been sitting on the stairs waiting. He held one finger in the air, a gesture she found very irritating. It was his acting-surprise pose, but who less surprised than William? He had been expecting this for the last five years and would have everything planned. Probably he was glad it had happened and relieved him of the worry of wondering when it was going to. It was the very first thing he had brought up during those "negotiations"—as her mother called them, not knowing what was being negotiated—five years ago, when the lease of her flat was being arranged.

"Germaine," he had said, "what about disability?"

"What about it?"

"We must consider it in the lease. Should your mother become truly disabled—one must be realistic—the flat would no longer be suitable. There must be a clause saying —saying—"

"Yes, William?"

"Saying that in the event of permanent disability the flat must be vacated."

"Will you show Mother that clause?"

"I thought perhaps you—"

"No, not I."

So there had been no clause. William had fretted and fumed, but in the end the lease was the most basic imaginable. Her mother had not expected anything else. She thought William welcomed her and would never have believed how near she had come to not getting the flat at all. If she had not called on William as he was about to write to her and then flee the country for a year, if she had not stood over him while he wrote to his solicitor . . .

"Hello, William," she said. "You've got a pretty kettle of fish on your hands this time, haven't you?" She saw William gulp.

"How is your mother?" he asked. He did not emphasize the pronoun, but then he did not need to, nor did she need to. They had played this out before.

"Very poorly," she said. "I should think it will be a two-month job at least. God knows how she's going to manage, though of course I will do my best."

"She needs skilled attention," William said, wringing his hands, "constant skilled attention."

"Hospital is out," Germaine said. "They don't have room for torn ligaments, not unless you're destitute, and she isn't, is she?"

"There are nursing homes," William murmured.

"Expensive," Germaine said.

"If it could be arranged—" William began.

"She wouldn't go. She's said often enough that she only intends to leave this house nailed up in a box. No, we'll all have to manage. It's very lucky you're retired, William."

"Yes, yes," William said. Then, very softly, "And very lucky she has a daughter so near at hand."

Germaine smiled. "You'll keep an ear open during the night, won't you?" she asked. "She seems very dopy, but she might wake up later on and need something."

"I do have a camp bed I could lend you," William said.

"William," Germaine said, "I'm a married woman. You seem to forget that. My husband doesn't even know I'm here. I dropped everything the minute you telephoned, and he'll be worried to death."

"I'm sure he'll be very understanding," William said. "She is your mother."

"Don't tell me my duty, William," Germaine snapped. "I've never failed to come throughout all her accidents and illnesses, and I've never complained about having to do it. I've spent weeks and weeks nursing her and never got any thanks for it."

"I'm sure Agnes has always been very grateful," William said in a trembling voice.

"I don't want that kind of gratitude. You know quite well what I mean. It hasn't changed how she thinks of me. I'm supposed to be the devoted ever-loving daughter, but she's

never been the devoted mother. Never. Anyway, William,
I'm not going to argue. I refuse to stay the night, and my
conscience is quite clear. As far as I'm concerned, you're
under as much obligation as I, and I wish you joy of it."

Mercifully, Germaine did not stop to clarify her parting
shot. She rushed out, banging the door viciously, and William was left to study the footprints on the black linoleum.
Someone wasn't taking their turn cleaning it. It was not his
own turn for another two weeks, but how could he complain
when one tenant was heavily pregnant and the other bedridden? If only he had been like Pullen and taken a housekeeper, years ago, someone who would learn his tastes and
preferences and cater for them exclusively, so that by now
she would have been not so much a servant as an ally. Pullen had told him to do it. He had said, "Get yourself a
woman or a valet or some dogsbody, William, and make
yourself comfortable." He could have afforded it as much as
Pullen, but he had been afraid—it was ironic!—afraid of
getting involved in other people's lives. How could he em-
ploy a servant twenty-four hours a day, have them living
under the same roof, and not be burdened with their problems as well as his own? Impossible. He was not Pullen, not
heartless, not cold; within weeks he would have been at
their beck and call instead of them at his. He would know
their troubles, and their family's troubles, and they would
become his and he would get no peace. William groaned,
out loud. He had no peace anyway. His house, with its flats
and leases, had not protected him in the way that Pullen's
housekeeper had protected him. His desire to be solitary
had only led him into a labyrinth of emotions, and he
longed for a servant, faithful and knowing, to whom he
could say, "Deal with this," and it would be dealt with, and
much, much later, when it was all over, he would be informed and say, "Well done. Thank you."

He ought to go down to see Agnes at once. Not to do so
would be inexcusable. It was no good pretending he

thought she had settled for the night. She could not go to sleep without the spectacle of the odious Germaine being blotted out. Nor could he go emptyhanded—not because gifts were so necessary for her well-being, but for the cover they offered. Lightly he ran upstairs, taking pleasure in his own well-being, and hunted in his cupboard for something to take. There was nothing very suitable. He selected and then rejected several things before choosing some beautifully colored hand coolers that he had bought one day in Peter Jones and then thought too bright for his room. He placed them in a blue-and-white china bowl, a favorite that he used each year for hyacinths, and, carrying the bowl in one hand and a bottle of vintage port in the other, he tripped down the stairs again and into Mrs. Joliffe's flat.

Already the air, in some subtle way, had changed, and William hesitated at the top of the green-carpeted stairs like a mole, sniffing and fearing a new scent. It was very hushed, quiet enough for her to hear him standing breathing and hesitating. Silly to be afraid. Making more noise, he continued down to the basement, saying "Hello there" at frequent intervals. At the door of her bedroom he put his head round and said, "How's the patient? Feeling better?" Her eyes were closed, but she said, "Come in, William," and he went in, and stood, his arms full, in the middle of the room.

"Well, now," he said quickly, blinking hard, "glad to see you looking so comfortable, very glad, just the place to be on a night like this, just the place, you couldn't have timed it better, you gave us a fright, you know, quite a fright, glad it wasn't as bad as it looked, very glad. Look, I've brought you some port and some rather pretty eggs, ha ha, not real eggs, of course, though by the way I've got plenty of those if you should feel like some, but I'll put them there, on your table, and you might find them amusing. Now I expect you feel like sleeping it off, so I'll say good night and run along."

"No," Mrs. Joliffe said, "don't go."

"Expect sleep is the best thing," William said, aware that he had begun to sweat, something he rarely did and regarded with horror. "Knits up the raveled sleave of care and all that, best healer there is."

"Sit beside me," Mrs. Joliffe said, "please."

"Don't think I really ought," William said. "You should rest, you know, plenty of rest."

Two tears slid from underneath her closed eyelids.

"That's right," he said quickly, "a good, good sleep," and fled.

Back in his own flat, William spent a wretched evening. Like Germaine, and knowing he was like her made his feelings all the more contemptible, he worried not about the horror of the present so much as of the future. His house was not suitable for a convalescent, far less a very sick woman. It was an inconvenient house, a selfish house, full of awkward stairs and twists and turns. Then the bathroom arrangements and the heating arrangements and indeed all the arrangements demanded fit, hardy tenants. Mrs. Joliffe was not a stoic. She did not treat illness as he did. There would be a lot of fuss and his telephone would never stop ringing.

Sadly William sat and ate up the broken Bath Olivers at the bottom of the tin and looked over the top of his tray at the gas fire. The house had been lovely empty, quite lovely. He could remember clearly the evening the painters had finished and he had watched them loading the tins and brushes and dust sheets and buckets, and all the paraphernalia he had lived with for two months, into their van, and he had crouched behind his net curtains until he was quite sure they had gone. Then he had gone out into the garden and looked up with love at each repointed brick, each white-painted windowframe, and he had smiled at them. The light in every room was perfect as he walked from one to the other. The basement was pink and warm and enclosed him comfortingly, the first floor was brilliantly sunny and inspiring, and his own flat was like an eyrie, a nest, perched on treetops. He had wished it could stay like that. Was it so wrong to love a house, to want to keep it to himself? Other people did that with bodies, human bodies. They loved the bodies and tried to stop other people entering them. His house had never quite been the same since Agnes Joliffe entered it, filling it with the smell of her wholemeal bread and the sound of coffee percolating.

She was old. The fact was inescapable. William knew he was not old, because he could still do all the things he had been able to do twenty years ago. Oh, not so quickly, he granted that, but he could still do them, he was still living within his capabilities. Agnes was not, but she did not seem to be marking her own decline. In spite of her leg, she had been able to walk in the park, go shopping, go to the theater, even garden with impressive results. She had not done any of those things for at least five years. She stayed in the house, his house, and did not go out at all. He had noticed, too, that mentally Agnes was not what she had been. Though sharp and quick-witted still, she did not stretch herself. Not so long ago, the green Harrods van had come twice a week to deliver a case of books. Now it came perhaps three times a year. Agnes had given up reading, given up everything except gossip. All the signs were there. If they had been his signs, William, lying down there instead of Agnes, would have committed suicide.

The telephone rang. William, suddenly very tired, took off his spectacles and went to answer the call he had been expecting. He had known Agnes would never lie and cry and shun him. That was not her way.

"Hello," he said mournfully.

"Oh, Mr. Bone," Sophie Hill said. "What news? I've been so worried, but I simply didn't dare come down, not when her daughter was there. She was so cross with me."

"Ah," William said, more cheerfully, "ah yes, news, well, let me see, oh, very good really, no bones broken, nothing really drastically wrong."

"I *am* glad."

"Rest and quiet should do the trick, though of course the house isn't really suitable for the bedridden."

"But it's perfect," Sophie said. "She has everything so easily to hand in her little flat."

"Of course, it's hard to get day nurses these days, let alone night ones," William said.

"Does Mrs. Joliffe need a nurse?" Sophie asked.

"That has to be gone into," William said.

"Well, if there is anything I can do," Sophie said, "I would be delighted. After all, I'm not doing a thing all day. Playing nurse would fill in this last month beautifully—it would be good practice, don't you think?" She laughed, but William did not.

"It is your—er—last month?" he queried delicately, his voice full of blushes.

"Mm," Sophie said. "March fifteenth it's due. The midwife is coming round tomorrow to look at the premises. She will keep calling our flat the premises."

"Is that usual?" William asked anxiously.

"What?"

"Visiting the home."

"Oh, yes. Well, she has to see where everything is—the loo and hot water and all that kind of thing. It might be unsuitable for a home confinement, and then I suppose they would just have to make room in some hospital, though it would be a pity in a way. Now I've got used to the idea I quite like it."

"But it's out of the question," William said, shrill with terror. "This house isn't suitable for babies to be born in— it says so in the lease." At the other end, Sophie was silent. "Are you there, Mrs. Hill?"

"Yes, Mr. Bone."

"Is your husband there? I should like to have a word with him."

"He's out," Sophie whispered. "He's been out for two days." And she began to cry.

"Please," said William, "there is no need to distress yourself, please pull yourself together, there must be a way out of this unfortunate situation. We have a National Health Service, do we not? It must be made to understand your circumstances. I shall look into it tomorrow."

She had put the telephone down still crying. William lay in bed and heard her sobs and saw the tears slip under Mrs. Joliffe's closed eyelids and cursed them both. It was all a dreadful mess. He would be unable to settle to anything at all with these vast problems on his mind. It wasn't fair, it wasn't right that he should be dragged into other people's affairs, when he sometimes thought most of his energy was spent trying to keep out of them. The irony was that his own link with both women was as weak as it could possibly be: he was only their landlord; yet one treated him as her father, the other as her husband. Germaine and Alexander Hill, the real next of kin, had flown. He ought to fly, but he could not. His house must be protected.

"Tuck the undersheet in tightly," Mrs. Joliffe directed, "but leave the top one loose. I cannot abide being strapped down."

"What pretty sheets," Sophie said.

"You're a good child," Mrs. Joliffe said, getting into the remade bed, "but you shouldn't be doing this. Stretching and bending is very bad for you at this stage. It might bring on a premature birth."

"Don't say that," Sophie protested. "Mr. Bone would have a fit. He's trying to get me into a hospital."

"He's trying to get us both into hospital," Mrs. Joliffe said dryly.

"Has he said so?"

"No, of course he hasn't. One day an ambulance will draw up, two men will plunk me on a stretcher and William will wave from his window as they cart me off."

"Oh, I'm sure you're wrong," Sophie said, playing with the hand coolers. "Anyway, it would only be because he thought it was for your own good."

"His good," Mrs. Joliffe said firmly. "William is frightened of sickness. He has a pathological fear of being ill. We once went together to visit a sick friend, and William vomited three times on the way there just at the thought of it. In the end I said, 'For heaven's sake, William, give me those grapes and go home.' Dottie died the following week, so he was spared another try. She had cancer, poor love. I felt like vomiting myself when I saw her—cancer of the skin, you know, very rare—but of course I didn't."

"But we aren't that kind of sick," Sophie said. "It isn't the same, is it? Why should he be afraid of you lying in bed till a sore leg is better, or me having a baby—a perfectly natural function?"

"Both mean bother, or so William thinks. We disturb his calm. With you in particular there might be scenes—screams, that kind of thing. And I might have a heart attack. William does not like drama."

"How callous you make him sound."

"You will see," Mrs. Joliffe said. "Now, have you heard from Alexander?"

"No. Actually, I must go now—"

"Sit down. You must not go. You are a silly girl. You must talk to somebody about it and there is no one else for you to talk to. Tell me."

"There is nothing to tell. He went out, to work, on Tuesday morning. He hasn't been back since."

"Is this normal? Abnormal in others but normal in him?"

"No. He's always come back at night, or early in the morning."

"What is 'always,' Sophie? How long have you been—together?" Mrs. Joliffe asked, pausing so that Sophie would know she had deliberately picked "together" instead of "married."

"A year, almost. He's always come back."

"Then I expect he will again. I shouldn't worry. Nothing can possibly have happened to him—bad news travels fast."

"That's not what I worry about."

"What, then?"

"I may have driven him away—talking about money, that kind of thing, wanting him to get a proper job, wanting things for the baby. I knew it was silly, Alex can't stand that kind of silly nagging and fretting. He gets furious if I won't take things as they are, him as he is. We had a dreadful row about what we were going to do."

"I didn't think lovebirds had rows," said Mrs. Joliffe.

"Didn't you hear? I thought you and Mr. Bone would hear every word."

"William may have done, but I certainly didn't. I must have been asleep."

"Didn't Mr. Bone say anything? Do you think perhaps he heard nothing too?"

"There is no knowing—William does not believe in tittle-tattle. Even if you murdered each other in front of him it is doubtful if he would tell me for fear of gossiping. But I expect he heard—sound carries upward."

"That sound would have carried anywhere," said Sophie gloomily, "and Alex swears when he gets excited. It was dreadful. I really don't know how it happened. It was our first proper fight and it seems to have changed everything. I can't think of him quite the same. I never thought he could be like that—not violent. He broke a jug, threw it at the wall."

"William won't like that," said Mrs. Joliffe dryly.

"It was meant to be a discussion, that's all," Sophie said.

"I even said, before I said anything else, 'All I want to do is sit down and have a perfectly reasonable discussion, but I just can't go on worrying and keep all the worry bottled up inside me.' I didn't raise my voice, nothing like that, I just spoke quietly, like this, but he started on me straight away, with a string of insults, and I was so angry—it was so unfair —and before I knew what had happened we were in the middle of this ugly row."

"Long overdue, I should have thought," said Mrs. Joliffe, sniffing. "Pass me those paper handkerchiefs, my dear. I seem to be getting a cold as well as everything else. Make a point of telling William if you see him. He will instantly visualize pneumonia."

Sophie passed the handkerchiefs and watched Mrs. Joliffe blow her nose and clean her nostrils most thoroughly. It was always the same—the way was prepared, confidences were invited, and then the minute they were given, a smack in the face followed. Should Mrs. Joliffe have chosen to tell her about some personal trouble that was clearly painful to re-late, she would indeed have sat with bated breath, hardly daring to move a muscle for fear of not appearing to attend properly. Every ounce of concentration she could muster would have been Mrs. Joliffe's.

"Now," said Mrs. Joliffe, "I interrupted. What were you saying?"

"Nothing," said Sophie.

"Don't sulk, child. I simply couldn't help blowing my nose."

"Of course you couldn't," Sophie said, "but I really was saying nothing."

"You are like Germaine tonight," said Mrs. Joliffe, "except that even now you are sweeter. Germaine is at her sour-est when she has a tale of woe to tell."

"That's rather natural, isn't it?" said Sophie.

"Well, yes, but she is always so ridiculous I have to strug-gle not to laugh."

"You are very cruel to your daughter," said Sophie. "I know it's none of my business, but I've wanted to say that for a long time."

"Oh, come!" objected Mrs. Joliffe. "You have met her now—you have seen what she is. How can you accuse me of cruelty?"

"I do. You made her what she is."

"My dear child, you have been swept along on the wave of American psychiatric rubbish that engulfs this country these days. I did not make Germaine, except in the purely biological sense. On the contrary, when I realized how untalented and unlikable she was I did everything in my power to help her. But she is what she is, and she would have been like that whatever her background."

"Perhaps if she had had a father—"

"Her father would have had her sent off to boarding school at the first possible opportunity. At least I kept her with me."

"It might have been better if she had been sent away to school. She must have been so under your shadow—she must have felt so inferior all the time."

"She is inferior."

"No, she isn't. Not basically."

"What do basics matter?"

"I don't understand that kind of verbal fencing, Mrs. Joliffe. But I still think you are cruel to Germaine. You use her as a whipping boy and it is a shame."

"Oh, dear," said Mrs. Joliffe, "She would be so angry if she knew you were her champion. Well, I will try, but it is a little late and you are wrong about her. She is so lugubrious, not at all like me."

"She is like you in some ways," Sophie could not resist saying.

"You are trying to hurt me," accused Mrs. Joliffe, "and I have never hurt you."

"You have, often," said Sophie, and then, hurriedly, "but

this is silly, isn't it? Is there anything I can get you? I think I will go to bed. I feel tired."

"Have a glass of sherry," urged Mrs. Joliffe.

"No, thank you. Can I shop for you tomorrow, and cook your lunch?"

"Only if you will join me and eat what you cook. We will have fillet steak. I need some good red meat. And fried potatoes—we will be really wicked. William hates the smell of potatoes frying. He once had the impudence to suggest a ban on frying potatoes being incorporated into the lease. I told him the reason there was any smell to annoy him was the bad design of the kitchen."

So they parted friends. Mrs. Joliffe was careful to see that they always did. She listened to Sophie trudging heavily upstairs, and though she felt sorry for her—she was a kind, affectionate, gentle girl—she at once rang William, to whom her first loyalties lay.

"William," she said, "come down immediately."

"Oh, dear," said William, "is it urgent?"

"Would I demand your presence if it were not?" snapped Mrs. Joliffe, and she put down the receiver. She would give the man five minutes and then ring again. Waiting, she trimmed a cigar carefully and cleaned out its holder. She was smoking in fine style when William crept in.

"Oh, I say," he said, "is that wise?"

"No," said Mrs. Joliffe, "but at seventy I can afford not to care. Now, look, William, I haven't brought you down to talk about myself, you'll be pleased to hear. I expect you know whom I do want to talk about?"

"Ah, Germaine," said William.

"Good heavens," said Mrs. Joliffe, genuinely amazed, "whatever gave you that idea? When, in all the years I've known you, have I ever wanted to talk about Germaine?"

"I thought it was her news," William said.

Mrs. Joliffe peered at William through the smoke she was

creating. He had his head on one side and she could not decide whether he was being sly or discreet. There was nothing to be gained by pretending that she knew the news.

"What news?" she asked abruptly.

"Perhaps—if she has not told you—I would not like—"

"Shut up, William. Tell me this news at once or I shall behave very unpleasantly."

Quite what unpleasant behavior she had in mind Mrs. Joliffe did not know, but fortunately she was not called upon to exercise her imagination.

"She and Homer are emigrating to Canada," said William.

"How typical," Mrs. Joliffe said, and blew an extra lot of smoke. She found her heart was beating violently, but she could not let William see her distress. Who would not find it amusing that she should be distressed at the departure of her openly despised daughter? Though it took a great deal of effort, she began to speak very rapidly, one hand flattened against her wildly palpitating heart.

"William, I wish to speak to you about Sophie Hill. I am very worried about her."

"So am I," said William dolefully.

"But I am more worried," said Mrs. Joliffe. "She is more to me than she is to you, and besides I know more about the situation than you do. William, that girl's husband has abandoned her. Worse, unless I am very wrong he is not and never was her husband. Now pass me that bottle. No, the other. Thank you."

William sat very still at her bedside with his hands clasped on his knees, his extreme outward composure matched by his extreme inner agitation. He hated Mrs. Joliffe at that moment. He knew she had calculated the effect her revelations would have on him, and he could not forgive her for nevertheless going ahead. She liked passing on bad news. She always had. There was an extra gleam in her eye when she intended to be vicious. He had seen it and ought to have left the room.

"Well, William?"

William said nothing. He knew she was enjoying waiting. Finally he took his spectacles off, and put them back on again and said, "As you said, she is more to you than to me."

"That has nothing to do with it," said Mrs. Joliffe smartly. "You are up to your neck in it and must decide what is to be done."

William stiffened and consciously sat very straight. "It is all quite simple," he said. "I shall consult my solicitor."

"Rubbish. Next you'll be saying you'll consult your architect, and a damned lot of good that will do. No, there's only one possible solution." She paused, but William was gazing into space in a most annoying manner. "You must inform the child's mother."

"I couldn't possibly," said William, startled out of his trance.

"Of course you could. You must. Take the rent, the little rent you have had—did you know Sophie's mother had paid that?"

"Yes," said William. "I did."

"Oh. Then there is no difficulty. You must ring her up tomorrow morning and make an appointment to go and discuss the matter with her."

"I refuse," shouted William.

"Then what do you intend to do, apart from shout at me?"

"I don't have to do anything at all," said William. "I have no obligation to take any action whatsoever. It is nothing at all to do with me."

"What about the rent? Has it been paid?"

"No, but I am not desperate for the rent, I do not need to go to such lengths to get it. I do not need to do anything at all. I am perfectly entitled to ignore the Hills and their business."

"Being entitled is one thing," said Mrs. Joliffe, "being wise is another. If you stand aside now, William, you will land in a worse mess."

"I am not *in* a mess," said William. "It is everyone else who is in a mess, not I. I am quite all right, thank you. My affairs are in order, I trouble nobody and all I ask is that no one should trouble me. Do you understand? I am all right, thank you."

"Don't boast," said Mrs. Joliffe. "You take a simpleton's view of the world, William, and always have done. You do not live on a desert island—but I do not need to begin a dissertation on political philosophy. It simply won't work— you are a human being living among other human beings and you cannot bury your head in the sand. Where is your compassion? Don't choke—I know quite well you want to say where is mine. Mine is with that girl. She is not wholly innocent, but she cannot help herself. She is alone, pregnant, friendless and among us. We are old, William, but through her we can be useful. She offers us a great chance to do good and be enlivened by the good we do. You can't not care about Sophie Hill—I know you *do* care. Now, let us plan, two old people who ought to have a lot of wisdom between them."

"I reject that," said William. "I do not agree with you."

"What don't you agree with?" asked Mrs. Joliffe.

"I don't agree with a word you've said in the last five minutes. I'm sorry, but I think it was a lot of sanctimonious humbug. Good night."

Mrs. Joliffe lay in bed and laughed till she cried, and then kept on crying, in earnest, for Germaine emigrating and leaving her with no one at all, and especially heartily for the sad human failings she had just displayed so disgracefully.

Ten

>>>>>>

WILLIAM, the next day, was determined to stick to his routine and drive out of his head all thought of the madwomen who inhabited his house. He would sip his tea, read the paper, not answer the telephone or the doorbell under any circumstances. He had thought everything out in advance. On his door was pinned a notice which read: "OAK UP! Desperately busy!!" That was in case Sophie was encouraged by Agnes Joliffe to come up to see why he was not answering the summons that was sure to come. When both of them were resting after lunch, he would slip out and go for a very long walk. He would go to a theater in the evening, and perhaps even ring Pullen before and arrange to take him out for a late supper, since it was his turn to entertain and his flat was not yet ready for entertaining.

Unhappily, the debt was not to be paid. William's tea steamed to a halt as he sat and stared at the announcement of Pullen's death in the *Times*. "Suddenly," of course. That was a very real blessing. His old friend was spared a long, harrowing illness. And in hospital—that was seemly. Pullen had probably arranged to be taken to hospital in the event of sudden illness. William wondered if he ought to do the same, but then how could he? Hospitals were funny places. They did not necessarily welcome you, and then one might get in their clutches and never get out. Pullen must have been very sure—he must have had some warning that made him determined to get to hospital and get it over without inconveniencing anyone. Death was a hospital's business, after all.

William put his paper down. One could not read the rest of the news on the day Pullen died. He got up and drew his curtains and sat down again. Silly gesture, but not meaningless. However hard he tried, he found that he could not seriously think about Pullen at all. He tried to think about him at school, in the Army, but it was no good—all he could think about was himself. Where did it leave him? Alive. Life was precious because every day it was taken away from someone. A simple fact, which William sat and thought about in the gloom of his curtained room. He was alive and ought to be relishing the fact, but was not because of these tenants. Must he go burdened with them to the grave? Getting rid of the Hills was comparatively easy—well, not easy, not for him, but manageable. It required firmness, but that was all. The Hills, however, were not his whole problem: Agnes was the other part. The thought of a totally crippled Agnes in his house for the next ten years almost made him want to join Pullen—and to think like that was wicked. What he ought to do was get rid of Agnes.

He had thought about it a great deal and had all the relevant points to hand. He could not turn Agnes out: she had a lease. He could not persuade her to go, because she was averse to all persuasion and in any case he was not one of nature's persuaders. Agnes, in fact, was not his responsibility. He was not a relative. Germaine was her only relative. Germaine therefore had a certain degree of power. She had rights, a voice in the matter, and though she would do no better than he at persuasion, if it came to the push, Germaine was not insignificant. Suppose her mother had to be in someone's care—suppose, medically, she was declared unfit to look after herself, Germaine would have the whip hand. If she would not accept the job, then officially Agnes had nowhere to go and must be sent somewhere. But Germaine would never do this. She was afraid of her mother and would do what she was told. How, William wondered, could he use Germaine? A tiny corner of an idea came into his mind, but it was so distasteful he pushed it away. Why, he wondered, was he sitting in semidarkness at this time of the morning? He got up, parted the curtains, sat down to read his paper, and remembered Pullen. Poor Pullen. He sipped his cold tea and thought how fortunate it was that he had nipped out to buy a paper that morning.

Who had put the announcement in the paper? It bothered William. Pullen had no relatives, no close friends. Perhaps his housekeeper. Ah, yes. William nodded. He was still nodding his approval when he absent-mindedly answered the telephone at the very first ring.

"William," said Agnes Joliffe excitedly. "I say, William, have you seen today's *Times?*"

"Yes."

"Is it your Pullen?"

"No," said William calmly.

"No? Are you sure? Weren't his names Arthur James? Wasn't he sixty-eight and a member of the Royal Society of Architects? Can there be another such Pullen? Are you sure it is not your Pullen, William?"

"Pullen has died, you are correct," William said evenly, "but he was not my Pullen."

"You are splitting hairs, William," said Agnes crossly. "You knew perfectly well what I said, what I meant. I was only going to offer my condolences. I know you must be very upset."

"I am not in the least upset," said William. "He was a very good friend, but we had no emotional ties."

"Is not friendship an emotional tie?"

"No," said William.

"You are pretending to be hard," said Agnes emphatically, "and I shall treat such pretense with scorn. I will leave you to contemplate what you have just said. Good morning."

After that, the day was in ruins. William was disorientated by rage, not grief. He stumbled around his flat, muddling everything up, knocking things over, getting in his own way, and then he rushed from window to window staring out at the sky with tense expectation. He was much more bothered by Agnes Joliffe's interpretation of his feelings than by the fact of his friend's death. Left to himself, without her malicious intervention, he might, as the day wore on, have fallen into a mood of not unpleasant melancholy. Certainly he would have eventually remembered most fondly times he had shared with Pullen, gone over conversations of significance that he had had with him, perhaps experienced regret that another line of communication was down, leaving that part of his life virtually barren. All that, but no more. He would not have wept. He would not have been too miserable. As it was, he hardly gave a thought to Pullen. Agnes Joliffe's assumption that he ever pretended anything obsessed him. She thought that because he was not a violent man he did not mean what he said. Many times he had kept silent, but never, never had he pretended.

Compelled by an overwhelming desire to show his tenants that he meant what he said, William, around noon, made two telephone calls. He first called his solicitor and instructed him to write to Sophie and Alexander Hill saying that unless the terms of the lease were complied with at once they must consider it terminated. The rent must be paid in full by the end of the week or the flat vacated on that day.

The Hills' troubles were nothing to do with him. If Agnes Joliffe supposed that he was actually going to ring up or visit Sophie's mother she was very much mistaken. He had been more than reasonable. He would not be involved beyond what he thought reasonable limits. Then he rang Germaine, sitting very straight-backed and with a pencil in his hand.

"Look here, Germaine," he began.

"You are not allowed to ring me at work unless it's a real emergency," said Germaine furiously. "Is it a real emergency? Has Mother died? Has the doctor sent for me?"

"No," said William, "but I have an ultimatum to deliver."

"Then deliver it and get off the line."

"Unless you make provision for your mother to go into a nursing home before you leave this country, I will demand my loan to be paid in full."

"Blackmail!" screamed Germaine.

"No," said William firmly. "I lent you that money twenty years ago on the clear understanding that I would never tell your mother nor ask for it back sooner than you could pay it."

"I can't pay it now."

"Then arrange for your mother to go into a home," said William.

"How can I?" wailed Germaine.

"I don't know. You will have to apply yourself to the problem," said William. "It is your problem, not mine."

"William," said Germaine tearfully, "dear William, this is not like you."

"On the contrary," said William, "it is very like me," and he put the receiver down.

Germaine found it impossible to continue working. Her job was not very arduous—she worked in a picture library—

but she could not concentrate and eventually left at two o'clock, pleading migraine. The migraine was not entirely imaginary. All her life she had suffered from violent headaches brought on by any kind of worry, and she could truthfully feel one beginning the minute William hung up on her. What worried her most was that he had not sounded the least bit hysterical or overwrought, but very calm and decisive. This in itself was an indication that William meant what he said. Usually he so stuttered and mumbled and trailed on that one couldn't hear the half of it. Nor had he been embarrassed, and since she had never known William not awkward, that worried Germaine, too.

Repaying the loan was ridiculous. William had surely turned it into a gift by never mentioning it during the last twenty years. Yet, uneasily, Germaine remembered his insistence that it should all be done legally "for the sake of everyone." Somewhere at home, in one of her drawers, was a piece of paper in a buff envelope with a sixpenny stamp on it saying that William Ellis Bone lent Germaine Agnes Joliffe five hundred pounds under the following conditions. She had never even thought about it since she signed it, and never repaid a penny.

Hurrying home, Germaine could not believe William wanted the money. Well, of course he didn't, he wanted her mother out of his house. She shook her now painful head irritably. William wanted Agnes out. He was using the money as a lever. But supposing the lever did not work, would he force her to pay the money? How could he? What were the legal rights in such a case? He could perhaps take her to court, and even though she did not have the money— that was an easily substantiated fact—he might be able to stop her leaving the country until it was paid. That, surely, was what he was about. She had been foolish to tell him that she and Homer were about to emigrate; she had known at the time that she was foolish, but had not been able to resist it, just to see his face as he realized her mother would then be dependent on him. But would William take her to court? Suddenly, as she got off her bus, the conviction hit her as hard as her feet slapped the pavement: taking people to court was exactly what William would do. It was probably the only line of action he would find easy to do, because it was remote and right and rigid.

Germaine's flat soon resembled a jumble sale as she threw the contents of every cupboard and drawer onto the floors. She hurled clothes and papers about especially viciously as she imagined William going straight to wherever he kept his copy of the agreement. Twenty years or not, it would be slotted away in some immediately attainable hole. The flat wrecked, she stopped and sat among the debris wondering why she had spent so much precious energy making so much mess. What, after all, did it matter? William would have it all sewn up. If she thought it made any difference knowing exactly what that paper said she had only to ring William and ask him. He would tell her every word. He would not lie, but repeat the entire document from beginning to end without once looking at it. She could see him in her mind's eye as he read it out to her all those years ago, pencil in hand, ticking each clause off as he finished it and she gave her impatient agreement. She saw herself sitting there, un-caring, not listening to a word, wanting only to get her hands on the money and off, off to Sweden and the six weeks' holiday with the abortion in the middle that no one would ever know about except William, dear William, whom she had turned to as being the only person she knew who had any money and who had so unexpectedly agreed to give her the money, even though he knew what she wanted it for.

Not even attempting to tidy up, Germaine moved into the bedroom and, lying on the bed, lit a cigarette. She lay smoking it, remembering, wondering why William had ever given her that money. It had seemed strange at the time, but it seemed much stranger now. William had not changed in twenty years, but she knew him better. Before her mother had gone to live in his house, William had been a father figure, someone she had romanticized and even idolized, someone she had wished with a certain degree of impatience that her mother would marry. The ins and outs of their relationship she had never concerned herself with. Once, she had asked her mother, quite innocently, why she did not marry William, and her mother had laughed and said, "Ask William." But she never had asked him. She had not, even after growing up with him always somewhere around, ever been able to talk to William about anything personal. William was a man whose whole being precluded intimacy.

Yet she had asked him to lend her the money for an abortion, knowing though she did his abhorrence of all things feminine and his inflexible standards of morality. She had rung him up, at his office—how could she have!—and asked him if she could talk to him about something very urgent. If she remembered rightly, he had taken her out to dinner that very evening and over a drink she had told him, in a series of dreadful blurtings out, the whole dismal story. He had sat and blinked, head down, attentive, nodding from time to time, and when she had finished he had simply said, "Something must be done. Can you manage to eat?" They had eaten, she ravenously, he picking and poking over the bits. He had said everything must be properly managed but he would lend her whatever she needed, and he had even suggested, urged and finally ordered her to double the amount so that she could have a really good job done. Such was his calm they might have been talking about her portrait. He had never once asked if she had told her mother, or the man concerned, nor had he advised her to have it, like most of her friends. But neither had he been sympathetic. There was no patting of her hand, or head shaking, nothing. He did not wish to know the details of how his money would be spent. As she left him in the street outside the restaurant she had said, "Thank you, William. I know you're only doing it for my mother's sake, but thank you all the same."

"Not at all," he had said, so sharply that she had peered at him in surprise. "I would never do anything for either your mother's sake or your sake. I do it simply so that an unwanted child may not be born into a world that will not love it. That is all, Germaine. I am not a misguided philanthropist—merely a realist. You will hear from my solicitor." And he had trotted off into the night.

In any case, she had got the money, with a lot of William-type fuss, and had the abortion. William, meeting her at her wedding six months later, had not asked her how she was, how she had got on, what value she had got out of his money. She had, she supposed, been quite hurt that he had not tried to contact her in the interval. Her welfare did not appear to concern him. She was never able to give him the harrowing account of the operation, performed without anesthetic, in a room so small and narrow it was hardly big enough for a lavatory, by a man who spoke only to tell his assistants to hold her down more securely. The pain she could not re-create, but the intensity of it remained with her for four, perhaps five years after, and when she learned soon after her first marriage that she could never have children, as a direct result of an infection after the operation, she endowed the pain with all kinds of symbolism. William, when he shook her hand—not even on her wedding day kissing her—did not know what his money had begun.

Homer, when he came in, was cross. He had recently given up smoking, so the smoke-filled bedroom filled him with self-righteous fury. The untidiness he was used to and minded about less, but that night it was so colossal that he was moved to include it in his general condemnation. Living with Germaine was a sorry business. He was not a demanding man, his standards were not high, but his wife neglected all the creature comforts that to a man of his disappointed years were so important. Homer had not been married before—nobody would have him—and was used to living in domestic upheaval. Dirty shirts and dishes were part of his life, canned food not something he objected to, but he had hoped for a little human spark. He had liked the idea of someone speaking to him in the evening, inquiring about his welfare, sharing his ups and downs. He was not an artist, so he did not need inspiration, nor a dynamo of business activity, so there was no unwinding to be done for him by a clever little wife. All he was, was a beat-up, faded, unambitious, ordinary salesman, and all he wanted was some assurance that he was still alive and even kicking. Germaine did not give him this; rather, he had to pay out to her, nurse her wounds, make her feel conscious. They were both slag heaps. Having thought this, he said it, and more, despairingly, in his flat American voice, bringing Gawd into it over and over again. He picked his way over heaps of clothes and rubbish, banged empty drawers shut, kicked boxes under the bed, keeled over a suitcase with his toe, all the time with his hands in the pockets of his baggy raincoat and his trilby hat on his head.

Germaine hardly heard him. She watched him, gray like smoke himself, and felt nothing but apathy toward him. Of all her three husbands he was the least prepossessing. There was between them a kind of fondness generated by their mutual recognition of the other's awfulness. They frequently remarked on this quality. "Isn't it lucky we're both awful?" they said to each other. It was almost the only form of closeness they enjoyed.

When Homer had worn himself out, he collapsed onto the bed beside her, smelling of the tube, and said, "Why do I bother?"

"You never thought to ask why I was home early," Germaine said.

"Are you home early?"

"You never even registered the fact, you were so busy criticizing me. Well, carry on, I'm used to it."

"O.K.," Homer said wearily, "so you were home early. I apologize for not noting it. You want me to ask *why* you were home early? Is that what you want me to ask?"

"I don't want you to ask anything."

"O.K., so I won't. Since you were home early, may I ask if you've broken a lifetime's habit and made something to eat? Huh?"

"No. I haven't. I've been much too upset."

"It shook you, getting home early, did it?"

"Clever."

"Get up now and fix me something."

"I haven't time. I have to go and see my mother."

"Christ almighty, what for this time? You haven't been away from the place in weeks. You won't be able to do that when we're in Canada, you know—you may as well get used to it."

"I may never see Canada," Germaine said, and began to cry, having enjoyed so much the sequence of revelations.

"Oh, come on," said Homer, "now why not?"

"Because if I can't get Mother to go into a home William wants his money back and I can't pay it and he won't let me leave the country till it is paid."

"*What* money? What are you talking about?"

She told him. Homer listened, interrupting her only to swear, and when she had finished he said, "Ridiculous. William would never make you pay that money. It wouldn't get him anywhere and you know it and he knows it—and even if he could, he wouldn't. Not William."

"He's changed," Germaine said.

"At his time of life? He hasn't changed. No, you've got nothing to worry about. Now let's eat."

He got off the bed and, taking off his crumpled jacket, put on an even more crumpled lighter one. Germaine did not move.

"Come on," Homer said. "Come on, come on."

"You are a bastard," Germaine said.

"Now what? What have I done? I've reassured you, haven't I? I've told you everything will be all right. What kind of bastard is that?"

"All you worried about was the money," Germaine said.

"What did you expect me to worry about? William's health?"

"You've hurt my feelings unbearably."

"I do that every day, so what's that to you? I don't close the bathroom door when I take a crap—that hurts your feelings unbearably. I empty tea leaves down the sink and that hurts your feelings. Hurting your feelings is impossible to avoid." He paused and, forgetting, took one of her cigarettes from the top of the chest of drawers and lit it. "But I know what you're getting at," he said. "It's this abortion bit, right? So you never told me about it before, so what do you want me to do? Break down and cry? Get hot about it? Faint with shock? Listen, Germaine, you're fifty-one and I'm fifty and we've only known each other three years and been married two and a half. We lived our lives before we ever met, right? If I worried about all the things that happened before we met I'd go crazy."

"Some things are important," Germaine said.

"Not to both of us," Homer said. "An abortion you had twenty years ago is not important to us here and now."

"I've never got over it," Germaine said.

"You've never got over being born," said Homer sourly. "That happening to you was the end. You and your dear mother—what a setup."

"I hate her," said Germaine.

"You love her," said Homer. "You're nuts about her, you'd do anything to get her to say 'Good dog.' She's fouled your whole life up and you love her, and William. I've never in my life seen such a setup. It's disgusting. You're like three old crows pecking away at each other all the time. Childish."

"You don't understand," Germaine said, "you've got no emotions at all."

"I'd rather have none than your crazy ones."

"I still can't think of my child—"

"Oh, shit, Germaine. This is the first time you've thought of that little bloody bit of flesh for years. Anyway, you'd have made a lousy mother—you'd have taken it out on that kid all along the line. It would have been 'I've never got over your ruining my life' every day."

"It was a terrible operation," Germaine said.

"You didn't feel a thing," Homer said.

"I nearly died with pain. I thought I really was dying, I didn't care what happened in the end."

"You were probably stoned," Homer said.

"I screamed my head off."

"That's the first true word you've said."

"I've never got over it," Germaine repeated, and shook her head and clutched her stomach and redoubled her howls.

"You think I've got over being run down by a ten-ton truck when I was twenty-four? Six months in the hospital, four broken ribs, both legs in plaster, on the edge of death for three weeks. You think I've got over that? But I've never told you about it, because it's got nothing to do with you and me. Like your abortion. It's finished."

"You're like William," said Germaine contemptuously.

"Thanks," said Homer. "I rate that a compliment. In this respect I agree with William absolutely. He lent you the money, but he kept out of it. Great."

"You're hard," Germaine sobbed, "you're both hard, unfeeling monsters."

"Everyone is hard," Homer said, "everyone only cries for themselves. Look at you—what about your mother? You'd put her in any home in the country if you could manage it."

"It's for her own good."

"Balls, lies!" Homer shouted. "It's because you put your own interests first. You're much, much harder than either William or I. She's your own mother, but you hate her and you won't look after her without making yourself a martyr. That is hardness." He stood and watched Germaine bawling and writhing around on the bed. "Shut up," he said. "I'll ring William, it'll all be all right. We'll get to Canada. Do you still want to come—huh? Do you still want to come with awful old me to Canada and meet a few Mounties, huh?"

Homer, coy and playful, eventually coaxed his lumpy spouse into the kitchen, where she managed to forget her worries enough to fry him some frozen fishcakes which, smothered with tomato sauce and bolstered up with bread, took the edge off his hunger. But she would not let him ring William, not under any circumstances. Instead she put on her hat and coat when she had made him some coffee, and drove over to see her mother. As she let herself into the house, warm and full of warm smells, she heard voices coming from her mother's bedroom and thought at first that William was with her, but then she recognized Sophie Hill's soft, rather low tones, and confidently she went on down.

The scene was one of domestic bliss so that she felt an intruder and stood hesitating in the doorway, large and black in her boots and raincoat. Her mother sat up in bed, her white hair brushed and shining, winding wool, pinkish wool, from a skein held by Sophie, who was perched companionably on the bed. The room was hot and both their cheeks were flushed. On the dressing table burned a stick of incense, a habit of her mother's which had never found favor with Germaine, and beside it a portable record player rested with a Bach quartet just finishing the first side. An electric kettle was beginning to spout steam in the fireplace.

Germaine thought they looked guilty. "This is unexpected," her mother said, her eyebrows raised and that look of amused tolerance already settling on her face. "To what do we owe this honor?"

"I just thought I'd call in," Germaine said, "but if I'm spoiling anything I'll go."

"Don't be ridiculous," snapped her mother, "and do take off that dreadful mackintosh. You look positively sinister. Now we can go on winding wool, Sophie. You have come just in time to make us some coffee, Germaine. It is instant, so you will have no difficulty."

Going through to the little kitchen for cups and saucers, Germaine heard her mother talking animatedly about porcelain figures. She told Sophie of collections she had seen, and Sophie made intelligent remarks that showed she knew something about porcelain, too. Germaine knew nothing about art, of any kind. Before she knew the meaning of the word she knew she was a philistine, because her mother had told her so every day. Was it her fault? Had her mother tried to cultivate her? No. It was always other people's daughters who were worthy of her attention. Jealous to the point of malice, Germaine wished Sophie Hill dead. She was such a prig, such a showoff. She thought that because she had known Mrs. Joliffe one month she was qualified to say what was and was not good for her. She had actually rung Germaine up, the day of the accident, and asked her if she didn't think she ought to move in to look after her mother —as if William wasn't enough. Germaine had replied in icy terms, telling her most effectively to mind her own business.

"How funny you are, Germaine," her mother said as she walked in with the tray. "You have chosen teacups, very large teacups, too, to have coffee in."

"I thought they would do," Germaine said. "I didn't think it mattered what we drank out of."

"Nor does it," said her mother, "but coffee cups are nicer, that is all. It is just strange to choose teacups. However, I do not wish to make anything of it. Give Sophie a cup first—no, no, Germaine, the child will put her own sugar in. There, Sophie. You deserve something more. Germaine, bring the madeira from the cupboard. Sophie has been working very hard."

"Holding wool?" sneered Germaine.

"Not just holding wool—though you could never hold wool for more than two seconds without fidgeting, Germaine, so don't underrate the ability. Sophie has been writing letters for me and reading to me and even doing my hair. I am very grateful."

"You'll miss her," Germaine said, "when the baby comes."

"Yes," said her mother.

"When is it due?" Germaine asked coolly. "It can't be long now."

"Oh, still five weeks," Sophie said, drinking her coffee quickly and not touching the madeira.

"I expect time is hanging heavily on your hands," Germaine said. "You must be glad of anything to fill it in."

"It isn't as bad as that," Sophie said, standing up. "I think I'll go to bed now, Mrs. Joliffe."

"You must need plenty of rest," Germaine said.

Sophie said good night and went and when they heard her reach her own flat Mrs. Joliffe said, "You are very unkind, Germaine. I was ashamed of you."

"How was I unkind?" protested Germaine. "I thought I was very sweet to her."

"Apart from the fact that you are never sweet to anyone, I was not talking about Sophie. You were unkind to me. You tried to make it look as though Sophie only visited me out of boredom. Luckily, I know that is not true. Boredom plays a part, of course, but not a major part. We are kindred spirits."

"You will miss her."

"Cruel again. Yes, but she will still be here and when I am well again I may be able to help her. I can have the child down here in its cradle when she wishes to go out."

"If she lives here still," Germaine said, "which I doubt. William will not like a crying baby."

"He cannot turn her out onto the streets and she has nowhere to go."

Germaine found herself listening to the words but thinking not of Sophie so much as of herself. Twenty years ago she had thought of going to her mother and telling her she was pregnant and asking her if she could have the baby, please, at home. She had practiced her speech hundreds of times, but the minute she opened her mouth to begin, her throat went dry and the well-rehearsed words would not come. No words would come. She felt her mother's cool eyes on her, amused, contemptuous, and she could not speak. What if she had spoken? What if an abortion had not been easier than telling her mother and begging her help? Would it have changed their whole relationship? Germaine did not think so. Twenty years ago she had been sure her mother would turn her out, and she was still sure. Not, of course, for reasons of convention. She did not care about that, flouting it herself. What would have incurred her wrath would have been the thought of her daughter having the audacity to have a lover she did not know. She would not have rested until she had found out everything about him. She would have demanded every detail of their union, and that Germaine was not going to give, to anyone. The fact that she did not know the man's name, nor where he lived, and would never see him again—this did not matter. She—even she—had had a half-perfect moment and it was too priceless to save her baby with.

"William won't worry about that," she finally said.

"Nonsense. William is kind and has a great sense of responsibility."

"If she went, how would you manage?"

"As I've always managed."

"You have not always had two useless legs."

"Nor will I always have them. My left leg improves every day. Dr. Barber is very pleased with my progress."

"And your heart?"

"Under no strain. You are suddenly very interested in my welfare, Germaine. Are you worried in case you are sent for when you are in Canada? There is no need to worry. I shall give explicit instructions that you are not to be informed until after I am dead."

"Did William tell you about Canada?"

"Of course. Did you expect him not to?"

"I was going to tell you myself, when it was all settled. It still isn't absolutely definite."

"I wish you and Homer every happiness."

"If we go," Germaine said, hesitantly, "I wouldn't like to leave you like this, not bedridden."

"I am perfectly content. The blow is no greater because I am bedridden."

"Oh, you needn't pretend, or maybe you were being sarcastic—anyway, you needn't. I know you couldn't care less about what I do."

"Don't be silly," said Mrs. Joliffe sharply, "of course I care. I was upset to the point of severe palpitations when William told me, if you must know."

"I can't think why," Germaine said, head bent.

"You are my daughter."

"You mean blood is thicker than water, that kind of thing?"

"No, I do not. You think in clichés, Germaine—do try not to. I mean what I said—you are my daughter. If you had ever had a child of your own you would understand me.

Besides, you are all I have, all I have had for a very long time now. Does that mean nothing?"

"We have never got on," Germaine mumbled.

"I am a cantankerous old woman and you are an insensitive young one."

"I am not young."

"Do not quibble, Germaine. When you are as old as I am everyone is young. What I was trying to say was that I will miss you very much. I take you much too much for granted and when you are gone I will be very sad."

"I think you should go where there are other people," Germaine said. "You won't be properly looked after here. Why don't you let me find you a nice place?"

Mrs. Joliffe poured herself another glass of madeira, drank it very quickly, then took off her wristwatch, removed her upper dentures and her earrings and lay down in bed. She closed her eyes and put out the light, smiling in the darkness as she imagined Germaine's consternation. The girl was such a bumbling fool—so foolish she could not take an opportunity when it was put in front of her. All her life it seemed she had been apologizing to her daughter, admitting she was to blame, asking for a truce, but Germaine veered sharply in the other direction each time and they ended up further apart than ever. Well, they could stay apart, however sorry she might feel about it. Germaine had responded to her confession of love with a crudely disguised attempt to make her go into a home. That she would never do. God knew what Germaine's motives were—certainly not the professed solicitude—but her intent was clear. She must be made to realize at once that there was no prospect of success. She would be carried out of William's house feet first only, and that was that.

Eleven

MRS. JOLIFFE made very brave attempts to overcome her disability, and Sophie was both touched and eager when she was asked to help. The doctor had suggested that the torn ligament would heal quicker if Mrs. Joliffe went to the physiotherapy department of the nearest hospital and had deep-heat treatment combined with very careful exercising. Accordingly, a car was hired—she would not use the ambulance car—and Sophie and she set off for the hospital.

At first it all seemed a treat, for them both. The hired car was very large and luxurious, and as Sophie sank into the back seat she sighed with contentment. Sometimes material comforts were so delicious. Beside her, Mrs. Joliffe, perfectly and elegantly dressed in a tweed suit and a magnificent fur stole, sighed too.

"Shall we tell him to take us to Brighton, for a blow on the front?" she said.

"Or Dover, to catch the boat train to Paris," said Sophie.

"Perhaps, after all, morning coffee at the Dorchester and a look in the V and A—such years since I've been there."

"Give him his head," suggested Sophie. "Just drive us anywhere."

In that short time they were there, sweeping into the gates of the hospital, a mere five minutes from the house. Their troubles began almost immediately. The car was not allowed to park directly in front of the front door, not even for a minute, but had to pull up five yards to the right. Those five yards were painful ones for Mrs. Joliffe, in spite of Sophie on one side and the driver on the other. However, she managed the distance and negotiated the steps. Inside the hall, the driver left them to move the car to the car park. There were no seats of any kind and acres of shining marble tiles to cross. Off Sophie went to get a wheelchair, which took her a quarter of an hour and left Mrs. Joliffe leaning on her sticks and trying to take the weight off her sore leg by moving onto her crippled one. She collapsed exhausted into the chair when it appeared.

They waited in the appropriate room, when they found it, for nearly an hour. The room was not even a room, but an open space where two corridors joined. With them sat thirty-four other human beings on slippery leather benches, only two of which had backs to them. In one corner was a vast array of machinery for dispensing drinks and chocolate. Toward this, half the migrant population veered, some actually inserting coins—dumbly watched by the knowing rest —before realizing it was out of order. Across this stage scores of nurses swept by, all beautifully busy, trim, aloof. Those who smiled seemed the most aloof of all.

Gradually Sophie began to feel sick. At her side, Mrs. Joliffe was silent, her eyes closed, only the hand on the cane, constantly groping, showing that she was not a statue. Sophie had looked closely at every face and they were all frightened to some extent. There were three other wheelchair cases, one of whom was a deaf but garrulous old man who shrieked aloud everyone's fears—hoping those little bits of things knew their job, hoping it didn't hurt, hoping they wouldn't finish him off this time, hoping they hadn't mixed him up with someone else, hoping he wasn't going to sit here all day, hoping his room wasn't burgled while he was away, hoping they'd bring some tea . . .

At last Mrs. Joliffe's name was called and Sophie wheeled her forward. A cool, bright nurse took over at the door of the doctor's room, and there was an awkward moment when Mrs. Joliffe told Sophie authoritatively to come in with her and the nurse equally authoritatively to stay out. She was glad the nurse settled it by appealing to the doctor, who excluded her. After ten minutes Mrs. Joliffe emerged, spots of red high on her cheekbones, and Sophie accompanied her to the treatment room, where this time she was seen straight away. Here the atmosphere was less desperate, and Sophie recovered her composure in time to stand the journey back through the hospital and into the car.

They did not speak till they were in Mrs. Joliffe's bedroom and she was in bed.

"Thank you, my dear," Mrs. Joliffe said. "It was a service I should not have asked you to perform if I had known what it meant."

"That's all right," Sophie said. "How do you feel? It was an ordeal, wasn't it?"

"A fearful ordeal, and I feel dreadful, perfectly dreadful. I would have done much better to stay in bed and rest. I cannot imagine what Dr. Barber was thinking of to send me there."

"Perhaps one treatment isn't a true test—"

"It is enough of a test and I have failed. Now go and rest, child, and I will see you for a sherry later."

Dismissed—increasingly, Mrs. Joliffe dismissed her rather than said goodbye—Sophie went up to her own flat, collecting an uninteresting-looking letter on the way. Old age went with her. She thought of herself in the outpatients' department, in a wheelchair, dependent on a neighbor for the to-ing and fro-ing, stripped of pride and dignity, an object to be rolled over and prodded and sent away—and sent to nothing, no one. There were tears of sentiment in her eyes by the time she sat down, and she went on from there to cry some more for her own plight. Perhaps, without waiting for old age, she too would soon be part of the flotsam of that hospital. Perhaps the antenatal clinic was only another version of the same story which seemed to her a sorry tale of lost rights.

Sophie was not a good clinic attender; keeping appointments was something she found hard to do. It was not so much that she was vague or absent-minded as that she was incapable of realizing that they were important. She felt splendid, she looked splendid, she was doing all the right things, eating all the right food. All the weighing and testing she considered fussing. She was not stupid. At the first alarming symptom she would consult the doctor. Otherwise she was content to look after herself and let the baby grow. At the bottom of her bag she had two antenatal cards, each in its polythene cover, pristine and unmarked. One had been issued by Queen Mary's, Hampstead, and the other by her doctor in Richmond. Every now and again she would come across them, examine the particulars set down on them, and put them back again.

On February fifteenth Sophie had noticed the date on the newspaper she was reading to Mrs. Joliffe. Later in the day, she sought out the neglected cards and saw that according to them the baby was due on March fifteenth. It did not seem long. Perhaps she ought to take in a clinic somewhere. Only where? She had rung the midwife up after William's outburst and canceled the inspection. She could not now have it in the flat. William had said all she had to do was claim that her landlord absolutely refused to let her have a home confinement and they would be forced to take her into hospital. Sophie tried. She rang the doctor she had seen only once and told him what William had said. The doctor was very rude and said landlords had no business organizing

people's lives and to ignore him. Sophie did not know what
to do when the doctor hung up on her. Eventually, after a
great deal of thought, she rang the midwife who had been
going to visit her, but before she could begin to explain, the
midwife flew into a rage, said she certainly wasn't going to
be messed about with, and rang off.

Alex would have said fucking cow and what the fuck. Sophie smiled. She had always found other people's rages
funny, especially when she recognized herself in them. Why,
after all, did anything have to be done? When she was in
labor, which she was perfectly capable of recognizing, she
would ring for an ambulance and ask them to take her to
the nearest maternity hospital and that would be that. They
could not refuse to take a woman in labor to hospital, and
once she was there no hospital could turn her away. If they
tried to, she would simply lie down on the floor and have
it.

She felt that if he had been there, Alex would have
wholeheartedly approved. Birth was a natural thing to him,
as it was to her. Conception was even more natural and it
was unthinkable to attempt to thwart it. He had always
been fair to her about this, telling her from the beginning
that he expected the act of love to bear fruit and if she
didn't want the fruit she couldn't have the love. Sophie had
not been quite so confident about this as a permanent pol-
icy, but in Alex's case, and in that instance, she had agreed.
Perhaps, she had ventured to say, if they had five or six and
she was tired . . . She, after all, knew what it was to be one
of a large family continually bearing fruit. Alex did not.
For an orphan, he had very strange views on the sanctity of
a baby. Though he had been so clearly unwanted himself,
dumped in a station waiting room at three weeks old without even benefit of any touching note pinned to his shawl,
the idea of any baby being unwanted, rejected, a disaster
was anathema to him.

Sophie suddenly felt swamped by tears at the thought of

Alex telling her all this and at the memory of her tears then as he had told her. "Babies are fucking marvelous," he had said. "I mean, who could not want one?" Now she was beset with doubts that he would ever see his baby, marvelous or not, and it was worse still to realize that he would not think that wrong. She was sentimental, he told her. The world was hard, life was hard, it was better to have it hard from the beginning, then you knew what it was all about. He would not experience a single qualm at the thought of her baby being fatherless.

But then perhaps he had not left her. It was only ten days, even if it seemed ten weeks. She must have faith, that was the important thing. He knew where she was and by sheer willpower she could draw him back again. Staying in this flat was the only important thing—staying here night and day ready to take him when he came, without nagging or chiding or scolding, but smiling, tranquil, happy that at last he was here.

It was difficult, all the same, to live on willpower. The middle of February placed her another month in William's debt, to whom she had not after all spoken. Since she had realized that to be in his debt was inevitable, Sophie had drawn every penny she had from the bank, all thirty-two pounds, and used it for the gas meters and food. She knew it was dishonest, but if one owed sixty-five pounds what was the point in saving a sum so far short of it? None of Alex's laboring money had gone into the bank. They had spent it immediately on a transistor radio and cigarettes and clothes. She had taken, greedily, everything Alex had brought her, knowing that to argue at the wisdom of his random spending was unwise. She now had a fur coat (rabbit) that she could not button over her stomach, a pair of incredible embroidered trousers that would not rise higher than her crotch, and beads of such weight and size that she could not wear them without hurting herself. But he had worked hard to buy these presents, they were offerings of love and could not be thought of in the same breath as rent.

She had never made the visit to William that she had intended, because somehow it had seemed unnecessary. He knew her circumstances, she was sure. He had eyes and ears and knew Alex had left her. Then, on February first, she received the letter from his solicitor and her heart thudded so much she had to sit down on the stairs, where she read it. She had never imagined him capable of it—he was too good and kind. Once the first mouth-washing shock was over, the conviction returned to her that William was only using his solicitor to threaten her because the solicitor had said that he ought to. Yes, that was it. Should she tackle William on the subject, he would bluster and stutter and curse, insofar as he was able to curse, and say, "That damned fool of a solicitor, don't you worry, my dear."

Straight away, Sophie climbed up to William's flat and knocked. There was no sound of him coming to open the door. Determined, she knocked again, very hard, and shouted his name, and after a decent interval of total silence she pushed at the door. It opened. She hesitated. Of course, as with their outer door, there was no lock. The inner doors had Yale locks, but they never used them. Nor, to her surprise, did William. Peeping through the open outer door, she saw that both inner doors were wide open.

For a long time, Sophie stood at the back window and looked out over the net curtain. Who could believe that another fifteen feet up made such a difference? From her own back window she could see the garden and other gardens and very dimly the backs of a terrace of houses. But William had that only as a beginning. His view soared beyond the terrace, taking in the river far below and the meadows and the bridge and the boats like acorns underneath. There was a sense of time and place that she had not. Hardly noticing the furniture she avoided, Sophie walked straight through to the front room and boldly drew aside the curtains there. It was like sitting in the sky. Although not as high as the highest trees, the house was on a hill and from the top windows easily outstripped them. She longed to throw open the window and lean out and scratch her hands on the wicked points of the bare branches.

Only slowly did the rest of William's flat make any impression on her. She felt no guilt as she moved about, examining the contents, even picking up cards to read them and plants to smell them. She did not believe that she defiled anything, as her mother and then her teachers had tried to tell her. A perpetual wanderer among other people's possessions, she intended no harm and could not see how she did any. On the contrary, her respect was enormous. She thought she handled their belongings with reverence, as a visitor to a church might turn over the hymnbooks or peep into the christening register. Her uneasiness began only when she unsealed, cleverly, something that was meant to be sealed, or uncovered, noting scrupulously the order, something that was covered with several articles in a drawer. Then her cheeks would burn and the back of her neck prickle, but with excitement, not alarm—excitement in case she was going to get an insight into somebody that she could not otherwise get. She kept their secrets always. Once, hunting through her father's desk, she had found at the bottom of a wooden box in the bottom drawer a birth certificate on which his name appeared as father of a boy, born the year she was born, by a woman she had never heard of. She had never asked her father about it, naturally enough, nor had she hinted at her knowledge to her elder sisters, who went through a prolonged stage around their early teens speculating on the sex lives of both parents. Instead, she hugged her information to herself, looking at her father with more interest while he was alive, and thinking of him all the more fondly when he was dead. Only once had she been tempted to use her discovery as a trump card, and that was when her mother had invoked her father's memory during their last scene together. In the middle of her mother shouting at Sophie that she was little better than a harlot and that her father would have turned in his grave and other faintly funny platitudes, Sophie had felt a great desire to say that actually Father had liked harlots, he had even borne a son by one, and she was sure his moral rectitude was a façade to please his wife. But she kept quiet, and knowing about her father's illegitimate son, of whom he had been unashamed enough to give him some legal standing, had simply made her feel happier.

Sophie sat down among William's heaps and very quietly began reading his letters and papers. She was touched to see that he had kept all her notes, neatly secured with elastic bands. His letters were boring in the extreme—either all business or circulars. Why, she wondered, did he keep circulars? She was just beginning to doubt if there was a single personal letter when she looked in the last bundle and found about half a dozen envelopes addressed in various handwritings. Smiling, Sophie carefully began to take out the letters and with the very first one revealed a secret of William's that excited her deliciously. It was from Germaine and said:

DEAR WILLIAM,

I am very sorry but I have completely failed to get Mother to go into a nursing home. I suppose, therefore, you will take me to court as I cannot possibly repay any of that £500 loan. Truly, William, I thought that it had become a gift—twenty years is a long time and you never once mentioned it. However, I shall just have to face up to it. If only I had known earlier that you wanted it I would have started to save.

I was very grateful at the time for that money. As you probably realized, it saved me from an illegal operation that might have ended in death. I would be even more grateful if you would not prevent me going to Canada with Homer. If he goes alone my marriage would not survive, and whatever it looks like from outside it means a great deal to me. Please be generous. I have no one to turn to except Homer, who is penniless, and Mother, who has always hated me.

Yours sincerely,
GERMAINE

P.S. Could you let me know quickly what you are going to do? Our tickets are booked.

Hardly pausing, Sophie went on to the next. The handwriting was very shaky, and she was not surprised to see it was from Mrs. Joliffe.

DEAR WILLIAM,

I find writing difficult but you never come to see me and you won't answer the phone. Something must be done about Sophie Hill. Have you thought about what I said? You must contact her mother at once.

AGNES

Frowning at the thought, Sophie took up the next letter. The thick fawn-colored envelope was familiar.

DEAR MR. BONE,

Thank you for your letter. Please do not apologize for writing—I quite understand the position. Briefly, I ceased to pay Sophie an allowance on January 1st of this year. I am distressed to learn she is already in debt but I suppose I expected it since that scoundrel (who, by the way, is not, and never was, married to her) could never support her.

This is what I propose to do: I will pay you the rent due to cover the first half year. After that, no more. I shall inform Sophie of this and meanwhile hope you will take this opportunity to give her notice. There is always a home for her here—without her lover, of course.

Yours sincerely,

ARABELLA LANDELL-MILLER

Somehow thinking that the other two letters would also refer to her, Sophie found them puzzling. One was signed "Graham" but had a doctor's name and address stamped on the top. It said:

DEAR WILLIAM,

I've been trying to phone you without success, so this is just to order you—yes, it's as vital as that—to come in and see me the very minute you get this. I shall not answer for the very grave consequences to yourself if you do not.

Be a good chap—

GRAHAM

Biting her nails, Sophie frowned and read the last. The notepaper was lilac-colored and scented.

DEAR MR. BONE,

Mr. Pullen asked me to write to you if he should pass on before you and tell you to go to his house and take anything you want as a memento of your friendship. He has arranged it in his will and you are to get the keys from his solicitors. Everything is to be left to charity except a very kind legacy to me.

May I say, sir, how very much I enjoyed meeting you at Mr. Pullen's house? You may not remember but it was on June 1st nineteen thirty-two when we first met.

With every good wish,

ELSPETH MORLEY

Sophie put all the letters back and replaced them in the bundle. A box on the floor was full of old letters, but her enthusiasm had waned. She did not now feel like unearthing Mr. Bone's past. As she stood up, she heard the sound of the house door closing and quickly ran out of the flat and sat down on the top stair as though she had been waiting hours. The letters she had just read flashed and reflashed through her mind, and in the middle of the anger her mother's aroused in her she tried to compose herself into a state sufficiently coherent to use them to advantage.

Mr. Bone came up the stairs bald head first. His arms were full of packages and his vision was obscured, but Sophie somehow felt certain that he could see her and was preparing to be visibly taken aback, so she spoke first.

"Good afternoon, Mr. Bone," she said. "I hope you don't mind me waiting here for you, but I did so want to see you."

"Ah!" he exclaimed, dropping two parcels. "Ah, yes, now, let me see, yes, of course, come in, do."

He led the way in, then turned back to get the dropped parcels, and they had a mild collision before getting themselves safely inside, where William was all bustle and instant hospitality. He had the kettle on as quickly as any housewife determined to be neighborly, and lectured her nonstop on what was in the flat so that there was no need to say anything. He appeared to like to have her there, delighted to be making tea, delighted at the thought of her waiting to see him. But Sophie knew he must be in a panic. He must be desperately trying to stave off what he imagined would be a self-pitying outburst, one long solo story about having no money and nowhere to go. Or perhaps he was frightened she had come to accuse him of meddling in her personal affairs. What right had he to write to her mother— did he fear she would shrill that at him? Poor Mr. Bone. He knew so much that he thought she did not know.

"I love your view," she said in the first pause, "may I look at it properly?"

"Of course, of course," William said eagerly, "let me take this curtain down—a sad necessity, I fear, when one also washes in this room. Yes, a fine view, bought the house for it, took this flat for it. Of course, it wasn't a flat then, just a couple of rooms, you know—"

"Mr. Bone, I got your solicitor's letter this morning."

"Ah, yes. Well, of course, they sometimes can't be avoided, difficult business, has to be handled by solicitors—"

"I quite understood," Sophie said sweetly. "I don't know how you've managed to be so forbearing up to now. All I came to say was that if you let me stay here till the baby is born I'll move straight after. It's no good hiding things from you, Mr. Bone. Alex appears to have deserted me temporarily and there isn't anything I can do about it. I don't know where he is. But he knows when the baby is due and he'll come back for that. And the rent, Mr. Bone—I hate to do it, but I shall ask my mother to pay you that. I'm sorry to have brought you all this trouble, I'm so sorry, it's simply dreadful, after all your kindness, I'll never ever be able to repay you." And quite genuinely Sophie cried, thinking, How can I be so unscrupulous, how can I do this to him?

Wearing an expression of painful distress, William said nothing but stood by the kettle waiting for it to boil, and when it had done so he made the tea and carried it over to the fire. Still saying nothing, he gently led the weeping Sophie to a chair and put a cushion in the small of her back and a footstool under her feet. Then he poured the tea and sensibly waited for her to stop crying before he pressed it upon her.

"Consider it settled," he said at last, "just as you said. No need to go over it again, I think. I shall write to my solicitor tonight. The summer should be a good time for you to find another flat, more suitable for a baby, a garden perhaps and on the ground floor for perambulators. That's the trouble here, I'm afraid—impossible for those with small children and for invalids, it's so inconveniently laid out. I'm afraid Mrs. Joliffe is finding the struggle is getting much too hard, a great shame but there it is, built for a different way of life."

Sophie sniffed and searched for a handkerchief up her sleeve. Not finding one, she asked William if he had some Kleenex, but he insisted on presenting her a magnificently white monogrammed square of cambric. Sophie said it seemed a shame to use it.

"Oh, plenty of those," William said. "I'm very well stocked up. My nephew's wife gives me two dozen every Christmas."

"Is he your brother's or your sister's son?" asked Sophie, hoping that a nephew was a suitably innocuous relation to feel curious about.

"My cousin Bertie's," said William, quite easily. "He's really a cousin, but I've always taken an interest in Rupert and I think of him as my nephew. Nice young chap with a nice young wife."

"Any nice children?" asked Sophie.

"Two, both girls, rather jolly little things." He paused and then rubbed his hands and repeated, "Rather jolly little things," so that Sophie knew she had asked enough and he wanted her to go.

As she put her teacup down and stood up, she saw him flinch from the sudden arching of her back and the throwing forward of her huge belly. He could not keep the distaste from his face and she felt angry and humiliated. He saw her to his door with a great deal of muttering and mumbling, and when he had closed it she heard him running backward and forward like a little mouse. Very slowly, she went back down to her own flat.

She sat the rest of the evening staring into space, thinking about the letters she had read. Germaine's story she could reconstruct well enough except for the reason why William should want his money back. Why should he? Was he hard up all of a sudden? She wished there were a library where one could do research on ordinary people, for how else could one find out why his doctor wanted to see him and who Elspeth Morley was. Well, in this case, there was a library of sorts—Mrs. Joliffe would know everything and be only too willing to tell. But she did not feel inclined to seek Mrs. Joliffe out. She interfered and that was unforgivable. She had no right to make William write to her mother while at the same time pretending to be her friend. Sophie remembered all the occasions on which Mrs. Joliffe had professed herself eager to help, and yet no help had ever been forthcoming. She was all talk. Furthermore, she undoubtedly did dislike and abuse the lumbering Germaine, making unkind jokes about her and holding her up to ridicule all the time.

Neither of them was any good. Sophie cried a little with self-pity and wished they had chosen a house with other young people in it. She was sick of old people and their devious ways, sick of their problems and dependency and dreariness. She wished they would both drop dead and be discovered to have miraculously left the house and belongings to her. Her mind ran on the lines of euthanasia, and she fell asleep and dreamed that William and Agnes were removed from the house in a black van and exterminated.

The van was white and extermination not intended, except so slowly as not to count. Sophie helped Mrs. Joliffe into it and got in herself, with difficulty. William was nowhere to be seen.

The driver drove very carefully through the London traffic onto the North Circular Road. Their destination was somewhere on the way to Harrow, but otherwise Sophie was ignorant and had not even worked out how she would get herself back from St. Ursula's Home. She sat, very uncomfortably, on the edge of the hard black leather seat facing Mrs. Joliffe, who was perched hardly more luxuriously on a

canvas contraption supposed to be designed to support her
legs. This was the last thing it did. The newly broken one
stuck into the air encased in plaster, and the other crippled
one was left lolling under it.

Mrs. Joliffe's color was very bad. Sophie saw that she had
made herself up as she always did, but the hand that held
the powder puff had gone mad and rubbed powder into ears
and nostrils and all the way round the hairline. She was
dressed, but not so smartly as usual, though there was a
cameo brooch clipped onto the collar of her dress and she
wore gloves. At her side was a small leather case that Sophie
had packed. The rest of her belongings were to follow later
in the week.

Sophie had no idea how her companion was feeling. It
seemed cruel to ask, and she was afraid of unleashing un-
controllable fury. It had all happened so quickly: testing
her leg out, as the doctor had said she could, she had immediately fallen and broken it. When she came home from the
outpatients' department of the hospital it was to find that
William had arranged for her to go into a nursing home. He
told her so himself. At first she thought she had not heard
aright, but William rapidly repeated the information. Germaine had that day left for Canada, Sophie was in no fit
condition, and he was too busy to look after her. He had
told the doctor she would have to go somewhere and the
doctor had suggested this very good home. There had been a
dreadful scene. Mrs. Joliffe had shouted and brought Sophie
down, and William had then disappeared.

There was a note from Germaine which Mrs. Joliffe had
made Sophie read aloud and then torn into tiny pieces. It
said:

DEAR MOTHER,

William says you have broken your poor leg and I feel
all the more awful about not saying goodbye, but Homer

and I and William thought about it a lot and decided it
would be kinder if we just upped and went. It would be
the day you broke your leg! Poor Mother—I am so sorry
but William will look after everything. I will write soon
and we will work hard to get a nice place so you can come
and visit us in the summer. Get well soon, all my love, in
haste—

GERMAINE

Sophie looked out the window. They were still passing
endless little shops and cramped, dull houses. She thought
she heard Mrs. Joliffe say something, and said, "I beg your
pardon?"

"I didn't say anything," said Mrs. Joliffe clearly.

Sophie was sure she had. "A conspiracy," she had said, as
she had many times in the last few hours. Sophie had tried
to close her ears and mind to the genteel abuse she had
hurled at William, but the word "conspiracy" kept coming
through. Mrs. Joliffe believed William and Germaine had
plotted to have her put away, and there was no reasoning
with her possible. Emphatically she refuted the suggestion
that the timing of Germaine's departure was accidental.
William was quick-witted when it suited his interests, she
said. The minute she broke her leg he was on the phone
hatching this plot with Germaine. She even said she
wouldn't be surprised if Sophie was in it, too.

"I know I've become a nuisance," she said, "but you need
not have encouraged them."

"I didn't even know," Sophie pleaded. "I told Mr. Bone I
thought you were quite all right here, and said I would do
anything I could to help."

"I am grateful for your help," Mrs. Joliffe said. "You do
not need to keep pointing out that you give it. One day you
will need it—perhaps sooner than I."

"How can you?" Sophie said.

"Quite easily," Mrs. Joliffe snapped. "I am bitter, I am a realist. I know quite well that though you have been exceedingly kind you, like the others, want no responsibility. Perhaps if I had money it would be different—I expect I could bribe my way out of this mess. But I have very little money and what I have I spend. I do not suppose my bank balance makes good reading, there cannot be more than two hundred pounds in my account. Now, William Bone is rich —moderately. He has thousands of pounds to his credit, pounds he is about to happily diminish paying for this nursing home he is condemning me to. Doubtless people will say, 'How kind.' Doubtless you will agree. How kind of dear, good Mr. Bone to pay for my—what shall we call it? retirement?—instead of sending me to the workhouse or the knacker's yard. Doubtless you will pat him on the back and applaud and marvel at his generosity. Won't you? Won't you do that the minute I've gone?"

Luckily Sophie had not attempted to argue, but had set about packing and had said she would go with her.

They had turned onto the Harrow Road before Mrs. Joliffe said, "It is very good of you to accompany me, Sophie. I am very appreciative."

"I'm pleased to," Sophie said, smiling.

"You are a kind girl, most kind. You've meant a great deal to me the past weeks."

"And you to me," Sophie said.

"Nonsense," said Mrs. Joliffe, but without her usual vigor. "What have I meant to you? A nuisance, somebody you felt obliged to pass the time of day with out of pity. I daresay not wholly out of pity, either—I probably bullied you into it and there was no escape."

"I refuse to listen," said Sophie, "because you know perfectly well none of that is true."

"It's irrelevant," sighed Mrs. Joliffe. "It's over, finished. Every time I meet someone agreeable they are snatched from me."

"I will come and see you," promised Sophie, "and I'll take care of your flat till you come back."

"I will never come back," said Mrs. Joliffe.

"Oh, yes, when—"

"No," said Mrs. Joliffe, "never. William has got me out. He will find excellent reasons to keep me out. It's nothing new, this rejection. William has been rejecting me in one way or the other ever since we met, and do you know why? He's afraid. He knows, you see, that he loves me and I love him. So he rejects me. He destroys his own happiness, out of fear. Have you ever heard of anything more ridiculous? Well, have you?"

"No," said Sophie, stunned.

"Well, now you have, and you can tell William that he doesn't fool me, not for a minute."

She sat erect and proud for the rest of the journey, a triumphant flush on her face, and Sophie, jolted and shaken in the van, tried to absorb a love that, rejected, had lasted fifty years and still went on, rejected, to the death.

Twelve

>>>>>>>>>>>>

THE HOUSE was very quiet. William reflected that since Alexander Hill had taken himself off it had always been quiet, but this was a quietness of emptiness, which was different. The house was empty. He did not know where Sophie was, but she was not in the house, and Mrs. Joliffe's flat was, of course, empty. So William was all alone in his house, as he had not been for years, and he relished it. For a little while he savored the feeling, beaming to himself, relaxing, and then he took some old sheets from his linen cupboard and put on his workman's overall and went down into the basement. Outside the basement door were some large crates that he had kept for many years in the garden shed in case he ever moved. He dragged them into Mrs. Joliffe's little hall, glad that he had been so farsighted.

William was painstaking and careful. Before he began, he rolled up all the carpets, tied them with string, and slipped them into long polythene bags, securing the ends with thick, strong elastic. These he stacked in a corner of the hall after he had affixed a descriptive label to each. Next he swept the floors and covered them with newspaper, and then he

dragged in the crates and put them in the center of the dining room. He was ready to begin the real work. On his left
he had a pile of newspapers and on his right a box of wood
shavings. Kneeling on the floor, he opened the door of Mrs.
Joliffe's china cabinet and slowly started removing the contents.

She had some nice stuff. William could remember eating
at some time or other off everything he packed. The willow-
pattern dinner service was the first set he recalled, the blues
slightly faded but otherwise intact. It had rested on a
starched white cloth in the big dining room in Cambridge,
and if he remembered rightly everything in that room had
been blue and white. Agnes had been very proud of that
room. Only forget-me-nots and lilies of the valley ever
graced the willow-pattern table. Wrapping each plate in
newspaper, William remembered the incident of the gravy
and searched in the cabinet for the gravy boat. It was not
there. Broken, or could Agnes not bear to remember and
have thrown or given it away? William smiled. The fat had
congealed so quickly that each guest had had a plate swimming in grease and Agnes with not a cook in sight to blame,
since she had never stopped telling them from the minute
they arrived that this was all her own work. Matthew had
still been alive—it was the second year of their marriage
and the eight guests had eyed Agnes' white-gowned figure
with interest. It had just been whispered among the ladies
that Mrs. Joliffe was expecting a happy event shortly. William, of course, had not known, not that way, but his eyes
had traveled too, and he had realized and felt very emotional and happy. Agnes had been vivacious as ever, but
there was about her a softness William had never seen before. He saw her touch Matthew's hand as he carved and the
look they exchanged—a perfectly respectable, inquiring
look, but intimate all the same. William had felt excluded,
not just from their happiness but from the convivial life. He

had walked home on his own afterward and wondered what he could do about it. If he seriously wanted marital bliss—and that night he ached for it—he must look around.

He had looked. Between dinner parties and sherry parties and coffee evenings with Agnes and Matthew he had looked. Quite in vain. Sometimes he had seen a girl he admired, but his admiration precluded action. It was always the same. He would see such a girl and instantly want to withdraw to a great distance, the better to examine her. The last thing he wanted was an introduction. He would not wish to hear her talk. That would spoil everything. And if by chance the talk began before he could stop it his panic was so great that he literally ran away.

Finishing the willow pattern, William moved on to the Wedgwood, which evoked memories much more disturbing. He pursed his lips—he was always wary of sentiment. As he lifted the cold white plates, chosen by an Agnes more sophisticated, he deliberately pushed to the back of his mind the oval table and the candles and the merry, wicked (he had thought then) eyes of his hostess as she served him. Often they had eaten alone during the Wedgwood era, he at one end of the slippery, treacherous wood and she at the other, accusing him of thought and actions that never entered his head. He remembered a nightgowned Germaine pattering in, fat and plain at seven, and being harshly rejected and told to go to bed. Once, he had broken a tureen —yes, here was the lid, cracked and held together with metal pins. How? He could not exactly remember, which surprised him, but it was something to do with Germaine coming in and his distress at the role he had been pushed into.

At the back of the cabinet William found what he had been dreading. There, each wrapped in rose-pink tissue paper, were the champagne glasses. At first he covered each glass in its wispy cocoon with newspaper, but then, as he was

about to put them into the packing case, he took one out
and took off the paper, both layers, and very carefully held
the glass up to the light. The pink tinge around the base of
the bowl of the glass was only just discernible. In Agnes'
drawing room it had seemed all pink, but then that was the
fire and the one lamp and her dress—velvet, he thought. He
had given her the glasses, an odd number, only five, which
had been given to him, only five, by his grandmother. They
were priceless, but he had not needed to say so. Agnes had
known their worth, or so he hoped. He had given them to
her on the occasion of . . . William did not speak the
words, even in his own head. He wrapped the glass again
with more speed than was wise, put it to join its fellows, and
moved on to the Georgian silver. With this he made rapid
progress. Knives and forks were not romantic objects,
though the feel in his hands of the heavy crested handles
was familiar. He recognized the grip, tight throughout most
of Agnes' dinners with nervous anticipation of one sort or
another.

Soon the cabinet was empty and only the glasses in the
room upstairs needed similar treatment, but William
thought he would leave those and deal with the kitchen. He
was interested to see how little equipment Agnes had—
quite ordinary mixing bowls, white pot ones, and very few
pans. Those she had were battered and much dented, and
not of very good quality. Now, William himself had always
believed in good pans—good pans and good luggage,
though lately he had rather forsworn the luggage in favor
of the rucksack. How funny to find Agnes with inferior
pans! It amused him and he giggled as he packed them.

The kitchen and the dining room, when he had shrouded
the furniture in each with the sheets he had brought down,
he now locked. He did not quite know what to do about the
bedroom. The thought of stripping the bed was curiously
distasteful to him, so he left it with the counterpane thrown

over it. But the cupboards and drawers could not be left. Agnes would want her clothes almost at once. Really, it was a job for a woman—Germaine or Sophie, but of course Germaine had gone and he did not like to speak to Sophie about it. He did not like the very hostile way in which the girl had looked at him when she had returned from St. Ursula's. Firmly, William opened the wardrobe door.

There were a great many clothes, some of which hadn't been worn for years. Never an expert on clothing, William took pleasure in the fact that he could visualize Agnes in most of the dresses that hung there. Some she could have kept only for the associations: at least four ball dresses, in bags, took up space when Agnes had not been to a ball for twenty years or more. But what shocked William unutterably was the discovery, at the very back of the wardrobe, on the side where the door had been so bolted down that it would not open, of a white muslin frock with brown stains on it. The idea of her keeping the frock in which she had had her accident made him feel sick. Why? Surely the memory brought back only pain. He would have thought she would have burned it rather than have to look at it again. But there it was, on a hanger, gray-white, soiled, limp. William left it where it was.

Agnes' old big brown case held all her clothes with such ease that William realized she must after all have given away a lot. She had always loved clothes. Once she had appeared in a different dress every day and had followed fashion with zest. He had rather despised her for it, and she had teased him for being a miserable puritan. She liked, she said, to look nice and there was no harm in that. William, who loathed the necessity to clothe himself, was not so sure there was no harm in it. Narcissism was harmful, in his opinion, and should be avoided. Agnes had laughed and twirled round in her dress and asked him if he didn't all the same like her in pretty clothes? Even latterly she had always looked smart, but remarking on it to cheer her up he had been contemptuously slapped down. Old rags, it appeared, were all she now wore.

William locked that room too. He had closed the shutters but not taken down the curtains. Agnes might want to leave them, and in any case he had a pain in his side which, though he was busy ignoring it, made the idea of stretching unattractive. The crates he left in the rooms, where they were safest. On his way up to the drawing room, he thought about taking up the stair carpet, but decided against it. Uncovered stairs meant noise and he might want to use them to get to the garden. In the drawing room he at once drew the curtains, though it was the middle of the afternoon. Agnes would not have net and he could not endure that huge blank area of glass. Here he followed the same procedure as below, first rolling and wrapping the carpet and then covering the larger objects with sheets. He sat for a while in the big velvet Queen Anne wing chair that had always been his seat, then he leaped out and threw his best sheet over it. He had reserved one crate for books and he now lined it with an old green baize cloth and prepared to deal with the books. Before he began, he took a pair of thin cotton gloves from his pocket and slipped them on; he hated touching dusty books and he was sure Agnes' would be dusty.

The bookshelves were in the right-hand alcove between the fireplace and the wall. To William's annoyance, they had not been fitted as he had advised. Pullen had said pyrana pine was the best wood to use and he had sketched for William a way of putting the shelves in without damaging the wall. William had passed this information on to Agnes, but it had been ignored and the wall ruined by Homer Hooper, who had driven into it what William could only describe as metal stakes. Removing them would bring off not only paint but plaster. The shelves, instead of being adaptable, were nailed onto these fiendish supports and caused William much distress as the full horror of the work-manship was revealed with the removal of the books. His lips were tightly compressed and his frown was ferocious.

Agnes was addicted to what William considered rather dreadful historical novels. She had had several lady friends who had turned their hands to this trade, and several gaud-ily covered volumes were lavishly inscribed to her. There were also some travel books and complete sets of Jane Aus-ten, Dickens, Scott and Thackeray, but no poetry or biogra-phy or criticism. William had not realized quite how light-weight Agnes' taste was, and was rather shocked by it. For a woman with a good brain she did not keep much fodder for it.

The job done—luckily there were few ornaments—Wil-liam locked the sitting-room door and stood for a minute in the hallway. Already the flat smelled different—colder, less fragrant, slightly dusty. His feet left marks on the black li-noleum as he stepped into the main hall, and he took off his shoes and carried them as he went upstairs. On the way up, he stopped and washed his hands and face thoroughly in the bathroom, and went on his way refreshed. He could not help feeling pleased at his afternoon's work—pleased at the amount he had packed away in so short a time without a single breakage, pleased at the tidiness of the rooms he had left behind him, pleased at the successful way in which he had overcome all emotion, except for a very few seconds. He had been foolish to dread the job. To be apprehensive about what had been a perfectly straightforward job was silly. Agnes' flat was full of inanimate objects, not ghosts.

Tea was an almost gay affair. William sat before the fire and ate scrambled egg on toast and macaroons and short-bread biscuits and sipped lemon tea and thought how pleas-ant life was becoming again. It did enter his head that per-haps St. Ursula's might not provide such tasty fare, perhaps not even the joy of a fire, but he quickly got that into perspective. Agnes would appreciate the central heating, she had always felt the cold, she would not give a thought to a fire. And as for scrambled egg and all that—well, she had said herself she had lost her appetite and was not interested in food. It was a necessity, that was all. Her meals would doubtless be scientifically balanced, as they usually were in institutions, and that was of far more value.

William thought about the word "institution." It had been a mistake. St. Ursula's was not an institution, or rather not what the word implied. The doctor had been enthusiastic in his recommendation—he said it was a modern, attractive building, light and bright, with lovely grounds and views. William could not imagine any lovely views up the Harrow Road, but never mind. The staff were young and jolly, always smiling, and the other inmates, of whom there were not many owing to the high fees, extremely friendly and sociable. Each inhabitant had her own room with bathroom attached, and all the rooms had ramps to the garden for wheelchairs. What more could anyone want? What indeed, William had endorsed, trembling at the thought of passing on the description to Agnes and instantly resolving to do no such thing.

There was bound to be a difficult period of readjustment for Agnes. William nodded sagely as he washed up, and decided not to visit St. Ursula's for several weeks. Perhaps he would not visit it at all—it might be upsetting. For whom? For Agnes, of course. Very upsetting to see old friends who were still hale and hearty when one was dying, for Agnes was dying, he was sure of it. That second fall had been very bad. The doctor had said the bones in the leg might never mend, and her heartbeat had become wildly irregular. It was simply a matter of time, and since he was convinced she must know this deep inside, William thought it tactless of him to visit. He did not subscribe to the view that friends must rally round in times of sorrow or need. Rather, they must stay discreetly in the background and not flaunt their own exemption from whatever misfortune was about.

No, he probably would not go. It would be masochistic. He would not enjoy seeing Agnes so reduced, better by far to remember her as she had been. And he might be sick. Should there be any smell of disinfectant he most certainly would be, and how embarrassing it would be. He would not be able to converse in such a place, and why else go but to converse. He would not help Agnes that way. Far better to write her a long, interesting letter, send flowers and books, even telephone, though not yet, not for several weeks.

Preparing his tray for the evening, in the midst of this contentment, William was struck by terrible pains. He froze. Breathing very gently, he placed both hands lightly on his stomach and waited. It was quite hard and solid. The pains came again and decided him. He glanced at his watch and saw that there had been two minutes between attacks. In the next two minutes he managed to get to his bed, in the next to get back to his chair by the fire with two blankets, in the next to the sink, where he filled a jug with water. Two minutes by two minutes he methodically prepared himself for what he knew might be a long vigil, and before the intervals had been reduced to fifty seconds he was sitting in his chair, draped with blankets, a hot-water bottle on his lap, water beside him, aspirin and another bottle of tablets to hand, and all the doors and windows shut and locked and the fire reduced to the minimum safe heat. He removed his spectacles, loosened his tie and, lying back, began to fight— for that was how he saw it. Someone—Agnes—had once chided him for giving himself up to pain, but he did not give himself up, he *fought*. Every particle of his being was concentrated on riding the crest of each wave of pain, striving not to scream or writhe about or otherwise waste his energy, but fight, fight, fight. Very soon he did not know light from dark or cold from warm. He lost all sense of feeling and response, knowing only that he was battered by pain, squashing in on him from all sides, whirling in clouds with himself as the vortex, blinding, deafening, dehumanizing him.

He did not consciously think, except Is it time, time, time? His hands were too busy somewhere clutching the hard rock between his ribs to pick up that other bottle of tablets even if his brain had managed to achieve the miracle of sending messages to them. He could not have taken that lethal dose, hoarded for so long. His hands could not have got to it, his lips, slabs of gray cement, could not have opened to let it through, his throat could not have swallowed and his stomach, cause of this action, could not have received it. It lay there as he thought only, Is it time, time, time, and was useless.

William survived. His first non-pain-bombarded thought was, how long had he been there? It took him five minutes of fierce effort to raise his wrist and look at his watch, which partly for this reason had a mechanism working out days as well as hours, one of the few American abominations he had been delighted to discover. More staggering mental calculations were needed before he worked out that he had been in his chair two and a half days. Not so bad. He lifted a glass of water and drank a little, slopping the water over the blankets that had covered him. He wore cold sweat like a rubber suit, but a bath was impossible for at least another day. He lay back, grateful, free from the pain, dimly distinguishing the stars outside and the glow of the fire and thought, Is it time? Should he, now that he was able, take the one hundred sleeping pills, five at a time, steadily, slowly? Did he want to die? Did he want more pain like that? Did he want the attacks to become more frequent until he never moved from his chair and died like that, like an animal? Did he want to run the risk of being discovered, forced into hospital, treated and kept alive for fun? Did he? Did he? Or was he afraid to take them, was he after all like Agnes, greedy to cling on to life, any kind of life?

Another ten hours passed and William was strong enough to stand up and make his way to his bed, where at last he allowed himself the luxury of lying down. Here he slept, and woke the next day refreshed and decided. It was not time, not yet. As he cleared up the signs of his ordeal he felt proud that he had been calm and dispassionate. He had always sworn to himself that he would never commit suicide either when an attack began or when it had only just ended. His motive in both cases would be fear. It had to be done when he was able to weigh up the pros and cons. They had been weighed and he was glad. The tablets were locked away again, the doors and windows unlocked, and William prepared to live again.

The face in the mirror on the bathroom wall was familiar to William. He was always, against his will, impressed by it. So quick was he each time to assure himself the attack had not been too bad that his face, when he got round to looking at it, made a lie of his opinion. Even washed and shaved the face looked very little better, and William did not feel like presenting it to anyone. Luckily, there was no one looking for it. There was no telltale line of milk bottles outside, there were no newspapers, with luck no letters—he had nothing delivered regularly. Softly, he unlocked the bathroom door.

The click was very faint, but Sophie heard it and went onto the landing as quickly as she could.

"Oh, Mr. Bone," she said, arresting William, sponge bag in hand, in mid-flight.

"Ah," said William, embarrassed, trying to throw the bag up his own stairs and at the same time hide his face behind the towel draped round his neck.

"I'm afraid it was me knocking at your door," said Sophie, and she added defiantly, "and ringing your telephone. I'm sorry—I realized afterward you must want not to be disturbed."

"Yes," said William, starting up the stairs.

"But I felt like disturbing you," Sophie said, shouting a little. "I'd just got back from the place you sent Mrs. Joliffe to, you see, and I wanted to tell you what I thought of you. You'll think me very rude, but I still do. I'm sure you can't know about it or you wouldn't have sent her there."

"I didn't," said William. "It was her doctor's advice. He said it was quite impossible—"

"Come off it, Mr. Bone," said Sophie, deliberately choosing the most harmless and antiquated reproof she could think of but then spoiling the effect by her mocking tone.

"I must get on," William said, beginning to climb the stairs. He felt so weak he could not go on standing and he did not have the energy to deal with this cheeky stranger.

"But I've got a message," Sophie said, "from Mrs. Joliffe. She was most insistent that I should give it to you personally. Don't you want to hear it?"

Depressed, William trudged on up his stairs, not replying, incapable of stopping his tenant from following. He must at once get an estimate for building a lavatory into his flat so that he need never emerge. Council regulations must be bypassed—harassment by tenants was too much. He did not ask her to sit down, but somehow she was in front of him and sitting on the chair he had so recently vacated. The sight of her where all his pain had been made him smile.

"Mrs. Joliffe wasn't smiling," Sophie said, "she was crying. Not on the way—she just sat in the ambulance and seemed very composed and proud and I admired her courage. But then when we got there the matron was so ghastly and vulgar, cracking horrible cheap jokes all the time and pawing poor Mrs. Joliffe—it was horrible. Have you been there, Mr. Bone? Did you meet that woman? Did you see that room? When I thought of Mrs. Joliffe leaving that lovely flat furnished with all the things she's had for years and years for that slot—have you seen it?"

"No," said William.

"Then you must go today and bring her out."

"I can't do that," William said.

"Why not? It isn't an institution, she isn't committed, you must take her out at once, you don't know what you're doing to her."

"It had nothing to do with me," said William. "There is no one here to look after her and she is incapable of looking after herself."

"I would look after her," said Sophie.

"You will soon be otherwise engaged."

"Then you—you could look after her. You've been her friend for something ridiculous like fifty years, haven't you —doesn't that mean anything at all? Can't you spare a little time to be compassionate and help her?"

"I am a busy man—" began William.

"What lies! Your business is of your own making—you don't *have* to be busy."

"I am busy," said William distinctly, "and I am far from well myself."

"Oh, really," said Sophie contemptuously. "There's nothing the matter with you compared with Mrs. Joliffe. You're just trying to make excuses—it's disgusting. I know you hate me for saying all this, Mr. Bone, but it has to be said. You simply haven't used your imagination. Try. How do you think Mrs. Joliffe feels, unable to move without help, in constant pain, stuck in a whitewashed cell twelve by twelve. Would you like to be her? I just don't understand you. I don't understand how you can know and perhaps love—oh, I'm not prying—one woman for fifty years and then when all she needs is a little comfort and attention which you can give, you throw her on the rubbish heap. It doesn't make sense—it means you're a monster."

"Kindly leave my flat," said William, his back turned to her.

"Not till I know what you're going to do about Mrs. Joliffe."

"Nothing."

"You aren't going to see her?"

"No."

"Then what shall I tell her?"

"It is not your business to tell her anything. Please go. You are continually invading my privacy, which the lease specifically says you are not to."

"All right," said Sophie, "but I wouldn't have believed it. I shall tell Mrs. Joliffe what you've said and I hope your conscience gives you hell."

William trembled, and the sweat he had washed away was replaced by more rivers springing from the agitation in him. What the girl had said—and how could he have been so mistaken in her?—was irrelevant. He almost hadn't heard it. It was, as usual, her presence in his house that he found intolerable. When she, anyone, was actually in his room, among his things, giving off their own animalness he felt so violated he wanted to open the window and jump out. His limbs began to twitch, his eyes to blink, he could not keep still. And at the moment he was not up to it. He could not subdue his physical loathing and make bridges into other human beings. No man is an island, but he wanted to be, that was the point.

Bed again, though it was not yet evening. He felt odd twinges of pain as he lay there, but that was customary—he would have to be very careful for a week or so, keep himself quiet, mentally and emotionally as well as physically. He ought, of course, to go to the doctor. Graham had written to him most melodramatically, to frighten him into contact, but he was not frightened. He had undergone those tests in the summer only so that he would know once and for all, and the minute he had had them he had known. Graham would expect him not to. He would think he thought it was his old war wound, which William had always known it was not. Sometimes that wound did play him up, but the feeling was different. He undoubtedly was suffering from an advanced cancer. Possibly it was operable, but he had no intention of submitting to an operation. All men die, and he intended to die of what was intended to kill. He had the tablets, when the end proved too difficult, though he began to worry about the excitement of *not* using them.

Sophie Hill and Agnes Joliffe were well back in his thoughts. He could not be bothered with these poor women and their troubles. They rampaged and stormed and scolded and it was all so unnecessary, so repugnant to him. Lying there, half asleep, he suddenly thought of Alexander and applauded him in his head. That was the way to do it: walk out and go on walking out, all through life. He had an inkling that for all his antipathy toward that young man, they were alike, only appearing different. William hoped he did not come back. He hoped Sophie never saw him again. Allowing himself the luxury of malice, William smiled and his face was kindled.

Before he fell asleep, William felt all his ugly feelings drain away. That, he thought, was the point of growing up, maturing, call it what you liked. One gained a sense of perspective. The hurts did not hurt less, but they were gone sooner—one did not go on and on suffering agonies over a quarrel that was past. Already his row with Sophie seemed unimportant. To her it would not be so, and he must bear that in mind. She was young and obsessive, he was old and resilient. She would still be going over and over every word they had both said, still be trembling with rage. Poor soul. He wished he could show her somehow that it was all unnecessary, he wished he could do something for her to show her that, far from disliking her since their row, he still regarded her in the same light.

Thirteen

THE JOURNEY to St. Ursula's was a long and tiring one, and before she was halfway Sophie knew that she should never have undertaken it. When she had looked up the distance on her *A to Z* it had not seemed far, but then it was one of those cross-country journeys that meant going in to get out. Even using the electric train, the bus and the tube, it took her over an hour, waiting each time several minutes for connections. Waiting in the tube station was at least warm and she had a seat, but waiting for the bus was murder. Her legs ached, her back ached, and the biting early-March wind tore through her inadequate clothing to the baby itself. It never stopped heaving and turning somersaults in its endeavors, she was sure, to get warm.

But the ordeal had to be gone through if just to show William that she was not as disloyal as he, though a friend of much shorter duration. She had deliberately left a note for him saying: "Dear Mr. Bone, I am going to see Mrs. Joliffe tomorrow. Is there anything you would like me to take?"

He had replied, after what were obviously several hours thinking hard: "No, thank you. Pleasant journey!" She had it in her handbag to show Mrs. Joliffe, though she was not sure that she should.

The last half mile to St. Ursula's had to be walked. It lay at the top of a hill, and Sophie found it a hard pull. She discovered in the process of dragging herself up that she could no longer see her own toes, because of the size of her stomach. She tried breathing in, but it was no good—the great hard bulge stood between her and her shoes. This disturbed her. When had her toes disappeared? Did they always disappear in the last month? Not for the first time, she wished she moved in a circle where pregnancy was known and discussed down to the last detail.

Her face was worried as she turned into the gates, and Agnes Joliffe, watching from her peephole—she refused to call it a window—felt guilty. She should not have let the child come, knowing her condition as she did, and her financial circumstances. She had never thought of Sophie arriving in anything but a taxi or hired car, forgetting this would be unthinkably costly! She must pay for a car home. Quickly, before Sophie should arrive, she lifted her ghastly green phone and ordered a minicab to come to pick her up in two hours' time. She told the idiot secretary to put it on the account, and there followed such an argument on how the cab should be paid for that Sophie was in the room before she had finished.

"Sophie, my dear girl," Agnes said, and into the receiver, "I will not continue with this nonsensical conversation. Good afternoon. Oh, they are so stupid here, Sophie, so unbelievably stupid. You simply would not credit it. But how are you? Let me look at you—you're cold, aren't you? Oh, for my fire! This beastly central heating is dreary and uncomforting. Sit here—no, here. I feel I should get up and let you get into my bed. You look quite worn out and I ought never to have let you come, but I couldn't bear the thought of not seeing you when you offered."

"I should think not," said Sophie, glad, as she sat, to see her toes again. "I would have been most offended. Now, I didn't know what to bring—"

"Bring! I shall be furious if you've brought anything but yourself."

"—so I brought some Earl Grey tea and a lemon—very feeble. I thought perhaps they made that nasty thick stuff you hate."

"And they do," said Mrs. Joliffe. "I have very nearly stopped drinking their tea. You couldn't have brought anything better. I shall ring at once and get one of the idiots to bring a kettle of boiling water and an empty teapot. I shall not give the tea to them—they are not trustworthy."

She did this and while the kettle and teapot were brought they fussed with cups and the cutting of the lemon and felt the embarrassment between them. Meeting like this made everything quite different. Mrs. Joliffe, sitting up in the utility bed with its vulgar candy-striped green and purple and pink sheets, was not the same person. However gracious her manner and proud her bearing, she could not look anything but pathetic in the nasty little room. Even the few beautiful objects she had taken with her fought a losing battle with the hideous furniture. And Sophie felt different, too. She was for some reason ashamed of her size and felt indecent in front of the "idiot" who came in and out. Finally the tea was made and they were released, in the action of drinking it, from some of the tension.

"Well," said Mrs. Joliffe, putting down her cup very carefully on its saucer, "tell me how you've all been getting on at 109."

"All?" queried Sophie, laughing. "There is only Mr. Bone and me."

"Then Alexander has not returned?"

"No."

"Have you reported his disappearance to the police?"

"Of course not—why should I? He isn't missing, not in that sense."

"I do not want to alarm you, but surely you cannot know if he is safe and well? He has perhaps met with an accident —a slight one—and cannot get in touch with you."

"He'll be all right," said Sophie calmly.

"I wish I shared your confidence, my dear. But then if he *is* well and has not come home it is all the more disgraceful. He needs whipping."

"He's been whipped," said Sophie, smiling, "often. It never did any good. It's just the way he is—he's not ordinary, you see, like you and me."

"I am not in the least ordinary," said Mrs. Joliffe without the least humor, "whereas that young man does not appear to have distinguished himself in any way at all. He does not do any worthwhile work, he has no talents, his behavior is mostly disagreeable, yet you expect me to accept your word that he is a genius."

"I never said he was a genius," protested Sophie.

"Well, explain yourself."

"I can't—it's really very difficult. He has no background, you see, and his standards aren't like ours and he can't be judged in the same way."

"Rubbish," Mrs. Joliffe snapped, and sniffed. They were silent, then she said, "Come, now, don't take it to heart, Sophie. This place makes me more vicious than usual. How is William? I am amazed he hasn't procured a chaperone," she commented dryly, "but perhaps he thinks your condition allows such dangerous living to go unnoticed."

"I've hardly seen him," said Sophie. "He seems to stay in his room for days at a time."

"Silly man," said Mrs. Joliffe, expressionless. She pushed the checked folkweave counterpane away from her in one irritable movement. "I suppose he has all my things in bundles ready to be thrown on top of the coffin after me?"

"He has been busy," admitted Sophie.

"How he must have enjoyed it," said Mrs. Joliffe. "I'm glad I was able to amuse him for a few hours, if only indirectly. Well, he can just keep it all a little longer and go through agonies trying to decide how and when he should get rid of it all. That's his problem and he'd better be careful or he will be in trouble. I'm not above protecting myself legally if necessary. I'm waiting for him to get in touch with me and then we shall see."

"What if he doesn't get in touch?"

"Has he said that? Yes, I can imagine it—you must have provoked him unduly. Well, whatever he may have said, he will still get in touch. He has to. He won't want my goods and chattels cluttering his precious house up, and if I don't die he won't be able to avoid getting in touch."

"He's very unfeeling," said Sophie.

"Nonsense," said Mrs. Joliffe sharply, "William is not unfeeling. Rather, he has too much feeling, especially for me." She watched Sophie lower her eyes and start plucking strands of wool from the end of her scarf. "You don't believe me, do you? What did William say?"

"I can't exactly remember, but he didn't seem to care what happened to you. I thought he was very callous and cruel."

"Then you're a silly girl with no insight at all."

Sophie flushed and felt again the familiar fury she always felt when Mrs. Joliffe thought she could be as rude as she liked just because she was older. She said, very stiffly, "I'm sorry. I do beg your pardon."

"Don't be hypocritical. You know you do nothing of the sort. It is for me to apologize—I forget you know so little. I'm going to tell you something I've never told anyone else and you must promise never to repeat it. You promise? Very well. You know I was married when I met William and you know how I fell in love with him. We could do nothing until my husband died and then it seemed to me there was no obstacle. I was free to declare my love and William to declare his intentions. I found no difficulty in revealing my feelings, but William found it impossible to reveal his. You would laugh if I told you how many opportunities I gave him, how many times I set the scene, how I encouraged him and yearned over him. But it did no good at all. He never even kissed me, do you know that? Once, he came very near —but that was my accident. After my accident nothing was the same. But I know, I truly know, that William loved me. One night, he almost managed to tell me. He had given me a present, some beautiful crystal goblets, and in a very roundabout way, very involved, very William, he confessed that he did not know how people had the *confidence* to marry. He said, should he ever want to marry, the more he loved his lady the more reluctant he would be to expose her to what he felt was his perilous way of life. He asked me if I did not think sacrifice, self-sacrifice, was the greatest test of love. It was all ridiculous, of course—William was very secure, doing very nicely, quite unlikely to be in difficulties. But I spoiled it, you see. I misunderstood William. I looked him straight in the eye and said, 'William, live for today and let tomorrow take care of itself. That's what I believe.' I might as well have hit him."

Throughout her little speech, Mrs. Joliffe sat up very straight with her hands clasped in front of her and her eyes fixed on some invisible spot. Sophie felt acutely uncomfortable. She was aware that Mrs. Joliffe thought she was re-creating a magical scene, that she should be holding her breath with suspense, that perhaps tears ought to be in her eyes, but she was unmoved. If the roles had been reversed, Mrs. Joliffe would now have been saying, "What utter drivel." She would not say that, not because it was not drivel, not because she was too kind, but out of doubt. What did Mrs. Joliffe now remember about Mrs. Joliffe then? Hardly anything, probably. Oh, she might have remembered conversations accurately, but feelings? Sophie was sure not. The day her father had died she had told herself she would remember every detail of the following twenty-four hours forever. Now she could remember only the headings to the chapters, as it were. She sat and looked at the inspired Mrs. Joliffe and thought how she would like to have met the young Agnes. She had to take everything on trust because she was fifty years too late. What seemed to her now a tale of a hard, scheming hostess trying to ensnare a shy boy might have seemed otherwise then. Perhaps Agnes was the one her contemporaries felt sorry for and admired— perhaps William was the one that made them feel impatient. Whatever the truth, this dreary account of what had gone on was no good at all.

"How awful," said Sophie, though it did not seem awful to her. "Perhaps," she said, "it was just as well all the same. William isn't really the marrying sort, is he?"

Mrs. Joliffe stared at her for a full two minutes before she said, "My dear child, you have made some stupid remarks in your time, but that must be the most stupid. There is no such thing as a marrying kind of person, male or female. I was not what you call the marrying kind, but married I found a fulfillment I had never had before. I could have gone through life very happily unmarried—I would have taken up a profession, had lots of interests, I would not have languished. But I would have been unfulfilled just as William is unfulfilled."

"He seems happy enough to me," said Sophie sulkily.

"He is content. That is not the same. Sometimes I wonder if you know what marriage is about."

"Sometimes I wonder if you do," said Sophie quickly.

"Certainly I do," said Mrs. Joliffe. "I have had fifty years to think about it."

"But not to experience it," said Sophie.

"Unhappily, no. But had I had the luck to do so, my conclusions, I feel sure, would have been the same. Marriage is an extension of one's soul, of one's personality. William never knew it."

"He might have found it the opposite," said Sophie. "He might have been crushed and repressed."

"By me, do you infer?"

"No—by marriage, any marriage. He has found his own kind of happiness and he values it. But," she finished, suddenly repentant, "I am sure you would indeed have been very happy."

All the way home in the warmth of the minicab Sophie reflected on her own crassness. History had repeated itself and there was no need for it to have done. She knew Mrs. Joliffe and she knew what the old lady had wanted her to say and had not said it. She had been mean and spiteful and she was distressed by this darker side of herself. It had proved impossible to make amends. No matter how many topics they ranged over they were not comfortable together and could find no common ground. Both were glad when the arrival of the minicab was announced and Sophie was obliged to leave, with many protestations that a cab had not been necessary, in a great hurry.

She let herself into No. 109 and without bothering to put on the hall light made her way upstairs. In her own flat she did not bother to put on the light either, but stood at the window looking out onto the darkened park feeling depressed and miserable. She seemed for so long to have been in the same darkened state as this room, without any kind of inner illumination—but she had followed that train of thought so often that she was impatient with herself and abruptly went around switching on every light till she was dazzled. She made herself some coffee and toast and sat at the window as she nearly always did. As she watched, snow began to fall and she was delighted, for watching snow fall was an occupation. It fell very thickly and lay at once. Soon it reached blizzard proportions and the balcony outside was almost obliterated. Excited, Sophie searched for her transistor radio, which she rarely used, and tried to find a station that would tell her about the weather, but she had no luck. Only mindless music came from the set, and she switched it off. She dimmed some of the lights and lay on her side on the floor watching the snow. Overhead, William thundered backward and forward as though running a race from front windows to back. For so small and slight a man he was heavy on his feet, and Sophie smiled to think how outraged he would be if she were to tell him this. It had been a winter for snow—snow in November before the last leaves were off the trees, snow at Christmas when they had arrived, snow most of February and now snow in March, the heaviest of all. Her baby might well be a snow baby, though she had always imagined the daffodils would be out and the sun shining.

Busy thinking prosaic thoughts and wishing there were someone to share the prosaicness with, Sophie was not aware of any pain beginning. Stretched out on the floor with a cushion, she in any case lay awkwardly, and when her back became painful enough to notice she was sure it was because of the way she had been lying.

Too lazy to move, and still fascinated by her view of the snow, she rolled onto her other side and dragged a cushion from the chair nearby to lie on. The pain was no better. Sighing, she got up and stretched and sat down on the chair and yawned. She paused in mid-yawn as a very startling pain seemed to strike from one side of her body to the other, and at the same time there was a distinct pop and a small waterfall cascaded down the inside of her tights. Horrified, Sophie tried to bend to examine her wet legs and thighs, but as she bent another pain shot her upright and finally convinced her. This was labor. Labor not as the only leaflet she had ever read described it, but a galloping labor that had taken her from square one to countdown before she knew what was happening. It was like nothing she had anticipated. Where was the smiling Sophie, calmly telephoning for an ambulance? Where was the capable mother-to-be getting together her things? Gasping, Sophie tried frantically to order her thoughts although every movement was already an effort and her one desire was to go to the lavatory. Aloud she said, "Don't panic, don't panic," and inwardly remembered phrases like "They just drop them in the fields, my dear, and go back to work." She was going to drop it on the carpet borrowed from William.

Slowly, Sophie stood up. The telephone was across the room, a mere three yards away. She took a deep breath and immediately felt faint, and thinking she was about to faint made her really become giddy and she had to sit down. With the next pain came a wave of nausea, and in trying to overcome both the nausea and the faintness she ended up crouching on her side again. Her heart hammered not in her body but in her head as she made her second attempt to go to the telephone. This time she managed a little better and began to move across the room, feeling that she was swimming or flying. The distance seemed vast as she walked very slowly, in a daze, concentrating on the black instrument ahead of her that she wanted so much to reach. Like a man in space, her weightlessness troubled her and she took each step with exaggerated caution as though afraid she might end up on the ceiling or out the window. Her arms were outstretched, her legs stiff, and she swayed slightly as she went. In her head she tried to practice what she was going to say on the telephone so as not to waste time when she got through, but her throat was dry and she was sure no words would get past her cracked lips. Almost there, a pain that made her pant started in her thighs and spread over her entire body and she suddenly became convinced that this was not childbirth but some other horrible death.

The telephone would not behave properly. She could not get the dialing tone and could not be sure her shaking fingers had dialed 999—perhaps it had been 888. Sobbing, she threw the receiver down and lurched toward the hall door, where she clung on to the handle and tried to shout for Mr. Bone. "Mr. Bone!" she whispered, and sank to her knees the better to cope with the pain. Oh, Mr. Bone, please come quickly! She wanted to defecate but could never make the bathroom. The pressure was almost unendurable and she felt that the slightest push and she would empty her bowels on the floor. "Help," she croaked, on all fours, and could not even hear herself. She felt only just conscious, locked inside powerful rhythms that had taken her over, and the cry that came at last was an involuntary one and not anything she had attempted.

Sitting enjoying the snow, William heard it—a howl, it was, deep and low, and it made his skin prickle all over. Where had he heard it before? He passed his tongue over his lips and remembered. Agnes, Agnes had made that sound, lying trapped . . . But nothing could be trapped in his house, there were no traps, it was nonsense. All the same, he went to his door and listened and the sound came again, louder, more anguished, and William found himself sweating as he crept down the stairs. As soon as he saw Sophie, he shrank back round the bend. Cautiously, he put his head round again and took in the disturbing sight again. The girl was kneeling, her long hair tumbling down over her face, obscuring it, and her crouched body swaying, one hand beating the ground. Numbly, William looked at her. He would have to do something, though he wanted to run away and hide. He went closer and bent down also and said, "I say, are you in trouble?" The face that was raised to his was red and the eyes bulging. Little veins stood out across the forehead and the neck. She was quite incapable of speech.

"Ah," he said. "An ambulance, I think."

To step over the body seemed revolting, but there was no

other way past. He stepped and went to the phone and was upset by the dangling receiver. Quickly he replaced it, then lifted it and dialed 999.

"Ah," he said, "this is 109 Pendleton Place and I want an ambulance straight away for a pregnant tenant that appears to be in—well, in need of a doctor. It's very urgent."

"You should ring her hospital," the voice said accusingly.

"I don't know it and she doesn't seem able to speak."

"All right," the voice said, "but if she's that far gone you'd better roll up your sleeves and put a kettle on, hadn't you?"

The line went dead. Agitated, William went back to Sophie.

"Well, now," he said, "everything is under control, an ambulance will be here soon, nothing to worry about."

She seemed dopy and her breathing was rapid and shallow. Suddenly she sat up and whispered, "I think I'm having it," and at the same time she grabbed his hand and held on. "Don't leave me!"

"Ah," said William, "hang on, now, the ambulance won't be a minute and they have very experienced men." He tried to detach his hand, but her grip was strong. "Ah," he said again, "I think I will just go next door and see if I can get a woman to sit with you—much better at a time like this." But the grip tightened. She lay now on her back in the tiny hall, in semidarkness, and held on to him with both hands. "Oh, dear," muttered William. "Oh, dear."

"You'll—have—to—help," Sophie gasped. "It's coming, I've got to push—please help."

The last "help" was long drawn out and frantic. William realized the truth of her statement and shrank from what it implied, but he thought of his own pain and Agnes in the trap and he tried to subdue the loathing that filled him and said, "What must I do?"

Fumbling, William put his released hands up her skirt and groped for what he was to pull down. The whole area was sodden and slippery and he was afraid of hurting her. He found himself saying "Oh, my goodness" over and over again until at last his fingers closed on some elastic and in one movement he flung away the tights and underthings. Not daring to look, he hurled them over his shoulder. His ears sang with straining to hear the sound of the doorbell or the ambulance. Below him, Sophie was quieter and he felt more hopeful that she would hold on, but then she lifted her head and gave a huge "Oh!" and her face bulged alarmingly. William knelt beside her, his face averted, but in the pause that followed she said, "Get my dress up—up—out of the way." Dumbly, William pulled at the dress, and his insides turned to water as her knees fell apart and he saw the bloody, hair-matted opening. He felt he was going to faint and put a hand over his eyes, shivering like a dog and whimpering. Again he heard her push and hunched himself beside her, as though sheltering, though what protection she had to offer him he did not know.

"Can you see?" she shouted. "Is it coming? Oh, please look, tell me—oh!" And she pushed again.

"I can't," William croaked. "I really can't."

"Look!" she yelled and seemed to give him a little push and he was lying looking into the opening.

Lying flat on his face with the soft thick carpet under him, William wished himself in mud that he might sink into it and vanish under its oozing cover. He wished he were back in France, fighting, with wounded men all around him and himself wounded and in terrible pain, but alive and groping his way back through the mud to the shelter of the water-filled trench. Inching his way backward, hand after hand, bleeding body snaking backward, the blood blotted out in the wet mud. Other bodies passed him, swifter, on hands and knees, sometimes on feet, and he passed lumps of human matter himself, groaning and motionless. The wounds he saw were at worm's-eye view and thumped into sight with sickening suddenness. A couple of feet and he would rest looking into the stomach of a fat soldier, guts spewed everywhere. He would slide a yard or two and hang on to a hunk of grass and a head would come away in his hand. Then he had been touched, two large white hands had come from heaven like eagles and lifted him up and placed him onto a stretcher and he had clung to the hands, even when they were carrying him, and just the strength and sanity of them had made him cry, just the thought that there was still someone not bleeding and smelling and moaning, someone who would take charge and control, who would know what to do, who was there and whose presence meant one could give oneself over to the pain.

William put his shaking hands over his face, knocking off his spectacles, but he could not shut out the dark gap which moved and quivered like a species of jellyfish, and after a while he spread his fingers and peered through them and saw nothing distinguishable in the tunnel.

"I can't see anything," he said, but Sophie was off on her own, pushing and crying out and then pausing to pant, her arms braced against the walls. Hands dropped, watching, half his terror overcome, his sickness subsiding though all his senses still shrieked in protest, William saw a bulge appearing and then disappearing and then more appearing and he grabbed his spectacles and put them on with trembling hands.

"I think I can see it," he said, and at that minute Sophie gave a great roar and seemed to split and a strange blue blood-covered object was protruding from her, and then there was another roar and a slither and there on the floor lay what looked like the inside of a rabbit.

"Oh, God," William said, "your baby." He knelt over Sophie, but she was quite unconscious and a panic far greater than any that had gone before overwhelmed him. It was up to him to do something. Quite forgetting his disgust, he put on the main light and looked down at the baby, lying without movement between the white, collapsed legs of its mother. Far back in the recesses of his mind was a memory of an army manual which had included in its section on emergencies how to deliver a baby and had always caused great hilarity. But William had automatically read it and now he remembered, he could see the small black print in the green book and as he read it again he bent down and picked up the baby by its heels and slapped it on the buttocks. Nothing happened. He slapped again, and at last the body shook and the knees drew up and it gave a piercing scream. Gently, William cleared its mouth of mucus with his little finger and then he laid the baby down on the floor and, afraid to leave it for a single second, wrapped it in his cardigan. The thick cord, like a plastic washing line, was still attached to Sophie. Did he have to cut it? He did not dare. Instead, he pulled down Sophie's dress and sat on the floor and watched the baby, and at that minute the doorbell rang. Such was the trancelike state that he had now fallen into, he did not realize its significance and when the ambulance men began banging on the door his first reaction was a desire to tell them to be quiet.

"Where is she?" the man said.

Incapable of speech, William pointed up the stairs, and the man and his companion pounded past him. He heard their exclamations, but all he could do was support his exhausted body against the wall. A few minutes later, they began bringing the stretcher down and he heard them telling each other to be careful, keep her head up, a little to the right, more to the left. The men were both beaming.

"Well, you saved us a job, Granddad," one said. "Bet that took you by surprise, eh?"

William nodded.

"Doesn't happen often like that," said the other. "One in a million."

"Are they well?" William managed to ask, following them out into the snow.

"Placenta hasn't come away yet," the man said. "Bit

dodgy, that. She seems to have lost a lot of blood, too, but she'll be all right, don't you worry. You did a good job, and the little nipper's fine—a big 'un, wouldn't be surprised if he was a nine-pounder. Here, you can have this back now." And he handed William his cardigan and looked kindly at him. "You want to get yourself back inside," he said. "You look done in. We'll be taking her to Queen Charlotte's, but God knows where she'll end up."

They closed the doors and with great difficulty drove off, the wheels sliding in the snow. William trudged back to the house and closed the door. He stood with his back to it, looking at the many footmarks on the black linoleum, and then he went upstairs, very slowly, averting his face from the little hallway of the middle flat. In his kitchen, he dropped his cardigan into the sink. It was slimy and wet and stained with blood and he could not even think about washing it. Stiffly, he walked about his flat and found the brandy and poured himself a large glass and, sitting down, began to sip it.

Babies were born every minute, all the same way, all like that, with straining thighs and parted legs and bulging crotches. He had, he told himself, witnessed nothing extraordinary. Never before had he seen a woman naked, not below the waist, not exposed like that, and that was the shock, the revulsion, not the baby, no indeed. He was thinking more of Sophie than of the baby. And Agnes, who had had a baby, too, like that. To make love to a woman, to lie with her, genitals to genitals, had always seemed to William possible only if one was in the highest transports of passion, under cover, in the dark. The mechanics of doing it had always seemed to him impossible. Time after time he had told himself, and his body had told him, that it was a natural function and nothing to be ashamed of, but the truth was that he was ashamed. He had speculated about other people and been ashamed.

He drank the brandy and reflected that his admiration for women had not been misplaced. They had babies, like that. Queens, duchesses, women all had babies in that shattering way and yet lived to walk about and laugh and look people in the eye and appear quite unmoved by it. It was not something dignified done under the sheets, but a brazen act, basic and crude. William had heard it called beautiful. He shook his head. He did not suppose the birth of Sophie's baby had been any different from any other birth and it had not been beautiful. No, he could not subscribe to that view. He did not doubt that he would relive every moment several hundred times in the near future and his feelings would still be the same.

What, he wondered, would Sophie's feelings be? If it had been a traumatic experience for him, how much more so for her. He suddenly realized how brave the girl had been, how sensible, and how silly he had been, refusing to dispense with prudery until it was very nearly too late. He must beg her pardon at the first opportunity. The word "placenta" came into his head and he shuddered. What if the ambulance had never come and they had truly been cut off—what would he have done about the placenta, not knowing there was anything to be done? And the bleeding—what would he have done about that? Would she have died? Would he have had to look after the baby? First he would have washed it, in warm water, all over, removing the grime of birth, and then he would have found his whitest and softest towel and wrapped it up and made a bed in a drawer and put it there to sleep off its shock. He would have boiled water and fed it drop by drop into the poor little chap's mouth and then put him to sleep. The looking after might not have been too bad. . . .

The telephone ringing brought William out of his smiling and nodding.

"William," Mrs. Joliffe said, "I am worried. I was not go-

ing to ring you, ever, because you have behaved disgracefully, but I am worried. Sophie came to see me today and I
have been ringing to see she arrived home safely and is well,
and there is no reply."

"No," said William.

"Don't be a parrot, William. The point is, is she back?
Have you seen her or heard her moving about?"

"Yes," said William, "I have."

"Ah. Thank you. I will ring in the morning."

"She isn't here."

"But you just said—"

"She is in hospital."

"Good heavens! The baby is on its way, then?"

"It has arrived, here, in this house." William listened to
and enjoyed the stunned silence. He thought of what to say.
"I delivered it," he said.

"William!"

"A fine boy, lovely little chap. Now I'm a little tired, so if
you'll excuse me I must go to bed. Good night, Agnes."

Smiling, elated, William did a little dance round the
room.

Fourteen
>>>>>>>>>>>>

THE DAY that followed the birth of Sophie's son was one of those days William found too much to take. He knew that hopes of absolute peace and quiet, once so easy to count on, were bound not to be fulfilled, but he had hoped that fate, having subjected him to such an unlooked-for ordeal, would limit events to one happening. But no. From the moment he woke up, life was tumultuous.

Queen Charlotte's Maternity Hospital rang first thing, or rather Sophie rang from a bedside telephone, and William blushed down the line.

"Mr. Bone?"

"Ah, speaking?"

"I don't suppose you can bear to speak to me, Mr. Bone, but I *had* to speak to you just to say thank you, thank you, thank you, and sorry too—it's too awful to think what you went through."

Her voice was light and happy, and William tried to match her tone. "Splendid!" he said. "Glad all's well."

"Oh, very well," Sophie said, "we're both very well. And, Mr. Bone, I hope you don't mind—you probably will—but

I've decided to call my son William. William James."

"Good heavens," said William.

"Absurd, isn't it?" cooed Sophie. "But I thought it would be lovely and I've always liked the name and it's the least I can do—you know, after all that. Do you mind *very* much?"

"Mind?" echoed William. "My dear girl, I have never been so honored in my life. Dear me, it's quite extraordinary how pleased I am."

"Thank you," said Sophie sweetly. "Now I can put it in the *Times*, just for all my old friends to see. You will look for it, won't you?"

"I shall buy fifteen copies," said William, "and frame them all."

When the giggles had died away and the receiver been replaced, William found the desire to tell someone irresistible and so rang Agnes Joliffe. While the matron was putting him through, he almost hung up, as he felt the excitement die down within him, but Agnes answered and it was too late.

"Ah, Agnes?" he asked, nervously.

"Naturally."

"It's William here."

"I know. No one else would have rung at this barbaric hour. What do you want?"

"Oh. Well. Sophie Hill asked me—no, she didn't *ask* me, she—"

"William, I am not interested in your search for the precise truth. What are you trying to say?"

"The baby, her son, it is to be called William, after me. There."

There was a short silence. William listened anxiously. Surely Agnes could not be jealous? She could not expect Sophie to call a boy Agnes, or did she think Joliffe would have been included?

"I am pleased you have the grace to be delighted, William," Agnes said eventually.

"Good," said William. "I was afraid you might think the whole thing rather vulgar."

"Of course it's vulgar and trite and dreadful," said Agnes vigorously, "but that has nothing to do with it. You never knew, but Germaine would have been William if she had been a boy. I never told you."

"But I hardly knew you then," said William, astonished.

"Quite untrue," said Agnes, "and beside the point. Of course, mine would have been a gesture of a different sort from Sophie Hill's. You are such a simpleton where human behavior is concerned, William, that it may not have occurred to you that there is perhaps an element of cunning in Sophie's choice of name. Don't protest—let me finish, please. I am not suggesting she expects you to leave all you have to her son and heir, but she does have to leave that hospital at an early date and she does have to have somewhere to go and someone to stand by her. She has begun a softening-up process, I shouldn't wonder."

"If so, quite unnecessary," said William stiffly.

"You will not allow her to return?"

"Of course I will allow her to return," said William. "I have no option. The rent is paid until the end of June."

"By whom?"

"I am sorry, but that is a private matter. And I feel I must say that, quite apart from legal obligations, I would still, I hope, be charitable and not turn a young mother out. Bonds have been forged—" William cleared his throat—"and are not lightly severed."

"Dear me," said Agnes, "you have fallen hook, line and sinker. Before we know what is happening you will be forgetting a lifetime's habit and becoming involved. Remember, William? Your dread word?"

"Some things may need rethought."

"Well, when you've rethought them, William, do consider my case, won't you? I should hate to be left out of any general amnesty."

Even before he had begun to cope with the swirl of conflicting emotions that now beset him, William was aware of noises below. Still standing by the telephone, he heard doors crashing and a voice unmistakably that of Alexander Hill shouting for Sophie. His first reaction was to lock his door and hide, his second to go down and shout equally loudly, then run the odious fellow out of the house. He pulled his jacket straight and made his way, very quietly, downstairs.

"Good morning," he said.

"Christ!" yelled Alex. "You nearly stoned me, creeping in like that. Where's Sophie?"

"You may well ask," said William sternly.

"Oh, cut the shit. By the look of that floor there's been an accident—that blood looks fresh, the stain hasn't dried. What's happened to her?"

"Do you care?" asked William.

Alex, crossing the room, picked William up by the lapels and shook him. "Just tell me, little man, that's all—tell me."

"Put me down," said William distinctly. Their faces almost touched, Alex's long, thick hair swinging close to William's quivering nose. The minute he felt his feet on firm ground, William took one step backward, then punched Alex on the chin with a left uppercut. The crack rang through the room most satisfactorily and the young man went down with a barely audible moan that was almost a sigh.

"Bully," William said, "seducer, deserter." He walked jerkily through to the kitchen and washed his hands, then returned to the still prone body of Alex. Bending over him, he saw he was crying. His enormous black eyes were obliterated with tears.

"Now sit up," William said, "and listen to me."

Alex struggled upright and sat with his head resting on his splendid silk-covered knees.

"Sophie," William said firmly, "had her baby last night in this flat. She was alone and unattended. If I had not been there, she might have died. That blood is her blood. To say that you ought to be ashamed of yourself is a travesty of the truth. I cannot bear to think what you were doing at the time, when your place was with her."

"Nothing," said Alex.

"Quite," said William.

Alex wiped the tears away, sniffed and, standing up, lit a cigarette. He offered William one.

"I do not smoke," said William, with distaste.

Alex made a funny little gesture, half salute, half sneer, and began walking round the room. William had time to note the peacock clothes—velvets, silks, satins, all multi-colored and flowing—and the jewels on fingers, toes, belt, before Alex stopped at the stains on the carpet and said, "Why did she bleed?"

"There is a great deal of blood present during child-birth," William said severely.

"Is there?" said Alex. "I never knew. I'm glad I wasn't there—blood makes me pass out. Christ, just looking at that does." And he sat down on a chair, hand over eyes.

"I notice," William said, "that you have not yet thought to inquire after Sophie's health or—that of—that is—" he paused—"William's." His voice squeaked rather on the name.

"You look all right," said Alex, "and Sophie must be or you wouldn't have been able to resist telling me."

"I do not refer to myself by my own name in conversation," William said. "I was referring to your baby. Sophie has called him William James."

"You always used to address her as Mrs. Hill," Alex said. "No first names, ever. You've come a long way, William."

William frowned. "I don't know what nasty insinuations you are trying to make," he said, "but during your absence your wife—for want of a more convenient name—she had need of friends. In short, we became friendly. And naturally, bonds are forged during an experience like childbirth that make formality difficult."

"I'm glad you enjoyed it."

"I did not enjoy it!"

"Tell me about it—go on. Did it turn you on? What happened—inside you? How did it feel?"

"I prefer not to discuss it," said William primly.

"Oh, Christ." Alex lay back and laughed. "The one thing you've ever had to talk about and you prefer not to discuss it. Opt out, opt out, that's you, let nobody touch me in mind or body, let me touch nobody—no contamination, no contact, no nothing." He closed his eyes.

"You can open your eyes at once," William said, "and go, or I will have no alternative but to call a policeman."

"I don't want to stay," said Alex, getting up, to William's surprise. "I always hated it here, it really fouled everything up. Where's Sophie?"

"I'm not sure I ought to tell you."

"Then don't!" screamed Alex. "Christ, I can't stand your stupid moralizing cunt of a face. Do you think I can't find her? Do you think I can't walk through every hospital in London? Do you think I don't know her? Oh, God, you make me tired, that's all. Go stuff yourself, Mr. Bone—go and choke in your own spleen."

William had to admit to himself that he must have mishandled the encounter—it had not ended as it ought to have done. As he went back upstairs, he felt deflated. That was the trouble with being self-righteous; other people used it so adroitly, but he always ended up feeling deflated and rather ashamed. But he had nothing to be ashamed of. That young man had needed a punch on the nose for a long time. William was glad he had punched him, ineffective though this violence had been. He did not know how to deal with the Alexander Hills of the world, and increasingly he felt he ought to be able to. Now, Alex would have married Agnes, about that there was no question. He would have married her, or run off with her, and ruined her life. Would Agnes have really liked him to be Alex?

A little bit of the joy he had felt earlier crept back into William as he telephoned an order to a florist. He sent three dozen white chrysanthemums and then immediately canceled this and sent a posy of violets, then canceled that and settled on pink roses. The florist asked him coldly if he had finished and he had to say yes and did not have the courage to change again as he really wanted to. He wanted also to send something to his namesake but could think of nothing appropriate. Something silver was called for, but what? A christening mug, when he would never be christened? Or a tankard—but was that an encouragement to vice when he grew up? He would never see him grown up, of course. Even at a conservative estimate this was out of the question. Indeed, he would be lucky to see the young William walk and talk. Thinking this, William thought about the walking and talking that would be going on in his house, and sighed. Young William was bound to cry, night and day, it was inevitable. One would get no rest, and with only Sophie and him in the house he knew he might be called upon to come within uncomfortably short range of the crying. Did he mind? Was he prepared to endure it?

William endeavored to have a normal day. He did his correspondence, went for a run, did his exercises, read, learned some more Japanese—but ended up still arguing with himself about young William. He had watched the child being born, had indeed been instrumental in bringing him into the world. He bore his name, a deliberate coincidence, intended as a compliment if not an honor. Now, was this something to disregard or was it not? Was there a tangible connection he wished to preserve? And if he did, what was he going to do about it? Acknowledge it existed, for a start off. Acknowledge that he was not going to wash his hands of Sophie Hill and her son.

When it was dark, William walked through his empty house, ostensibly to see it was all locked up and safe. Agnes' furniture and the crates with her things in them bothered him. While they were there, he did not feel his house was freed of her presence. A sewing table he had forgotten to cover had gathered a thick layer of dust, and blowing the dust away he thought of Agnes using it. She had sewn a great deal. She had sat in this window, in the sunlight, the material of whatever she was sewing gathered in her lap, the lid of the table open to reveal the green-silk-padded inside punctured with needles and the narrow boxes stacked with many different-colored cottons. Her head high, she had raised needles to the light so that they glinted and with great delicacy and a sense of triumph at a skill mastered had threaded them first time. Something he had liked to watch, but a pleasure he had never confessed. He thought for a moment of sending the table to her, but it would be too complicated and anyway she could not now sew. Instead, he found a cloth and covered it and patted it and continued his tour.

He could leave young William his house, the house where he had been so unceremoniously born. Agnes would say Sophie had schemed for this, but he did not have to either believe Agnes or, if he did believe, take any notice. His house had to be left. As his will stood, he had left it to Rupert, the second cousin he thought of as a nephew, simply because he was the only one left who bore the family name. Rupert would sell it, William did not hope for more, but perhaps a family who loved it would buy it. The point was, it would stay a private house, whereas if it were left to charity it very likely would not—or so William conjectured. But instead he could leave it to young William. Since Rupert did not know he had been left the house, he could not be hurt.

By this time William was in the middle flat. Earlier, he had opened all the windows to get rid of the somehow rancid smell that seemed to hang around. William had not analyzed the smell too closely, but he was determined to get rid of it. Now he closed the windows, satisfied that the cold, crisp air outside had done its job. He knew he ought to do something about the stain on the carpet and stood and looked at it doubtfully. It was extensive. The only thing to do was to buy another two yards and carefully replace it. Tomorrow he would visit Harrods and order the necessary amount. One could not possibly scrub it out. Nor young William. Whatever one did, he was unscrubbable out.

William spent a week alone in his house and was indignant to find he did not wholly relish the solitude. True, it was pleasant to go to bed in perfect peace, not worrying about possible noises. Very pleasant. He slept the better for it. And baths became enjoyable again without the anxiety of wondering if he was holding someone back from their natural functions. All the same, he could not rid himself of a puzzling sense of expectation. He seemed to be forever listening and looking—not fearfully, not in the manner of a man afraid someone had broken in, but more as though something was missing. What exactly was missing was what made William cross with himself. Nothing was missing. He had never set much store by the sound of human voices—on the contrary, most of his energies had been directed toward either subduing or silencing them. He did not like company, especially female company. No, it was not that. More, he finally supposed, the removal of challenge. Other people in the house had been a challenge. They had had to be overcome, prevented from intruding, and William reflected that he must, without knowing it, have enjoyed this. Happily, once he had recognized his affliction there was then pleasure to be found in dealing with it, and to this end William threw himself into an orgy of paperwork and library visiting.

During this time, he heard twice from Sophie. She sent him a card thanking him for the simply beautiful flowers which were too beautiful and too many and too extravagant, and a card—a rather alarming card, William thought—announcing, officially, William James's birth, weight and date. This last card was festooned with sharp-beaked storks. On the back of it Sophie had scrawled, "Back on the 18th!"

On the seventeenth the last of the snow melted and spring arrived dramatically. William had always felt a great affinity with the mole who, disturbed in his subterranean passages by the warmth of the earth, burrowed to the surface and shivered with excitement at the headiness of spring. William always felt very heady. He spent a great deal of time, every year, trying to define precisely how the air changed, but the effort always proved abortive and he was left to be struck anew by the difference. In Sophie's flat he felt it particularly. The windows there were enormous, three times the size of his, and as he worked cleaning it the air rushing in overpowered him. He had to keep dashing outside to fill his lungs, and then back in again. The sun flooded the flat from back to front, bringing out colors that William had forgotten existed. He was very happy as he swept and washed and dusted.

When all was ready in the flat, William went shopping. He knew he was not a good shopper—Agnes had always told him so—but that day he meant to be good. He intended to buy nourishing food that Sophie would find easy to cook and eat. So he bought *pâté d'Ardennes* and fillet steak and salad and fruit and bread and butter and cheese. He sailed along, knapsack bouncing, a smile on his face, enjoying the new spring air. At the corner of the street he stopped and bought some daffodils for Sophie and some for himself and had to stand quite still for several minutes, disturbed by the smell, before he could go on. Once home, he put away the food and put the flowers into water, and then, because he did not know exactly when she would come, he began to write a note. He did not want to be around when Sophie and young William arrived—it would, he felt, be indelicate. She would want to savor being home first, and settle William. Suddenly a dreadful thought struck William—there was nothing ready for the baby. No cot, no cradle, no pram, no bath—had Sophie thought about all this? There he had been, thinking only of what the young mother would eat and see, not thinking of her child. William felt responsible for this neglect, but after several breathless minutes absolved himself of guilt. He had done his best. Solemnly he went on with writing his note.

He wrote:

Greetings! I hope you find everything satisfactory—there are a few provisions in your larder which I thought you might find useful (returning after an absence is always difficult). The sunshine is by courtesy of the spring, and not, alas, my doing! When my namesake is up to receiving company I shall be happy to pay my respects but am quite willing to defer this momentous meeting to a later date.

If I can be of any assistance do not hesitate to ring.

W.E.B.

He thought about signing himself "William" and putting "Dear Sophie" at the top, but old habits died hard. They would both feel easier if the formula was adhered to, for the time being anyway.

On the morning of the eighteenth, William was up and about very early. He had a bath, washing it out scrupulously before he left, and then dressed himself in clean clothes from the skin outward. His stomach felt a little fluttery, so he breakfasted on lemon tea and a dry cream cracker, then stationed himelf at his window with the *Times* of the day before. He did not, of course, know how Sophie and the baby would be coming home. Perhaps by ambulance? Was one brought back as well as taken by ambulance? He rather thought not. Surely she would come back by hired car, it being an occasion. Really, he ought to have organized transport, but he had been shy of turning up at the hospital or contacting it in any way. It would not have been seemly. Agnes, too sharp always, would have said it was his ridiculous hospital phobia. Maybe it was, but in this case it was more. He might have delivered the baby, but he could not have brought himself to walk into a maternity ward—absurd.

By lunchtime when she had not come William felt irritable. He was a bad waiting man, and the *Times* did nothing to allay his irritation. He could find nothing to read in it—these days it was all pictures. He was glad he did not have it on order. As he made himself an omelette he went over all the reasons why he thought the *Times* had deteriorated to see if they were valid or simply due to the petulance of an old man in a younger world he did not know. He was pleased to find that petulance did not come into it and sat down for his next vigil in a better mood, which was fortunate, as it was long. It was four o'clock and he had gone through every single share price before Sophie turned the corner carrying the baby in one arm and her suitcase in the other.

William could not believe it—how could the authorities let her *walk*, a mother of ten days? Was this the National Health? But even as he made up his mind to run and help her, she put down the case and he clearly saw her look around and smile and breathe deeply and with exaggerated care. He stayed where he was. Clearly, she had chosen to walk. Clearly, to be in the open air after ten days in hospital was irresistible. Watching her complete the hundred yards to his door, William was struck by the suitcase. Now, why? he thought. Ah! She had not taken a suitcase with her, that was the point. And it was new—blue and shiny, with clasps that shone too. Someone must have procured the suitcase, and whatever was in it, for her. Odd. Perhaps, William thought, a reconciliation with her mother?

She let herself in very quietly, and again William was disturbed. How did she come to have a key? She had not taken anything in the ambulance, no coat, no handbag, and the dress she had been wearing had had no visible pockets. He heard her walk up the stairs and into her flat. There was a pause—putting the baby down—and then the kitchen door opened. A chair was pulled across the linoleum, and she sat down. Now she would be reading his note. Smiling, he stood at his window and though it was unreasonable found himself glancing at his telephone. It did not ring. The window below was flung open and after a few minutes he smelled the steak cooking and the mushrooms. Nodding his approval, William took up a book and sat down.

The noises of someone moving about, living, below soothed him. Gentle clatters, hisses, water running, kettles singing—done so gently it was melodious. So melodious that it must have reached lullaby proportions, because William fell asleep. The sun woke him and he knew instantly that it must be six o'clock, because the glare was red. He got the setting sun only in his back windows and at this time of the year that was at six o'clock. Surprised at himself, William sat quite still for several minutes. The house was perfectly quiet. He remembered, in a rush, about Sophie and her baby—how good they were! The child had not cried once and now it must be asleep, and perhaps its mother too. Really, they were going to be no trouble.

Going down to the lavatory, William peered over the banisters into the hall and spied at once the note propped up on the radiator shelf. It could only be for him. Tiptoeing, wincing as a stair creaked, he crept down and took it. He thought, as he passed the middle flat door, that he heard the baby whimper, and he froze for a moment before stealthily climbing the stairs. In his own flat, he sighed loudly. It would have been dreadful to disturb them—he who set so much store by not being disturbed. Knowing that his floors tended to have loose boards, he made his way with great care to his working chair and, putting the fire on low, he settled down to read the note, reflecting that it was nice to have a note again, and how he had missed them.

DEAR MR. BONE,

To thank you for all your kindness is impossible—I am overwhelmed. I have never known anyone so kind or thoughtful and I cannot bear the thought that I might not always have been appreciative. Believe me, I am. The last few weeks would have been purgatory but for you.

But this is to say goodbye. We cannot trespass on your kindness any longer. Alex has found another flat—not one-hundredth as nice as yours—and I really only came back to pick up our things and for a last fond look. I knew you would not want to be embarrassed by any meeting.

When we are more settled, you must come and see dear little William. Until then, thank you and all my love—

SOPHIE HILL

The physical sensations, William noted, were not unfamiliar. First the pang, as though his heart sounded a gong to let his blood know that it must run more quickly, his brain work overtime and his flesh burn. He trembled and felt a little sick and his vision was doubled. Closing his eyes, he lay back, weary.

"It was to be expected," Agnes said triumphantly. "The girl was always besotted."

"Rather unusual case," William said absent-mindedly. "Lovely azaleas they have here—marvelously well looked after."

"They care more about the azaleas than the inmates," said Agnes scathingly. "You were duped, William, as I said you would be in the beginning."

"Mm," murmured William, vaguer still.

"And have you heard from her?"

"No. Settling down can be a lengthy process."

"Rubbish. That type never settles—they will have been in half a dozen different flats by now. In the end he will take up with someone else and she'll go back to her mother, which is the best thing that could happen. You won't see her again, William, nor your namesake. My goodness, I shuddered when I heard how much store you set by that empty gesture."

"Oh, it wasn't empty," protested William mildly. "It meant something, I think."

"Nonsense. What could it mean?"

"We were—together, you know, at a great—"

"Oh, shut up, William, you never stop boasting about your wretched great experience when you know and I know that it was nothing of the sort, and neither was the naming of that child. Now let us talk about something else—about finding me another home, for example. Since you are so frightened of my imminent death that I cannot be permitted back in your house, you must find me a more congenial doghouse before next winter."

"Yes," said William, "perhaps St. Ursula's is not ideal. When I return from Portugal we must search." As he spoke, he noticed that somehow his hand had been placed underneath Agnes' on the arm of her wheelchair. Thoughtfully, he stared at the little mound of fingers. His was on the chair itself, so Agnes must have put hers over his, yet he had not felt her touch. Should he take it away? Her hand was warm and his rather cool. Experimentally, he stretched his fingers apart. She stretched hers too. He tried to lift his hand, thinking that he would use it to take a handkerchief out of his pocket to blow his nose, but he was unable to do so, such was the pressure she exerted. He could not take his hand away without asking Agnes to release him and that would call attention to the imprisonment and that would never do. His hand would have to stay under hers.

"I cannot look," Agnes was saying.

"No, I will," said William.

"But I don't know if I can trust you, William."

Was she joking, being sarcastic? Did she squeeze his hand or did she not?

"Oh, I think I know now what you want," William said.

"Let us hope so," said Agnes. "We have been together long enough. Now, did I tell you about Germaine and the mess she is making of Canada?"

They talked, or rather Agnes talked—loudly—and William listened and made suggestions that were ignored and thought about young William. Yesterday his will had been duly witnessed and stamped, and there was no going back. To William Hill, born March 8, 1970, at 109 Pendleton Place, Richmond, he left his house and all its belongings on condition that the same was cherished and not sold into other hands, to continue in the said William Hill's family or, failing legitimate issue, to be passed into the hands of Rupert Bone of Surrey.

As Agnes forged on, William smiled and nodded to himself and felt perfectly happy. He was committed at last. Agnes, still holding his hand—he was used to it now, he did not mind—thought everything had returned to normal, but it hadn't. He had passed the point of being worried either by the past or by the present, and his thoughts were fixed resolutely on the future. He would not let his house again, not yet. He would find Agnes a nice place nearer to it and visit her often. He would be kind to her, perhaps even take hold of *her* hand, and let her remember the past as she wanted to remember it. What harm was there in love? None, William thought, none at all, whether the giver or the receiver. He did not reciprocate Agnes' love, but he could accept it gracefully, just as young William would. The quality of the gift was what mattered, and he would not have liked to die without doing his bit. Let the Sophies and Alexes do their own thing and he and Agnes and young William would do likewise.